DEVIL
LET ME GO

NATHAN
ROBINSON

To Jeremy

Happy Reading!

Nathan Robinson

CONTENTS

DEVIL LET ME GO

ACKNOWLEDGEMENTS

The House that Creak'd was previously published in Thadd Presley Presents Hauntings 2012.

Top of the Heap first appeared on The Dark Fiction Spotlight and as Snakebite Horror's story of the month. It has since been adapted into a podcast by www.pseudopod.org and was published in Thadd Presley Presents Murder.

Crack'd appeared in Winter Chills published by Static Movement 2011 and in Quakes and Storms, a charity anthology published by Panic Press (out of print).

Not That Way Home is previously unpublished.

In One Form or Another is previously unpublished.

If you ever meet a girl named Maisie Mae . . . was first published online at www.spinetinglers.co.uk when it won the monthly competition in May 2010. It was also published in hardback and paperback editions in Soup of Souls by Panic Press and appears in the Spinetinglers 2011 Anthology.

Banana Boxes was previously published on www.spinetinglers.co.uk and appeared in their 2011 Anthology. It also appears in Phobia, published by Black Hound Press.

Eat your Heart out Lorena was previously published in Tales of a Woman Scorned by Panic Press (out of print).

Brian of the Night has appeared online on www.spinetinglers.co.uk and was published in their 2011 anthology.

The Skeleton Tree appears in Carnivorous published by Static Movement.

The Chicken in Black gained first place in the www.spinetinglers.co.uk monthly competition in March 2010. It also appeared in the Spinetinglers 2011 Anthology.

Colder than Hell up here… appears in the charity anthology, The Undead that saved Christmas Vol 3 from Rainstorm Press.

Fallen appears in Ultimate Angels published by Knight Watch Press November 2012

FOR ALL THOSE THAT I'VE DOOMED.

DEVIL LET ME GO

The House that Creak'd

THE HOUSE THAT CREAK'D

Dismay creased across Broome's wizened features. They'd ruined his garden, the last of his summer crop had been destroyed, the remains now largely inedible. Every tomato had been squashed, the gory, pulped remains still hung from the vine where mysterious hands had popped them in place. Every pepper plant had been thrown about the garden and stamped on; even the burning Scotch Bonnets had been mashed to into a paste of red veins. The lettuce was shredded before its prime. The peas had their stems snapped, severing the flow of nutrients to their burgeoning, crisp pods. Another week and they would have been ready. Now all his crops had been destroyed in some way. Broome had hoped to get through the coming winter with the reliance of wholesome vegetables, jarred as well as fresh, to help comfort him and subdue his bitter and depressing loneliness.

With the insects gone, Broome had pollinated the garden himself with an old pastry brush. He'd let the grass grow long. One- to save on fuel; Two- hopefully encourage wildlife back to his garden, of which he held little hope after all the time that had passed.

The vandal/vandals had also taken their aggression out on the greenhouse too, smashing every pane of glass out from the metal frame; a show of strength had been portrayed where they had attempted to bend the framework out of square from where it was fixed onto the concrete base. Now it resembled nothing more than an insect-like skeleton of a robot caught in a pose of death.

A tear welled up in each eye, before cascading down in rivulets through the aged crags on his face. He wiped them away, offering no more sorrow on the matter.

He had heard them last night, whilst curled up around himself in bed, too terrified to move in fear of drawing attention to himself; they sounded like a low wind. Moaning and howling in operatic unison with each other as they vandalised his treasured garden, murdering his beloved crops. Animals. They must be animals. There was no other answer for the matter. Feral or diseased. Or both.

He needed a gun to scare them off. Tonight he'd wait up for them should they come back and blast a few shots in their direction.

But where to get a gun? It would take a lot of effort in finding one. Maybe borrow one from a nearby farm? Fireworks maybe? Huh, but where from? Make some? Make your own. He needed a deterrent of some kind. Broome guessed that fencing off the garden wouldn't be an option, as it wouldn't deter them much. If they were set on ransacking his abode then a simple fence wouldn't hold much defence.

Why him?

Of all the people in world, why did it have to be him?

Because . . .

Grey clouds hovered with menace like blurring waiting aliens on the northern horizon, threatening to daub out the bright blue sky with their dirty, encompassing shade. Broome could feel the approaching pressure building in his ears and gnawing at his antique bones. He had maybe half an hour of good daylight left before the rains came. He checked the water barrels. Barrel 3 was only half full; he adjusted the guttering so that the third out his four barrels would be replenished by the approaching wash of rain. He'd gotten used to rain water now, he didn't even have to boil it anymore, saved him the trip to town anyways.

Broome sighed, shrugged and turned, shuffling toward the back door of his home, thinking that he'd have the last remnants of the dusty porridge for breakfast.

***

When the rain had finished its mid morning assault on the homestead, Broome pulled on a jacket, picked up a brick from the reclaimed pile in the front garden and climbed into his car and headed for town, down the bumpy dirt track that led his home to the outside world, the London red brick his passenger on the seat beside him.

Upon reaching the T-junction that butted up to the main road, he slipped a CD into the slot, humming to himself the first harmonic bars as *'Trouble in Mind'* by Brownie McGhee and Sonny Terry pleasantly seeped cheerily voiced melancholy from the speakers.

As he drove, Broome ran a leathery hand over his scalp and felt the emerging fuzz on his head, deciding that it was time for another trim. Every two weeks, despite the fact he proudly owned a full head of hair, Broome picked up an electric clipper and shaved off the emerging growth; it was easier that way. Less trouble in the morning, this wasn't because of what happened. Broome had always treated his hair like that since his teens, he guessed by not messing with it too much, he'd given his hair a longer life.

'I'm gonna lay, my head, on some cold, old railroad iron,' he sang mournfully, *'let that two nineteen, pacify my mind.'*

Broome had to drive a little further today for his needs. He'd already cleaned out the shops closest to his home of what he needed, so he'd have to travel further afar. Not as far as Abcastle, but Powton should suffice his needs. He daren't even venture into Lincoln; he didn't even want to imagine what horrors awaited his weary eyes. Stick to the small towns.

In front, the line of trees that overreached the road like a natural tunnel finally cleared, the supermarket slid into sight.

As he pulled in he noticed that the supermarket had a few vehicles parked sporadically in the car park, litter rolled around on the tarmac, confident weeds crept out from any available crack in the surface. The unkempt grass bank surrounding the supermarket had overgrown, creating a protective fringe that boozily swayed with the refreshing morning breeze. Grass hadn't died, for the unruly lawns were pollinated by the power of the wind. After he had gone, he figured grass would continue to flourish, eventually overtaking every viable corner of the earth.

Broome eyed the scene with a careful stare. Knowing that he was probably the only one left did nothing to deter his cautious nature. You had to be sure. There might be others. He backed up to the front window of the supermarket and turned off the engine, pocketing the keys. '*My Pencil Won't Write No More,*' by Bo Carter abruptly ended half way through the second chorus.

Broome noticed the fuel gauge was tickling the top of the red; he'd need to fill up soon enough. These little trips to and from nearby towns were starting to add up to an empty tank.

Eying up the main entrance, which was caged in by a probably locked roller door brought upon him a mild sense of disappointment. Broome didn't fancy venturing through the confined darkness of the warehouse, so he decided on the front window as the best point of entry.

He put a dust mask on, then tied a rag around to doubly protect, pulled on a pair of gloves then got out of the car, taking the brick with him. Over to his right, in the centre of a disabled parking bay, lay a dead crow, its unused wing brought back to life by the cooling wind. It hadn't truly rotted, it couldn't. Some biological restraint stopped it from doing so. There were no more flies, no maggots or earthworms to recycle the nutrition down back to the earth. The bird simply dried up, and rotted as slow and unnatural as possible. No bacteria had broken down the proteins. Broome had figured, back when he had seen the multitude of fresh looking bodies upon the streets of Lincoln that something was biologically amiss. They didn't rot normally, as if the usual procedure in which carcasses broke down was missing or redundant. They seemed preserved. Even the lowest forms of life had perished.

Except him.

Broome surveyed the desolate car park once more; ripped carrier bags acted as tumble weeds, jostling about in whirls and lonely circles. Empty drink cans rolled to and fro, creating tinny susurrations upon the tarmac, creating an eerie soundtrack of unease.

He was alone.

But he knew that already.

He hoped for this in a strange, misanthropic manner. Why wish for loneliness in a world like this one? For the fear that a new stranger might bring, what psychosis would a fellow survivor harbour.

Broome was relatively sane, he guessed. But what of his night-time vandals, clearly they held some form of derangement. He shivered at the thought of meeting them, trying his best to bury the fear.

Winding his arm back, he threw the brick at the front window of the supermarket, the glass blinked into a mosaic of ice-white diamonds. The brick fell and tumbled to the floor. Broome picked it up and threw it again, tearing a hole through the frozen white collage of glass, replacing it with a gaping black hole that the brick disappeared through, swallowed by the dark internal chasm of the supermarket.

Broome casually retrieved a garden rake from the boot of his car, and began to smash the shattered glass to the other side, creating a way in, a viable doorway to the other side.

He'd brought a head torch and a hand held one for back up illumination. He clicked both on, and stepped inside, his boots crunching down on the shattered sugar-like fragments. Outside he could hear the low, mournful howl of the wind. The weather was changing; he was merely in the midst of a reprieve from the rain. A storm was brewing yet again, Broome wasn't too much of a fan of the rain as it kept him inside when he wanted to bask in the ever-healing sunshine, he wasn't looking forward to winter at all, the coming one even more so. His olden bones pained in protest at the inclement weather, he could always feel it coming before the sky told him so.

Broome turned his back to the light and headed into the dark cave of the unwelcoming store. Finding an abandoned trolley, he pushed it with an alarming squeak down the first aisle.

A stench of rotting vegetables flooded his nostrils, a musky, eye watering odour that did nothing but offend the senses. He passed the dairy aisle as he made his search, the shelves fully stocked with rancid milk, curdling into an inedible cheese in the mould of their plastic containers. Some had burst with the build-up of gases, creating a foul stench that mercilessly permeated his olfactory senses.

Broome was thankful that the aisles were free of any bodies. It seemed that people didn't come to supermarkets to die. Most stayed in the comfort of their homes, or died in the crowded, hellish wards of hospitals. Like Jessica. Like all his family.

He wondered if this place had a pharmacy as well; he needed tablets for the heart attack he had three years ago. The last time he'd officially picked up his rations of Rampiril, Simvastatin and Atenolol had been over a year ago now, when the world started to fall apart around him and countries died one after another, Broome had made his pills last for the six weeks he refused to leave the house. Eventually he left the confines of his shell and ventured into the world where he plundered the first pharmacy he found, relieving it of all heart medication. He had to ration that supply too, now he'd spent the past month with no medication is his system what so ever, so finding a fresh stash of tablets was pretty high on his list. He'd watched his diet, eating well and avoiding cholesterol-laden foods as much as he could. Broome raised his head torch and read the sign that labelled the aisle.

Home and Garden.

Pushing the trolley down aisle 7, Broome began to search the shelves for seeds. He wasn't going to let vandals ruin his crop. He was here to replenish what had been lost in the night. They'd left the potatoes, as they'd been underground. If he could get the greenhouse fixed he still might grow a few toms so he grabbed the remaining packets from the shelf and slung them in the trolley. He needed strawberries, even though it was too late in the year to begin growing, still he took all the seed packets for next year's crop. Runner beans, parsnip and every variety of pepper he could find. It wasn't long before Broome had pretty much emptied the shelves of most of the seed packets in a gathering frenzy. Everything but flowers; the flowers had always been Jessica's department.

A tin hit the floor a few aisles over. Broome guessed it was a tin. It sounded like a tin; they had tins here, so by rationale, it must have been a tin. However, what was in the tin would forever remain a mystery. Broome froze; fingers clenched the handle of the trolley like the neck of a despised enemy, his knuckles drawing white. It had been loud, breaking the still silence as a gunshot would do so. Every hair jumped to attention, standing up straight, an army of follicle warriors ready to fight a keratin war. A river of sweat burst from his back, greasing the strain of adrenaline he felt invading his arteries.

An explosion.

Boom boom boom boom. Not John Lee Hooker or an approaching cannon friendly army. Just his heartbeat preparing to fight, flee or fuck. He prayed it wasn't anything, just the wind taking down a precariously balanced tin, stacked by some careless, spotty oik those few moons ago, now pushed from its delicate position by the influx of a freshening wind.

It must be.

Another clattered on the floor, the unreality of the situation made Broome jump a little out of his saggy skin. Broome rarely jumped at anything, he'd never had the chance. He held his fingers to his mouth to suppress a scream that clung to his throat like treacle.

Two more tins were removed from their designated place on the shelves and dropped deliberately on the tiled floor of the supermarket, the clatter echoing doubly this time. An animal had followed him in, a dog or fox or deer or something and was now investigating this new seam of a food source.

He was wrong.

Broome shivered.

He never shivered.

They're no other animals. Just him. Him and the grass, the full breeze, the unpolluted sun and the dark, dark, dark. The only things that differentiated the days from each other were him and the weather. Everything else was a constant. The loneliness was a constant; it couldn't even be measured any more. It was a bottomless sinkhole that he threw the days and nights into.

A waterfall of tins collapsed to the floor in a tinny, metallic clatter, a puddle of sweat escaped his worn and stretched skin. The urge to piss started to overtake him. Even the fluid in his body was trying it's best to abandon the situation and escape the supermarket.

A dilemma clouded up in Broome's head. Take the trolley or leave it. Someone or something was in here with him, even though he couldn't hear the direct presence of another mortal being, he was 100% sure that he wasn't alone. Even though he knew he was. He had to weigh up his chances of facing danger.

Broome decided to take the trolley. Take it as far as he could, then if anything came after him, he'd dump and run.

Pushing the trolley forward, a burning built up in his lungs; he'd forgotten to breathe. He gasped; annoyed at himself that he'd allowed the breath to resonate so loud. He stopped and took another, almost automatically holding his breath; again, he had to remind himself to keep breathing in order to not black out. A malignant tightness squeezed his chest.

Broome pushed forward again, the trolley squeaked, loud and proud as if to say *coo-eee! Here I am. Come and get me!*

He broke into a loping run, his ancient knees betraying him and refusing to let him travel at the youthful speed he imagined. The squeak chirping faster. More tins fell from the shelves, until it became a jarring waterfall of noise. Battered tins rolled out from the affected aisle. Then the aisle next to it. Amongst the cacophony, the smash of glass, as jars joined the assault on the floor.

It wasn't the wind, Broome thought as he absent-mindedly crashed the trolley into the low frame of the smashed window. With the speed he was going, he torpedoed over the top of the trolley, then tipped off the front left hand side, falling down hard, his elbow smacked into the concrete outside firing a lightning bolt of pain brighter than the sky through his entire body. The trolley tipped over with him. Tins started to hit the trolley with a rattling smash. He looked back into the gloom of the supermarket and saw nothing but tins and jars cascading themselves from the shelves. Because of the gloom he couldn't make out who was causing the disturbance. Pushing himself raggedly to his feet, Broome left the seeds in fear for his own life, got in the car, and drove away with an impatient squeal and the boot still gaping open. '*My Pencil Won't Write No More*' started up, continuing the last verse of the song. The spare torch he'd brought now missing from his person had been dropped in the madness of the moment. Broome left the supermarket scared; his hands quaking as if overnight he'd developed a severe case of Parkinson's. He daren't look back. He headed up the hill of Browswater Road, towards the cemetery. 'Gallows Pole' by the late, great Odetta began to boldly blast forth its tale of desperation and depression, the next track on the mix CD that Broome had made for his wife. He liked the old tunes; they meant much more to him than the drivel they used to play on the radio.

***

'Who are they?' he asked Jessica, who wasn't there, 'or what are they?'

Like the supermarket, the grass was long and unkempt; dandelions grew tall, but the nettles were sunk in a depressive state, not as adept at pollinating as their Lion's Tooth cousins. No insects investigated the lonesome petals of their flowers. Broome had already figured, no pollination, no flowers next year. This would have distressed Jessica greatly, but she wasn't around to weep. It was just him.

'Tell me now, or tell me in a dream, who were they?'

Jessica didn't answer. She wasn't even here, in body or spirit. Broome didn't know where to even to begin to look. What was left of her could be anywhere. A secret urge, a definite humane frustration that willed him to plunder and search every hospital in a fifty mile radius, hell a hundred miles, just to take her mortal remains and bury them here in the plots they had chosen together, on a high hill that overlooked the town that they had both been born in, grew up, met, married, lived and died in. She was out there somewhere, in truth rotting away on a hospital bed or a place less respectful than this all too peaceful shade.

He had accepted her death as just, he only wanted to lay her to rest, her final spot of sleep. Well supposed to be, if things panned out the way they should've. But they didn't. Not for anybody. Not even him, yet the world was his for the taking. He didn't want it, Broome wanted to bury his wife, like they had both planned. But nobody could have planned what happened, and if they did, they were very sick minded indeed.

Broome talked a while before tiring, speaking of his restless days and insomnia buzzing nights. He told her of the vandals and the crashing tins in the supermarket and what he planned to grow next year, even though that seemed like a faraway dream at this particular moment in time. He wanted to have a go at sweet potatoes this time round.

Broome sighed. Jessica wasn't here, she wasn't anywhere because she was dead; a lump of rotten coal in his vacuous heart told him that, it was the truth. She was in a feverish coma when he last saw her. The paramedics loading her frail near-corpse into the back of the ambulance that was parked on their drive in the snow swept depths of winter. Nine months ago now. Winter was coming round again. He wasn't looking forward to it.

In a frail and flimsy theory of spirituality, the majority of Jessica's spirit, if it could even be measured, should she be listening and should she hear him, would be at their home. In truth they had only been up to this patch of grass once, when they'd viewed and put down a deposit over three years ago now, to reserve this serene pitch to a vista for themselves. He always imagined that they'd die together, heading off to bed one night after an Ovaltine spiked with sweet rum, and not wake in the morning. Comforting arms laced together in a romantic tangle, the warmth leaving their bodies as their souls departed bound tightly as one.

In the very least they could have died days, weeks or months apart. But fate was selfish, and it kept him on as the lone caretaker of the world, the gulf of time ever expanding their time apart, but time was nothing but a brief blink compared to the vast, empty chasm that had replaced his heart when Jessica was lifted into the ambulance and taken away for good.

Suicide had been an option, but he once read that those who commit suicide don't get into heaven. Now Broome wasn't exactly a god fearing man, but with a possibility of an eternity without seeing his Jessica again, he wasn't taking any chances what-so-ever. He'd live a pious life, busying himself in his garden until fate stole him away from this earthly bounding. If he even contemplated suicide or made preparation to do so, he knew Jessica would never forgive him, and that would be another sweet soul damned as well as his own. He had his children to think of, his grandchildren as well. Would he see them on the other side? He wanted to. But death had to be natural in order to get a ticket to the further station of reality he so desired. He had more to gain in believing in the afterlife than dismissing it as bunkum. The way for him to go would have been by natural causes. No cars would knock him over, no mugger would stab him for his pension, and no planes were dropping out of the sky towards him. The only way Broome was leaving was by his body giving up, not his soul.

Broome sighed once again and sloped off to his car, treading carefully around the gravestones, weary of the at-peace dead. Unaware that despite his loneliness and forced solitude he was being watched from afar; a blackened spot, the cool cavern of a chapel, swathed in darkness, sheltered from the still bright grey daylight, angry, ashy eyes burned upon him.

***

Broome got home, and boiled the kettle for green tea. He hadn't drunk it before the world tipped sideways and everyone fell off but him, but Jessica had. So now he did, because the sweet earthy aroma brought even sweeter memories of her. He'd gotten used to it, even enjoying it more than his morning coffee. Coffee wasn't the same without real milk, and green tea didn't require such sought after ingredients to finish the product, just hot water and a bag, maybe spoonful of honey to take away the stringent earthy taste. Plus it was healthier, better for his heart as a whole.

Broome took his hot cup of tea outside to enjoy what was left of his garden. Leaving the tea on the low wall of the raised bed he had built himself from reclaimed bricks, he busied himself with clearing up the mess that the vandals had made; composting the decimated plants, trimming back what he thought could be saved and sweeping up the spilt soil. It was here he noticed that there were no footprints human or animal upon the scattered soil upon the patio. None at all, aside from his own.

He knew that it had rained last night, so he checked the muddy patches of the lawn; he found no evidence of trampling or disturbance. Broome took his cooled tea once he had finished his chores and leant against the raised fish pond, again a product of his own design and recycled materials. He gazed into the murky dead waters, the fish long dead from the disease, just after they took Jessica away, now buried peacefully at the bottom of his garden. Only green algae lived in the confines of the walled pond, the vibrant, natural green covered the polythene sides like a furry wall, truly making the place their own.

Broome pondered his day.

The Vandals.

The noises last night.

The supermarket.

Somebody else had survived. It was the only conclusion he could even begin to imagine.

An idea formed.

A scare tactic.

He was sure that they'd come back tonight, even if they didn't, he still wanted to be prepared. So he went into the garage and set to work collecting what he needed. Even though Broome didn't feel the need to wear a watch anymore, he guessed it was about three pm when it started to rain again. It didn't matter. Broome was ready and waiting, hours before they were due to turn up. He guessed that they'd come with the darkness.

They did.

***

Broome couldn't stomach much for his tea, a tin of beans, mopped up with the crust of some long stale, homemade bread. He needed more supplies first. Another supply run to a different town. Brigg maybe? They had a camping store there; he needed more Calor gas as well as batteries as he didn't like to rely on the generator too much. Brigg was a little bigger than the other villages and he hadn't ventured that far yet.

Anywhere but Lincoln.

He'd tried searching after the plague had first decimated the world. He hadn't seen a soul for a week and decided to head out and search for any survivors. No one was talking on the radio so Broome realised he'd have to find somebody.

Anybody.

The loneliness was excruciating, he even made himself jump a few times when he spoke aloud to himself. His ears were used to the chatter of human kinship. The silence was unnerving.

He had taken the car to Lincoln, stopping on the last roundabout before entering the city. He got out of his car, and sniffed. The smell was horrendous; the city had a population of close to 100,000. Judging from the vile vapour that tinged the air, Broome guessed they were all dead.

Nevertheless, Broome climbed back into his car and drove into the city. A minute passed and he wished he hadn't. Death was everywhere, bodies in the road, people rotting behind the wheels of their cars, animals, children, everyone.

Staring faces stretched with the fixed gawp of death.

Broome span the car at the next roundabout and headed home, immediately washing himself down on the patio with shampoo and cold water to remove the stench. Yet somehow it remained in his mind, festering away, the odour resurfacing whenever he considered returning to the city.

Their staring, hollow sockets still haunted him.

That was why he preferred living in the country, in the open air the stench of life passed was diluted by the vast empty spaces. He could tolerate the little towns and villages, but the cities were a no go.

No one knew what the plague, or virus as the news reported it at first, was. They first suspected that it was terrorist built, as it didn't respond to any known treatment. Some suggested that Bird flu and Swine flu had combined forces. The ever sick minded media, in its delivery of the news, jokingly referred to it as Flying Pig Flu. The jokes soon stopped when the television went off the air and newspapers stopped appearing in shops.

Rumours were abound that it originated in Africa, the distinct possibility that AIDS had finally become airborne manifested itself with the death of millions in a week. Then billions by the end of the overly eventful month . . .

Jessica was propped up in bed, her face pale, wan and seeping with a sickly sweat. The TV had said to keep loved ones quarantined. How could you do that when they couldn't even walk, let alone look after themselves Broome had thought.

He took her some soup, knowing full well she wouldn't eat it. He had to try to make an effort. It made him feel better at least. To do nothing to aid a loved one was pure hell.

'I'm fine,' Jessica pleaded, 'I'm not hungry that's all.'

'Please eat something, I'm worried about you. I've heard a few people in town are ill as well . . .'

'Charles, darling, don't worry it's only a bug going round. It's not the end of the world.'

Later that evening, Jessica started throwing up blood. He called an ambulance. After a fretful night, it arrived the next morning, the dark and hollow eyed paramedics took a comatose Jessica away, while Broome screamed blue murder at them for being late, they didn't wait for him to follow in the car. Seeing as his rage had taken over, he forgot to ask where they were taking her, thus he never saw Jessica again, not for trying. But then the phones went out and the TV showed nothing but blank screens, automatic technical error messages or eerie shots of empty studios devoid of human habitation. Radio was next. They didn't possess internet access so that wasn't a worry to be had.

Before the world went kaput, he tried calling Greg, his eldest son, then Guy his second youngest and finally, Sammy, his daughter. Of course, he got no answer; he tried their mobiles, which wouldn't even connect. He knew that his grandchildren possessed mobiles, but he knew none of the numbers. He was left alone in the world not knowing their fates.

The last human he had contact with was an army lorry that drove through the village whilst he was trying to break into the local Co-op. A young soldier was behind the wheel, a feverish worry marked his face. He didn't even consider Broome with the brick in his hand. He drove straight down the high street with the engine roaring. Again, Broome never knew what his fate had held . . .

Broome awoke with a start, gasping and struggling for breath as if he'd forgotten how to breathe. In his ears, the army truck rolled past him and the soon-to-be broken window of the Co-op in the bitterly nostalgic dreamland.

Silence hummed, loud and all together deafening his old ears; maybe it was tinnitus, maybe it was prolonged isolation from any other beings.

Broome was alone in the dark.

He caught his breath and waited.

Reaching down from his position in the comfy chair by the back patio, he searched with blind fingers, checking the battery by his feet, and the cable that had fallen from his sleepy grasp. Thankfully, he hadn't let it fall upon the primed terminals. A bizarre sense of patience prevented him from flicking on a torch and exposing himself, even though he knew that they knew he was here.

Waiting.

Broome stole a gaze outside, peering round the curtain to peek upon the nothingness that was once his beloved back garden. Cloud had covered any shadows; he could see nothing but the night. Outside, the sun had bid its burning bright farewell and let darkness cloak the earth. An unnatural inkiness that former dwellers of the civilised world had ceased to fully experience before the world turned itself off. It would have been a good night for stars had it not been for the cloud cover.

The Impossible Black.

The more he stared at it, the more he could see colours bleeding out from the challenging deep palate of obsidian; real or imaginary, a definite presence pulsed beneath the shadowed veil, pushing it towards him as if whatever was out there passed by close to this world. He felt like he was missing an important point or perhaps a key to unlock the vision that wanted to burst out in front of his eyes. The darkness was a galvanised sheet that hid them from him. He concentrated and peered further in; he could see low laying stars out in the gloom, then immediately dismissed the notion. There was low cloud out there tonight; he couldn't see any stars, some looked bunched together, almost like . . . eyes.

A sea of grey eyes stared back at him, thousands blinking out from the black haze. It must be his isolated imagination playing cruel tricks on him, the more he concentrated on a set of eyes, they quickly faded into the black, as he flicked his gaze to another pair, they too melted away. He wanted to see one. Just one of the bastards.

Growing impatient, he retrieved from his pocket a slim piece of plastic. An MP3 player that his daughter had bought for him two birthdays back, already preloaded with all his favourite blues staples. 5000 of them, and with room for more. Sammy had shown him how to navigate the simple menu. From then on, whenever he took a walk, he would always have his music with him. He wanted music. The silence grated on him, shredding away strips of his soul and lust for life. He wanted music to fill his world with something.

Broome thumbed the switch, the screen glowed green to life, automatically the last song played; '*Wade in the Water*' by The Charioteers, resonating a tinny, mournful, though almost derelict harmony from the bud like speakers still in his hand.

Broome was seconds away from placing the left bud into place in his ear when he stopped.

A creak came from upstairs, a foot depressed on a warped floorboard.

Broome paused, stalled his breath and waited.

Another creak, this came from the front of the house; loud and deliberate almost, yet it carried no weight, he couldn't hear the step or the planting of a foot, the impression of a floorboard creaking guiltily under pressure.

Every grey hair upon his person, prickled with fearful anticipation, a thick, almost syrup like sweat sprouted like escaping slugs down his back. Despite his many layers, Broome shivered.

Another deliberate footfall pressed down hard, this time above his head. Broome looked up, as if expecting to see some kind of reasoning on this side of the room.

They were in the house.

Whoever vandalised his garden was in the house with him.

But it was impossible as he'd locked every window and door, compulsively and obsessively checking each handle three times with a secure, mind-easing tug.

Impossible.

Another creak. This time it was louder, this time it sounded as though a hundred different people had shifted weight at the exact same moment.

Moonlight broke through the thick black covering of sky, enlightening the garden from the lawn to the pond and partially the patio.

Broome saw them, partial figures in the gloom, but still, they hadn't been there before.

Lots.

Panic set in, a defensive measure took over him. Fight or flight, yet reasoning told him to do both. He leant forward and kissed the jump leads to the battery terminal, a spark jumped outwards that shocked his dark adjusted eyes. An electrical charge shot through the jump lead, seemingly at the speed of light, into the cable that Broome had run out of the window, across the patio and into the hidden bucket of petrol beside the tomato plants.

Broome had meant it as a shock tactic, and as the fireball punched upwards into the midnight sky, the only person that it had shocked was him.

He saw more of them, staring at him with empty grey eyes; the fire illuminated them, as did the moon. The back garden was full of thin, ash-like forms.

One of the shadowed trespassers kicked out at the erupting bucket, it tipped and burning hot fuel spread down the patio, vaporising what was left of his garden.

He'd destroyed it himself.

Seeing the flames spread towards the house, Broome dropped the jump lead and ran. Upstairs the creaking became more of a constant groan, akin to an old ship, doomed against the jagged, shallow rocks.

He daren't venture upstairs; neither did he wish to meet the strangers that waited outside for his eventual company.

They had a cupboard with a key in the utility room, stumbling in the darkness, this was Broome's destination, and knowing his house well, in darkness as well as light, he found his way there, unlocking the cupboard just as an orchestra of hands beat down upon every window pane that the house possessed. A frantic drumming that seemed to mock his fear.

Whatever meagre items remained in the cupboard, Broome reached in and pulled them out with a sweeping arm, clearing a space for himself, then he stepped into the further gloom of the cupboard, locked the door from the inside, then crouched down low, burying his head in his hands and wept.

They were on the roof now, whoever they were, their numbers had allowed them to occupy the roof, for now he could hear roof tiles being thrown down onto the driveway and patio below. He could hear some puncturing the upstairs ceiling.

I hope they hit one of their own! Broome prayed with bitter vehemence.

All at once, the crashing, creaking and banging ceased, almost convincing Broome that it was all part of his lonely imagination.

When he concentrated, he could still hear the fire that he had caused, crackling happy and ever-hungry outside.

A sigh of final relief escaped his lungs, his shoulders sunk as the stress melted away, relieved that the ordeal was over. Maybe he'd dreamt it all . . .

The cupboard door rattled violently and didn't stop. Broome felt his body automatically press itself into the wall. He cowered, his breath quickened and that disgusting sweat heaped back across his skin. It had become a machine like rattle now, inhuman; no mortal could so violently shake a door.

He still had the MP3 player in his hand. Broome slipped the ear buds in and turned the volume up as high as it would technically allow. He wanted the last thing he heard to be a song he loved. Not the thumping of his own demise.

'*Baby Please Don't Go*' by Big Bill Broonzy, blasted out a pleading demand from the speakers, Broome revelled in the sweet escape it offered.

He could still sense the rattling of the cupboard door as a rapid vibration close to his head. He rightly imagined fingers seeping like venomous ink through the door jamb and pulling at the flimsy door from the inside. A crack became audible over the line.

'*. . . you know I love you so, Baby please don't go. . .*'

Broome felt a gust of movement across his face, then a punch shocked his face into tightening up, another bore down, hitting his arm this time. Before he could think, another hit his leg, then it came down like a battering rain. Soft, feeble punches impacting with every area of his exposed body. Soon it became a constant drum. Broome tried to scream as Big Bill stopped singing. They'd torn the ear phones from him. Now Broome heard himself scream a deathly high pitch falsetto.

The violence was immeasurable, Broome tried to look up at his attackers, but the gloom betrayed him a glance of their faces. He could feel them, yet they remained forever invisible to him.

He ducked his head to shield himself from the downpour of blows, immediately he felt a presence on his cheek, then the other, then his eyelids. Then beneath them as a stranger's fingers broggled their way in, violently pulling his eyes open as wide as they would go. He felt someone scream into his face, yet it felt impotent, devoid of any physical power or sound, but somehow he still felt its effect upon his face. Not breath, but a sixth sense of the close electricity of another being before him.

He had an image in his mind of the screamer's mouth; rotten teeth that more resembled festering wooden pegs than human dentures. Somehow, by a strange psychic connection he knew this to be the truth. Broome screamed back and into himself, a torturous gurgle that hurt his throat.

He retreated into his mind, burning out his brain with trailers of happy thoughts, times past and dead yet still all too sweet to him. Birthdays, Christmas with the family, the party he had when he retired with all his friends and family gathered round him, smiles bursting with obscene joy.

Somehow, he smiled defiantly against the punches. They didn't like that, so increased their assault tenfold.

Broom went further inside, to sexual pleasures with Jessica, images of her youthful body after they got married, she bent, she arched and they accepted each other. Broome smiled again, despite the violence that was inflicted upon him in the real world.

Keep thinking of Jess. The good and the fun times; the 'baby making practice' as she so called it. One of the best private pleasures a loving couple can keep from the world and only share with each other.

Somehow Broome managed to transcend so deeply, that he soon forgot all about the beating and slipped into a dreamlike state, a place where not even they could get him.

**

He'd dreamt of birds tweeting to wake himself up from his forced slumber. As he cracked open his eyes, Broome could make out familiar objects, yet they seemed strange from this angle. It was the kitchen, I've never seen it from down here, he thought.

Confusion bled from his mind and Broome crawled out of the cupboard with a new set of aches upon him. Feeling bruised, he pulled up his sleeve, not a single violent blemish marked his skin, yet he felt like he'd been thrown from a high speed moving car and down a mountainside.

A musty overpowering vileness hit his senses, a weird clinging sensation stuck to his crotch.

He'd pissed himself.

From the fear perhaps? Or had his bladder and kidneys given up during the psychic beating?

Had he passed out? Was he knocked unconscious? Did last night really happen?

Broome made his way through the kitchen. It had become a mess from the usual orderly nature that he possessed over it. Pots and pans had been thrown about the floor; some even had dents in the polished steel from impacts with the edging of the worktop. Every jar had been smashed, every tin popped open and smeared over the walls. Any food left was now inedible. Broome continued outside through the smashed glass of the patio doors and into the garden.

The patio was charred black from the fire, yet it had a washed appearance like volcanic ash upon a beach. He looked over to his water butts; each had melted from the flames, now a depressive, green and gloopy mess that resembled the remnants of giant candles

All the windows were smashed, he could see that his clothes had all been torn from the wardrobes, a few refugee shirts clung to the smashed glass of the bedroom window, cuffs waving hello and goodbye in the wind.

Broome kicked something at his feet; his beloved MP3 player, the screen smashed, the earphones missing, presumed snapped. He sighed and went back inside.

He noticed the message first.

It was written in a ragged smear of bean juice and ketchup, maybe meant to look like blood.

He knew what it meant. Arbour was a place, a fishing pond to be precise, across the way, maybe a mile or so down the road. He'd fished it a few times, but never had much luck so he went further afield.

Beneath the ominous message was an unbroken bottle of whisky and a large packet of pills, upon approaching closer he realised they were sleeping tablets. Jessica's to be precise, from a few years back now, so they were probably out of date. Dr Broome prescribed a foot massage instead, which soon melted his love's stresses away. The tablets had remained unopened in the medicine cupboard, and out of sight and mind. Until now.

The whisky was a large, two litre bottle of Famous Grouse, that he'd gotten from a now long deceased friend a few years back. Broome rarely touched the stuff and had saved it for a special occasion which had never come. Again the bottle had been stashed away, out of sight, out of mind. Until now.

It was a clear message. He knew who had written it. But there had been more than one. Who, or whatever had been in the house last night, wanted him to overdose and kill himself. He guessed somewhere at the Arbour fish pond.

Well if that was what they wanted . . .

Broome washed himself down with a flannel and what water he could find, searched through the wreckage of his life for some half decent clothes, then picked up the pills and whisky and took a meandering walk down the road towards the Arbour Ponds.

***

It was a little wooden platform that fishermen used to throw their lines off, offering more security than a wet bank and a little closer to the water, enabling them to be nearer to their prospective catch.

Two deck chairs sat on the end.

Either someone had left them there, or somebody had put them there. Broome didn't know which; in fact he didn't care, but he took it as a sign, and sat down in the one to the right, easing his aching form in gently, then he rested his head back and dozed, letting the nuzzling sun warm his cheeks, the pills waited in his pocket, the whisky warmed on his lap.

Basking, Broome let the day pass around him, erasing all worrying thoughts from his mind; he kept it a black slate. At this moment he didn't want to think about anything. He simply wanted to be. Exist and breathe, savouring every breath.

He let noon pass whilst he simply said and did nothing. He waited. He had no instruction other than to come here to this even lonelier brief expanse of water. So he did just that, letting the hours waste away, time became like sand through his fingers, his to waste where he so wanted.

He slept a little, nods and snoozes every so often. He was a patient man, yet he had realised why he was here. The figment of time pressed on.

As sundown approached he opened the whisky, and took a sip, then he took a pill from the box and politely slipped it onto his tongue. He took another sip of whisky.

He rarely drank nowadays. To drink alone would mean admitting he was lonely. Which he was.

He repeated this process, nibbling away at the bottle.

It took a few hours, but the elated buzz he got off the cocktail made him smile dopily, a free string of escaping dribble slimed down from his mouth. Clumsily he wiped it off.

The moon made itself known, peeking over the trees at the same time as the goodbye sun.

Goodbye sun, Broome waved drunkenly, bidding farewell to the celestial orb that had warmed him his entire life. Time to go. Time flies. Onwards.

He'd started to nod his head a little as he started on the second packet of pills. As he popped the first one out and pressed it firmly onto his tongue, he saw the first one.

Across the pond, beneath the darkened shade of a crab apple tree stood a mere wisp of smoke in the vague form of a man. He was staring at Broome with those empty grey eyes.

He felt more eyes burrowing into the back of him. Broome turned, another stood up the bank. This one was clearer this time but a different shape; a younger man or maybe a woman. She was smaller.

Every time Broome moved his head, shifted his eyes or blinked, a new form appeared, each a figment of arranged ash, there and not there, a coincidence of light at most.

Broome watched for an hour, enjoying the show lit by the fat, rising moon. The brighter the moon became, the more of an eerie audience he got. The sky was clear tonight, a billion stars winked at him from the incredible depths of the obsidian sea. Broome smiled giddily; he popped another pill in his mouth and took another swig of whisky, making his stomach growl and his heart glow a warming fire. He felt tired, but was too engaged with his emerging audience. Some of the wisps even stood on the still pond water, offering no reflections. None of them moved. They simply stared at him with their empty grey eyes that illuminated brighter as the night closed in darker.

Broome dropped the empty bottle; it clinked and rolled with a plopping splash off the deck and into the pond. A slowly increasing ripple pulsed out across the pond. Broome watched and waited, expecting the apparitions to bob and sway with the wake on the water. They didn't. They remained completely still, free of any physical anchorage to this realm, unaffected by the conditions that surrounded them. More of them faded in. Broome wasn't scared. He was drunk, he had no need to be scared, he didn't have the capacity.

He finished off the last five sleeping pills, swallowing them hard and dry. He wondered if the drugs and booze had caused these figments that stood so ethereally before him. Then he removed all doubt as he remembered what had happened last night. The punches seemed real. He hadn't trashed his own house. It had been them. It must have been.

He was alone, not crazy. But then, who could tell him otherwise.

The booze cancelled out the fear, the pills gave him an edge of giddiness that elated him strangely, took him beyond the situation. Outwards.

He laughed to himself and no one else. They couldn't hurt him. They hadn't the capacity to cause him any harm. They'd tried and failed sorely. That's what they wanted of him. They wanted him gone. Hence the pills and booze. An invitation to suicide. Well suicide would be the last thing he ever did, he reasoned giddily.

But Broome was here for another reason.

A voice made him jump, it seemed like a whisper, yet he could hear it loud and clear, akin to watching a foreign television channel then suddenly and inexplicably being able to understand the language.

'Hello Charlie.'

'Evening Jess, it's been a while,' Broome turned his groggy, booze dampened head. His wife was sat in the deck chair beside him as clear as day. The moon illuminated her beautiful, ageless form. Emitting a sense of youth, yet she looked as gorgeous as all her years put together. Every fantastic quality about was personified by this angel before him, an anthology of all her most stunning moments compiled into a single, beaming being. She looked like the day she'd left him, but wrinkle free and not crippled over with disease. The light that illuminated her came not from the moon high above, but from this wondrous vision of his wife beside him.

'I recognised your writing. That's why I came.'

'It was the only way I could get through to you. I've had a lot of interference,' she smiled and gestured to the massive crowd. Broome couldn't even count the eyes that glared at him. Thousands, yet he had a sense that they queued for miles in the deft moonlight.

'Why me, why can't they let me be?'

'They're angry that you were left behind. To them, you're a symbol of what they all once had.'

'They're jealous of me?'

'You have the world to yourself, why wouldn't they be jealous?' Jess smiled; her teeth were white and perfect, not a blemish marked her. For some reason, Broome couldn't concentrate on what she was wearing, it didn't matter anyway.

A headache formed in the centre of his brain. Broome ignored it; he wanted to talk more. Lots even.

'I'm sorry I lost you Jess. I wanted to look for you.'

'I know. There are some things in this world you can't control. You may not want to, but you have to accept these things. It all pans out in the end. Everything does There's a greater plan at work here.'

A brief tickle of pain flowed down his left hand side as a butterflies danced in his veins. Again Broome ignored it. He had Jess back and that was all that mattered. A warm, rising rush echoed through his body like a shiver, physically manifesting itself in a full body tremor, he kept control though, keeping his loving gaze fixed upon Jess.

'How can I trust you?' he asked, rubbing his shoulder.

'You don't have much choice. I know where you're going Charlie. You're coming with me. But first we have plans for you. Big plans that'll change the world.'

'Huh?'

The tingling tickle vanished. A feeling akin to his ears popping filled his entire body. Broome closed his eyes then felt an all enclosing blanket fall around him. He felt the surging rush of water in his ears then looked back at his glowing wife.

'You're supposed to die today. Here to be precise. All the others wanted you gone. They were jealous, it was understandable, but a lot of us have bigger plans.'

'I'm not following you,' Broome asked quizzically. The wet feeling around his head faded, an encompassing chill prevailed.

Jessica pointed to the water. He followed the line that her finger cast out to the pond.

He was looking at himself. Well, his back to be precise. One of the Ashen men stood hovering an inch above his shoulders as he floated face down in the water, riding him like a corpse surfboard.

'Am I . . . gone?'

Jess nodded, 'Easy as that. I made it as painless as I could with the pills and whisky. It was time I'm afraid. I knew you were lonely. You had to go sometime.'

Broome nodded along with her. He agreed, whether he liked it or not. Secretly he was pleased. He had Jess to talk to now, which was all he wanted. He gave the world up for her.

'Where will I go?'

'With me, I have a garden, with sun every day and rain at night. The soil is fine and moves like oil between my fingers. It's paradise. You can taste the nectar in the air. I grow every flower that's ever bloomed . . .'

'I mean, I died by my own hand. Don't I go . . . y'know . . . down?'

'You mean Hell?' She said it as if it was a normal place. Like Hull.

Broome nodded, his face worried at a fate worse than death.

'I made an agreement. We needed you gone for things to change. You were anchoring us all to this place. We all need to move on and we couldn't. We're all connected to this place.'

'So . . .?'

'What happened on earth, the virus I mean; it was beyond the control of this side. We couldn't do anything. Like I said, sometimes you just have to let things be. You can't control everything. What happened just happened.'

'What's this agreement?'

'Your body for your soul. You sacrificed yourself for the good of the earth. It's honourable, believe me.'

'I still don't understand.'

'This pond, your body. You were immune to the virus. Fate's Ace in the pack, a contingency method. You are the Ark. Whatever potential life that is left on this earth is still inside your body.' Jess tapped a finger on his chest. 'From this pond, life will flourish once again. They tell me it's happened before, many a time. Life has to come from somewhere,' Jess said cryptically.

'Am I . . . life?'

'You will be. It'll be slow, but we'll get there. We can watch. Forever. It'll be good. The world is our garden. Time doesn't matter much anymore. Time is a figment of the imagination, a human device to count days and seasons and the circling stars. We'll see sorrow and joy. In the grand scheme of things there's little difference between the two.'

Broome nodded, casually accepting the situation for what it was. He was the carrier of future generations. It might be only the bacteria which somehow had survived extinction inside his mortal form, but it was the start of something at least. Progress would be slow, but all progress is slow relatively.

Somehow, Broome felt his wife's hand slip into his. It was warm, like sunlight on his skin. She was real now, now that he was in her world.

He looked around the pond. The ashy figures had faded away. They'd got their man. They were happy, it had taken time, but he'd died for the better. They all were happy.

'We can go now,' Jessie said.

And they did. Upwards and outwards into the ether and the far twinkling and burning stars from where they came; now close enough to touch from the deep heavens and the numerous skies beyond.

The mortal vessel that once carried Charles Broome floated with a sense of morbid peace across Arbour Pond. Soon the sun would rise as it had always to knowledge and would continue with reason, warming his corpse, slowly releasing the lively bacteria and amino acids within into the expanse of the pond which would become their nursery, their new universe. It would take time, as all good things do. But life would flourish again.

As it always had, and always would.

TOP OF THE ʜEAP

Menu
Files
Recordings- (13)

It was Genaro and Miguel who found this place, only 10 miles from the city as well, so of course they told the boss, Alphonse Marcone, who you must have heard of. Pretty soon after he visited he'd send us stickmen out here to dispose of the unwanted. Now here I am. I want to record this as I'm bored and I don't know how long my battery will last

I have my driver's license in my wallet along with five hundred dollars or so in cash, so I'll be identified, a few cigarettes, my Zippo, my flick knife and my Glock. And my Blackberry, which thanks to God I charged this morning. No signal mind, at least I can tell you this.

Christ Jesus it stinks.

Cool though.

Miguel and Antonio and I, Ernesto Blanco, the poor soul whose words you hear, came out here with a young Pendejo named Pablo, a skinny little runt if I ever saw one. He cut some powder, too much, took the profit and didn't share. Marcone didn't take too kindly to this and put a price on his head.

Now, Marcone doesn't just silence those who disappoint him, nor does he bury them. He doesn't want the family to find the body; he wants everyone they know to suffer. He likes people to vanish from the face of the earth when they piss him off. Rival dealers, Federales, prison wardens and guards, the families of these aren't even out of bounds. You take a man's wife, tell him she's dead, dropped down some hole in the middle of nowhere, if he doesn't tell you where the goods are, his kids will be next. If he does tell you, you'll tell him where his wife's body is. We never did, but it got the job done, and no body, no evidence.

It stinks like hell down here. I'd take a picture, but if you're hearing this then you'll already know what I'm talking about. Somewhere between rotting meat and a shitty Culero. Every so often I gag because of the build-up of gas.

I'm off track.

The three of us brought this kid out here, naturally we had him cuffed, didn't want him hitting out at us. We'd already beat him up a bit, broken nose, cut off his little fingers. So he was sullen and quiet as most people are when they're about to be executed. We got to the hole, I've been here maybe twenty thirty times, usually we stand them on the edge then pop a bullet in their heads. Down they fall, gone for good. It's quiet round the entrance, surrounded by trees and in the middle of nowhere, so no one hears gunshots round here. There are farms so no one cares so much. They'll think it's just a farmer scaring off wild dogs.

Miguel was feeling experimental, brought his new shotgun along, says he's never shot anyone with a shotgun before and says that he'd like to see it. The little kid, Pablo, by now he's crying his eyes out, he'd pissed his pants and was pleading with us to change our minds. Miguel laughed in that demented way of his and shot him in the chest. None of us jumped. After a life of living with gunshots, you become accustomed to the suddenness of the blast. Pablo vanished in a blur, a misty cloud of blood remained for a second or two before settling on the ground. Once the blast of the shotgun stopped echoing in our ears we listened for a thud or impact or anything. We heard nothing.

Then Miguel turned the shotgun to me, told me to step to the edge of the hole, I thought he was joking, but his stone face told me otherwise. I edged over to the hole and peered into the hungry blackness below. He told me that he knew what I'd been up to with Liliana, Marcone's wife. Said that Marcone knew too, he said that I should disappear too. Said that I should be made to suffer. I laughed, at least trying to break the tension. I turned to Antonio, one of my oldest friends, his face told the same story as Miguel.

I begged them to reconsider, reminding them that I have a wife and young child, consider Elva, my baby daughter and my wife, Rosalita. Miguel said that they would be taken care of, and then fired the shotgun at my feet. The explosion of dust spat up into my face. This time I jumped, but I held my ground. Miguel fired twice more in quick succession, either side of me and then closer to my feet. This time I fell, but not before calling them both cara de conas and pair of jotos.

The dust I kicked up fell with me, invading my eyes, blinding me from the dark. I held out a hand as I fell, scraping it along a jutting rock. I hit, I rolled, my leg smashed into something hard and ever so brief, the pain lighting up the darkness as I screamed myself hoarse. I rolled again, holding out my hand again to slow down. My fingers gripped at mud and stone, at my speed I ripped out a few fingernails, waving goodbye to them in the gloom.

I stopped, my head kept rolling, even though I had free fallen for a few seconds. I was on my chest, breathing in dirt. I spat and cursed, my eardrums cleared from the shock. I could make out those two cabróns, with their fading laughter. Wet hit the back of my head and ran down my cheek and into my lips; I tasted a salty, bitter hotness, the steamy liquid somewhat soothing before my disgust. They were pissing on me. Urgency made me turn, the shooting agony made me scream. I felt down to my leg, somehow, I don't know how, but my right foot was now up near my hip. I screamed for a long time.

***

I always carry some painkillers with me, I get these terrible headaches, blinding flashes, but the tablets keep them in check. I reached into my jacket pocket and popped six dry into my mouth. Then I gritted my teeth until the pain subsided a little.

Of course the first thing I did was to try my phone. But no signal down here. It figures. I managed to turn on to my side so I was facing the wall of the shaft. I screamed at Miguel and Antonio for a while, but I knew that they'd left me, grinning like Maricons. If I ever see them again.

I spent some time looking at photos of Elva and Rosalita on my phone; I love that black and white one I took of us all together after Elva had been born. Christ I can smell her perfume; it's like she's here with me, I can only pray that she will offer me forgiveness. I was stupid to cheat on her with Marcone's skank of a muchacha Liliana. She was beautiful, on the outside only. Inside she was a whore of Satan himself. I wouldn't be surprised if it was her who told Marcone about us. She was the kind of woman who liked drama to surround her. She was a good fuck, that was all.

Rosalita must have called the Federales by now. On paper I'm a carpenter that works at one of Marcone's furniture factories. The cops will ask there and no one will know me. My life is one big sham.

***

Night falls, I can hear the insects on the surface, chirping and mating all through the night. I don't know if I have slept or not. With a scream or three I manage to turn on to my back, so I now face the stars at the end of the tunnel above. I must have fallen at least fifty feet. The shaft falls down at a steep gradient, and then it gets to the mass of bodies and levels out. It looks like a mineshaft that has partly collapsed from above. A thick dark timber lines the edge of the meeting point between the tunnel that heads off to nowhere and the shaft above. Definitely a mine. A lot of silver deposits round these parts. Well, used to be. The ground had long been raped dry and the companies had left leaving behind unemployment and a thousand sinking holes that swallowed up wandering animals and men who needed to disappear.

Curiosity gets the better of me and I take out my Zippo and lighter, the tiny flame seems gigantic before my eyes and it takes a while for my eyes to adjust to the gloom before me. Then I see faces. I recognize Pablo's yellow t-shirt; he's slumped over, thankfully facing away from me, a hollow mess of gore missing from his chest. More bodies, dark arms and bones sticking up from a mass on the floor where I sit, they stretch into the dark, many more beyond the reach of my lighter I'm sure. I'm sat on top of a woman I think, she's naked and her fleshy buttocks are my pillow, her arm has twisted up, now my head rest. I can't get away from them; my broken leg stops me crawling anywhere. If I had my legs still, maybe I could follow the mineshaft further, maybe find the original entrance. It's a thought, a painful one.

I turn off the Zippo.
I don't want to see anymore.
What a horrible place to be.
I cry.
I'll turn off the Blackberry to save the battery.
Then I scream at the stars for a while.
Hopefully I'll sleep further through this nightmare.

**

The harmonious tweeting of birds wakes me. I smile, hoping to roll over and see Rosa smiling at me, asking me what I want for breakfast. Do I want Huevos Rancheros or Pineapple Tamale Muffin if she's feeling sweet.

I open my eyes and the dead smile back with bare teeth. In the fresh, sparse daylight I can see the bodies beneath me. I want to reach out and touch their faces, close their beseeching eyes. I recognize a few of them. Some I don't, either through decomposition or the fact that I didn't dump them here. Marcone has a lot of guys and a lot of enemies, so a few strangers sit down here with me.

The thought of food rumbles my stomach, making it ache. I keep my eyes up, away from the bodies; I look up the throat of the shaft, towards daylight, towards hope. I chew my thumb nail.

I check my jacket pockets. I find some gum, happily popping a piece in my mouth, I chew for hours. Breakfast of Champions.

**

Around four o'clock it starts to rain heavily, it takes about half an hour for the water to really start to flow down here. I worry for a minute whether the tunnel will flood, then stop. What's the point? It may be the rainy season but it'll take a while for the tunnel to flood completely. I wonder. I hope it doesn't. I really want to see my daughter again.

I scrape a channel through the mud, forcing the falling water into my hands. I manage three handfuls of dirty water. It's cool and fresh so I don't mind. It pacifies my rolling stomach somewhat, making me happy. After the rain has stopped, fat earthworms start to fall from the walls. I grab one without thinking and pop the wriggling pink thing in my mouth. It squirms while I chew. It squirms down my throat as I swallow. It's like me now. I find a few more. I'm not in the least disgusted with myself, if anything I'm happy at my ingenuity. Again, it pacifies the hunger. I take six more painkillers, and hope to sleep for a few hours, I have ten more in this bottle, after that I have a full clip in the Glock if the pain becomes too unbearable. But that'll be my last resort.

***

I awake in darkness. The dead are speaking. I sit completely still, listening to their voices, caught fragments of a distant conversation in the next room, the next life. The harder I concentrate on the words the harder they become to understand. I must be hallucinating; maybe it's the worms.

I feel my twisted leg. It's bent the wrong way, the ankle up near the hip. Should I straighten it? I know it'll hurt so I won't bother. My cotton trousers have ridden up near my foot. The skin is whitish green. It doesn't even look real, more like dirty wax. Not much blood, though. A little near the knee, my only saving grace. A broken leg, sorry a snapped leg, the bottom half floating freely in the bent swollen sack that my leg has become. Every breath in and out makes it ache. I burn up every so often.

I look at the pictures on my phone for a while, staring for about an hour trying not to cry - as I need the moisture - and failing miserably. I watch as the battery drops down a bar. Two bars left. I'll turn the phone off.

Five more painkillers for supper, then I chew the ends of my fingers, cursing myself for keeping my nails short.

***

I had a visitor before sunset. It was Antonio. When he called down at first and I recognized his voice, a hateful instinct took over. I pulled out my pistol and fired a couple of shots up the throat of the mine hoping to Satan that I hit him. I should have saved my bullets, really. Antonio called for me to cease, throwing down a parcel. Goodwill he called it. I asked him why and reached over for the thrown parcel, wincing in the process. Couldn't he have used some string or something?

I pulled it closer to me, ripping into the brown paper covered shoebox. Inside was a bottle of cheap tequila and a big bottle of painkillers. Antonio shouts down that he thought I'd be dead by now. I tell him to fuck off.

He says he'll throw me down a ham and cheese sandwich as well if I tell him where Liliana has run off to. I say I don't know and tell him to fuck off again. He says he'll be back tomorrow, and then he fucks off.

I open the tequila and take a deep drink than take the rest of my painkillers. The agonizing hum in my legs slowly melts away.

I smile.

I know where Liliana is.

A motel far away.

She's pregnant with my child.

She wanted me to run away with her, leave Marcone's craziness behind. I said no, time with her was fun, but I love my wife. Liliana left the other

36

morning, telling me about the Desert Sands Motel, close to the border. I told myself to act normal and dumb as she left Marcone and me to fight it out. So far he is winning.

***

I awake hungry and pissed that I'd slept leaving my phone on. It's dark. I strike up the Zippo, setting fire to the brown paper and shoebox, the warmth makes me smile and hungry for worms. I think of Rosa and Elva. Of summer barbeques, cook outs at my cousin's place and lots of cold, cold beer.

My stomach groans, I take a swig of tequila, using the fire to calm my own burning hunger. I should have eaten the paper. I should have eaten the brown paper, hell and the shoebox. I tear the label from the tequila bottle and eat that. My dry mouth compacts it into a stodgy blob. A mouthful of tequila helps wash it down. I take out a twenty-dollar bill and eat that, then another, until I've eaten two hundred dollars. I open the painkillers that Antonio brought and take six. My leg has started to smell, the ankle skin is now green. The pain stifles the hunger, yet the hunger enhances the pain.

I'm so starving and yet I'm surrounded by meat.

Beautiful rotting meat.

I'm thinking about taking the leg.

I need to piss so I piss. I smell bad anyway. Isn't urine sterile? Maybe I should have pissed on my knee for all the good it would have done.

I burn a twenty-dollar bill, and then wish I had eaten it instead. Heat or eat, I don't have many choices left. But at least I have some.

***

Morning comes and I'm starving. There's no more hard skin on my fingers and my nails are raw nubs, I've been chewing them half through stress, half through hunger. I need something. Before I can stop myself or defy the reasoning, I've taken out my knife and cut into the woman I'm sat on top of. I cut into the top of her leg. The skin is dry and tough as I peel off a slice. I chew, I gag. I retch nothing but air. I try again, cutting her up into smaller pieces. Better this time. Tastes like old steak or dried up chicken, not that I've tried such dated meat. I manage a handful of morsels and keep them down. It feels morbidly wonderful to eat despite the menu. I have some more painkillers and down half of what is left of the tequila.

I feel good.

So good I'm gonna take the leg.

***

37

The remaining bullets in the Glock came in handy. Using my knife I fashioned some bandages from the arms of my linen jacket. I tied it as tight as I could round the bottom of my thigh, then pressed the Glock against my kneecap and fired. It took three bullets and a few slashes from the knife but it came free. I am now an amputee. I threw the leg away. It's caused me so much pain I don't want to see it again. Legless. I passed out after throwing my limb away, only for 2 hours though. Thankfully the tourniquet worked, and the bloodletting had slowed some. I waved the flame from my lighter over the stump in effort to cauterise the open vessels. I smell burning bacon as I cook myself to health. I pour tequila over the blackened stump then cover it with the remaining bandage. It feels weird, as it would, it feels liberating. I'm gonna rest a few hours then try to move now I've severed my dead weight. Ten more painkillers should do the trick.

Am I dreaming this? I can't tell.

***

Before nightfall, Antonio came back. He brought Marcone and Miguel. They both have a laugh and toss some more tequila and painkillers down. They land further away this time; hungrily I pounce for them and draw them near, tearing into the paper. You've gotta get what you can, I remember thinking.

Neither Antonio nor Marcone nor Miguel said anything, although I thought I heard Marcone say "Enjoy."

Then they threw Liliana in with me. It was strange hearing her fall. She was already dead when she hit the floor, looked like she had been strangled as her neck was peppered with dark thumbprints. She was fresher than my current squeeze I reasoned, so I edged over and cut a slice from her toned inner thigh. I didn't even cry this time. I ate in silence, more than I should have. I didn't realise I could get this hungry.

***

I'm losing my voice. After screaming and crying so much I don't think I'll speak again. Marcone has to die, same for Miguel and Antonio. Fuck it, I'll take them all on. I only fucked his wife. She didn't love him anyway.

From my new position on the other side of the shaft, I sat idly flicking my Zippo on and off as darkness surrounded me. My eyes cast over to my old resting place, my meal before Liliana. The shadows cast a familiar glow over this woman; my heart raced so much it felt like it was going to burst free. With Zippo in hand I crawled over and turned her.

Rosalita, with Elva snuggled with a face of terror beneath her, clasped in a death throe to her mother's breast. I didn't recognize them, but it was.

All this time.

Her perfume.

Miguel's knowing comment about taking care of her.

They were already here. Marcone must have killed them the morning I was thrown down. I held on to them for a long while, I didn't mind their smell. I was hunting for a trace of their living aroma or even one last sweet sense of Rosalita's perfume.

***

I had sunk the rest of the tequila and the pills when it started to rain. Really heavy. The wet season was in full flow now. I drank a little rainwater that cascaded down from the valley above; I turned down the worms for I was already full.

The rain was refreshing for so long, then I moved away and struggled over the army of corpses and into the depths of the mine. It was dark, but I didn't mind. Further in the thundering beats of rain seemed to subside and a new noise, a pulsing gurgle came to my ears. The downpour collected in the mine shaft seemed to flow away from the death pit. I flicked on the Zippo to prove to myself I was right, and I found that the shaft turned into a river. Clinging onto the wet wall, I followed it until it came to waist deep. I reckon I can swim out, it has to flow somewhere. If it flows to deeper hell, then so be it.

If you're listening this, I leave you here. You've found this statement saved to my Blackberry's memory card, stashed away safely in the waterproofed safety of the painkiller bottle. I leave this behind as my last, desperate message in bottle. If you find this, I beg of you, give my wife and daughter a decent burial; that is all I ask. I'll do the rest.

It's time to leave hell.

Devil Let Me Go

Crack'd

CRACK'D

Hilda Tock awoke in the early hours when her home began to shake. That morning, the radio buzzed with excitement regarding the tremor that struck at two minutes past three am. Now, as Hilda Tock looked out from her back porch onto her snow-strewn garden she could confirm to herself that an earthquake had occurred; disaster had struck her beloved county.

Lincolnshire had suffered only minor tremors in the past, nothing registering above a six on the Richter scale as the BBC newsman on the radio had said. But this was different. Out in the distance of the nearest town, chaos now seemed to reign. In the crisp December air even her blitz battered ears could hear the sirens of the emergency services trying their very best to control the situation, while otherworldly, snaking fingers of black smoke loomed upwards towards the bright white morning sky, ascending from people's homes and businesses. She dreaded what damage had been caused in the local village; she once had friends there, all gone now, long dead before the quake.

A slight aftershock vibrated through her old bones, then faded to nothing.

Hilda Tock's farmhouse stood in the midst of a barren field on a snow swept landscape. She'd let the fields go fallow for years now. She'd had offers from local farmers to sell on the good land, or in the very least rent it out. She refused, not through spite or mean spiritedness. No, she wanted to be left alone.

John Tock, her husband of sixty-three years this June, had passed on four years back, the memory remained; the touch didn't. The memory of him haunted her night after night, bringing joyous days of their youth, living on the farm together, whilst at the same time torturing her, reminding Hilda Tock of how lonely she really was.

Memories, it seemed, were sweet as well as bitter.

She missed John, not having him was worse than death. In fact, it was death to her, death of love, death of everything. She was already dead to herself, but the cool breath in her lungs and the pathetic beat of her heart betrayed that fact, her own heart was punishing her for not moving on after John died, she couldn't let go. She didn't want to anyways.

John's passing had been the most eventful time in her later years, but today that would change. She'd lived; she'd seen things. She'd survived the Blitz when she lived down in London as flower girl, she'd met Clark Gable when he'd been in London for a play he was acting in and back then she'd been married to the most wonderful husband a wife could want. But today, this cold and lonely December day, the particular kind that really made her wish she was dead and gone, rotting in the ground or cast like a seed to the wind lost in the ether. Hilda Tock would remember today.

From the back porch of her crumbling farmstead, Hilda's usual winter view would be of the one hundred acres of Tock's North field, with the pylons that the electric company had erected in the Sixties cutting across the middle, paying her husband a thousand pounds for the privilege. Behind these would be the main road that led up to the bumpy lane that led to her farm, behind this would be a small rise that hid the tops of the closest houses in the village. Then she could see trees, beyond this factories sat on the outskirts of town, then nothing but sky.

Today, however, those factories burned with hellish plumes of acrid blue/green chemical smoke that she could already taste on the breeze, the flames of which had spread to the line of conifers that bordered the industrial estate. Sirens wailed and more smoke pumped up into the air from the village, shouts and screams competing with the reigning chaos. The steel pylons had toppled like fallen giants; each now drunkenly slumped at difficult angles from what they were originally set.

The biggest change, however, was what was in the North field, well what used to be the North field. It had gone, replaced by a gaping chasm of which her home hung precariously on the precipice. The farmhouse had suffered a little damage during the earthquake as her husband had hand built their home with his own two hands and had formed it from a timber frame over forty years ago. He wasn't keen on the traditional brick house; besides, wood had been cheaper back then. And he wanted to build it near the ancient oak tree so that his future children had some garden shade during playful summers. So whilst all the other homes in the area had shaken to dust and rubble, the Tock's homestead had withstood the vibration of Mother Nature, except for a few broken windows and a crack that ran along the upside of the chimney stack constructed from weather blown red bricks.

The chasm ended near the bottom of what she considered to be her garden, although the once blooming flowers were now hidden beneath the death white blanket of winter. With boredom outweighing the cold, Hilda Tock slipped on her late husband's twenty year old work boots and traipsed out into the snowbound yard.

Although the snow had ceased falling, the northerly wind still continued its icy breath upon those who felt brave enough, or stupid enough, to face it. Although the dear Mrs Tock was one such brave soul, she still pulled her old coat closer around her, wishing she'd the sense put to on gloves before venturing outside.

She was eighty-six and, despite being in her depressive state, was still reasonably spry for her age and even though she languished in loneliness, she felt she had nothing else to complain about. Hilda was grateful for the life she had lived and wished for nothing more; except for Josephine, Derek and little Lilly to be back with her. She missed them all very dearly every day, maybe more than John, probably because she'd more time with John, lived a life and more, being happy together. With the children however, the happiness was brief, the anguish everlasting.

As she shuffled further down the garden, the snowdrifts grew deeper, spilling frozen space over the top of her unlaced boots, chilling her already aching toes. Not that she was complaining, she never complained about the cold, a lifetime of hard work had taught her that. Do what you can with what you've got, because the only way through hard work is by doing it. There isn't any other way round it except through it.

Hilda Tock stopped as she didn't dare step any further. The chasm gaped before her, sloping down into a bottomless pit, dark soil forming a deep wall into the heart of the earth. She guessed it was easily over three hundred metres across to the other side where she could still see Larson's windmill teetering on the far edge. The earthquake hadn't caused the ground to crack; it had collapsed into a vast uncharted lower chasm. Had her husband chosen to build their home north of the old oak tree, then she and her beloved farmhouse would be miles underground by now.

Hilda turned and smiled at the tree; it had been her idea to build south of the oak tree, that way the house would never be in its shade.

She turned back to the deep scar that had swallowed the North field. It worried her, there could still be an aftershock and the entire Tock property could disappear into the deep of the earth never to be seen again. But all this concern, any worry that Hilda Tock had held for herself or any other victims of the earthquake, vanished in an instant. The instant when she saw the egg.

It was ten feet away, down the slope, sat on top of the freshly torn earth, placed amongst fragments of what used to be her picket fence. No new snow had fallen, so the egg stuck out in contrast to the dark soil. Although she didn't know it was an egg, she was sure it was. It looked like one, but bigger. The same shape, the same eggshell colouring, it had to be.

Hilda looked round. She was alone. Her home was alone on this plain of farmland.

Without further thought for her own safety, Hilda Tock stepped into the mouth of the pit, carefully stepping sideways down until she reached the egg. It was the size of a rugby ball, maybe a little bigger. It wasn't smooth, the surface was rough like that of a stone, but it looked formed, not carved, not shaped by the wear of time or the tools of man, but moulded by nature itself. Hilda bent down and stroked the surface with her cold exposed fingertips. It was warm to touch, almost pleasant. Rough but not offensive; much like John's cheek when he'd forgotten to shave for a few days.

Again, without thinking, Hilda picked up the egg. It wasn't as heavy as it looked, holding it close to her chest as carried it back towards the house, her eyes not registering the scurried footprints that had left the pit for the snowy yard.

Once back inside, Hilda kept her coat on, she had yet to build the fire and as the electric and gas were cut off due to the quake, she had no other form of heating. She'd build the fire up in a minute or two. First she had to take care of the egg.

She snagged a couple of coarse old towels from the cupboard beneath the stairs, dropped them on the kitchen table and formed a makeshift nest, gently resting the egg in the middle. It was safe, this made her happy.

With the egg secure, Hilda headed back outside with her fire basket and filled it with cut logs and tinder from the woodshed which, despite being ready to collapse, had survived the earthquake due to its rickety structure.

In the kitchen she built up the fire and lit it with a wick made from an old newspaper. Within a minute heat was pouring into the room, warming it by a few welcome and pleasant degrees. The kitchen window hadn't survived the quake, several panes had splintered and shattered, sending deadly shards into the sink. Hilda ignored the shards, gathering a handful of drawing pins from a drawer and secured a towel over the window frame to keep out as much of the bitter cold as she could. It blocked a portion of the daylight, but it made the place cosier. She closed the doors, keeping as much heat as possible in the kitchen. With a little effort she pushed the old breakfast table closer to the wood hungry fire, but not too close.

The egg was now warm; this made her happy.

The thought of food passed through her mind. She didn't get hungry anymore. It was old age, you lose your appetite. Little morsels sufficed, a little bit at a time. She hadn't had breakfast, so she headed over to the biscuit barrel that lived in a cupboard near the cooker. The barrel as well as the other sundries had tipped and spilled their contents. Hilda reached in, grabbed a biscuit and popped it in her mouth. The sugar rush was welcome after the morning cold. She thirsted for a cup of tea, but with the power and gas off she had no means to boil water apart from the fire. She'd have to wait until help came. She couldn't very well walk into the village, the phone was out and she didn't feel confident driving the Land Rover anymore, not with the way her eyesight was deteriorating. Not worth the danger.

Grabbing one of the last remaining glasses that hadn't broken or shattered, Hilda filled it up with the cold water that was still left in the system. It came half way; she emptied it into her mouth. It hurt her gums, but the refreshment was welcome.

A crack, louder and closer than the snapping fire, resonated in her ears.

She turned. A line had appeared across the egg, three inches long. Temptation told her to slip a gnarled nail under and prise the section off. But no, it wasn't time. Nature had to take its course.

Hilda took another biscuit from the cupboard, poured herself a glass of milk from the carton in the fridge, fed the fire some more wood and then sat down on a chair near the egg.

After half an hour, the egg cracked a little more; on the left side this time. A squeak came from inside, followed by a dribble of yellowish fluid from the crack. The cracked portion moved, rising and falling as if something inside was breathing. In fact, Hilda Tock was sure of it.

An hour passed, the lunch hour continued, a pang in her stomach temporarily haunted her before passing. She didn't need food. She needed this.

As the hour reached one, a tiny bony finger poked through the shell. Hilda Tock smiled triumphantly, giving a little clap of congratulations, usually she wasn't this giddy.

The finger became a hand, the hand became an arm, bone white and spindly, weak and in need of nourishment. Hilda couldn't resist any longer, hobbling forward she drew close with the egg. The firelight had subsided now and with the insulating blanket over the window, light was minimal. With the nail of her little finger, she prised off the portion of cracked shell near the baby white arm. It tensed and half retreated back inside in shock. Hilda shushed and made a cooing noise. This seemed to calm it down at first, before whatever was inside kicked out in joy, the egg split in half and folded open. A thick yellow slime oozed out, soaking into the towel nest. From inside the split portions came a tiny squeak. Hilda peered inside. A tiny being with little dark eyes peered back. In a way, it smiled at her.

She didn't have her glasses on, she'd forgotten as to where she put them, losing them in the madness of the quake, but she could see well enough to see what it was before her. It was a child, a baby. Not a human baby, but humanoid. That was close enough for her. Her lifetime of prayers had being answered. Hilda reached in and plucked the sweet little thing from the amniotic gloop. It squeaked again, not quite a baby's cry but close enough.

Grabbing the least soiled of the nest towels; Hilda carefully wrapped the egg baby in its folds then held it close, moving closer to the fire.

Even in the dwindling glow she could make out the strange baby's features. It had a flat nose, tiny dark eyes that more resembled obsidian marbles than an organ to see. The skin was grey white, almost translucent and a little red road map of veins ran over the convex of its fragile little skull.

Hilda cooed and shushed, rocking the egg baby to and fro, basking in the fading comfort of the fireplace. The egg baby squealed with joy; it had teeth. A full set of fine pointers, small, thin and deadly.

He seemed to smile at her again.

She liked it. Revelled in it. How she had longed to be needed. It had been so long.

Hilda moved over to one of the cupboards and felt around in the dim light with searching fingers. She was sure she had some dried milk in there somewhere. She pulled out a tin of beans and some Ovaltine and then found the powdered milk. Using the remainder of the kettle water she had boiled the previous night, she poured a little into her glass, then added two spoonfuls of powdered milk.

The egg baby cuddled into her, nuzzling the warmth of her cardigan.

She swirled the mixture round with a spoon. The little thing bundled close to her chest, shifting his head towards the noise, half startled, half curious.

Hilda sat back down with the glass of milk and the egg baby; she held the glass to the creature's non-existent lips and let it sip. It managed to drink about half of what she had made before it pulled a face of horrific realisation and vomited the milk over her cardigan. Then it began to cry. Not a baby cry, but a beseeching terror, high pitched like an alarm, as if she'd poisoned it.

Hilda attempted to shush the Egg Baby but it carried on crying. Soon it began to wiggle free and claw at her hands as if caught in a mire and hungered for escape. Hilda grew frustrated and went back over to the sink to pour out the wasted milk. A tiny claw reached out and tore a wicked red line across the back of her hand, causing her to drop the glass. It shattered against the faucet, sending further shards into the steel sink and one into her hand. Brilliant red blood pooled over her hand, droplets cascaded, splattering over the sharp glass.

Hilda cursed, the first time in an age.

The egg baby stopped crying; then clamoured for her hand.

She resisted at first, then realising what he wanted, she relented and moved her hand towards him. He sniffed at the air and a crack of what appeared to be a smile curled up at the side of his mouth. Then his black tongue pushed out from that lipless mouth, hunting for the source of the plasma aroma. Hilda let a drop of her precious life force dribble out into his mouth. The Egg Baby snapped and licked his chops, another grim smile. She let it flow until the Egg Baby closed his eyes, seemingly content at his fill.

She moved the fluid soaked towels away, leaving the dry ones, then gently, as if he were a volatile explosive, Hilda placed the Egg Baby back into the nest, fed the fire and went upstairs.

***

John never understood. Never realised what she wanted meant so much to her. Her life's dream was to have a family, a happy one, with singing and dancing, trips to the park, the zoo, anywhere family friendly.

It wasn't to be.

She sat on the chair by the dresser, dust motes her only moving company. The afternoon filtered through a little, the snow filled clouds blocked out the rest. She didn't sleep in here anymore; too many things got in the way, much easier to bed down in the spare room where she could sleep soundly.

The wind had got up outside, more snow would be falling tonight, she was sure.

John never comforted her after Josephine, treated her mean. Blamed her for it all, said she was weak when she was anything but. She knew she was strong; she'd lasted eight months with child and tried not to let the death get to her too much when she saw them take that pathetic little body away. Soldier on; it's what people did back then. Derek lived a little longer, three months of bliss. John was made up, proud to have a son, despite being sickly. John cried a lot, his face was red raw with emotion, he even hit her again that time. Derek had been gone only a few days when John struck out after a week of silence. She wanted to talk; the first thing he said was "you…" then knocked out three of her teeth. She told the doctor she had insomnia and fell down the stairs, so he'd given her pain pills for the swelling. It was a different time back then.

Lilly was three when she went missing, they found her the next morning at the top of North field, drowned in a muddy ditch. She'd been held under, the police found skin and hair under her fingers. They never caught whoever did it. John was quiet for about a month, hardly talking, barely eating. He became a solid ghost of his former self, fading each day into a deeper and darker depression. That was when he started to neglect not only her but also the farm.

After everything, after all he'd done, she still loved him. He was still her husband; it was what she was supposed to do.

She moved over to the bed, a smiled creasing across her greying face.

'I have a child, John, He's funny looking but he's beautiful and I think I love him.' She paused, entwined her fingers nervously, looking at them knotting together.

'I know I do. Angels brought him to me. I think they want me to look after him. You're not taking this one away from me. Not this time.'

Hilda leant forward, her back popped and her hips strained like old weather warped wood. She planted a wet kiss on the forehead of her husband, the damp smudge of her lip print making the grey skull glisten.

She pushed herself off the dusty bed and moved for the door, turning back once. She smiled again. She hadn't ventured in here for well over a year, maybe two, she was happy that it didn't smell as bad anymore.

***

The Egg Baby awoke as darkness came, cooing and stretching its little white limbs within the confines of its makeshift nest. It had started to snow again, Hilda busied herself by clearing up the kitchen as soundlessly as possible and keeping the fireplace well stocked with fuel. Again the fire dwindled to nothing, eating through her wood supply as it fought off the attack of the unforgiving cold. She needed more wood, a lot more to get through the night without electric or gas.

After pulling on her old frayed coat and John's old work boots, Hilda quickly checked that her baby was content and secure. She placed a fresh towel across his body, tucking him in. She picked up the wood basket and ventured into the cold.

48

It was ten feet from the back door to the woodshed, even through the swirling almost magical flurries that besieged the back garden; she could still see the ominous emptiness of the vast pit in the North field. She shivered, but not from the cold.

Plenty of logs remained in the wood store, enough for another month or more, she'd have to get that young fellow from the village to come and chop some more after the snow had melted. Twenty pounds and he'd fill the woodshed to brimming. He was a good lad.

Meticulously but with haste brought on by the inflicting cold, Hilda filled the wood basket, stacking it as high as she dare. Her back strained and pulled tight as she stood, heaving the basket up into her arms close to her chest. Her already weary shoulders started to burn with the overloaded burden pulling at her. She took her steps carefully, the danger of slipping and breaking her neck played on her mind as she hobbled back towards the back door. The wind caught up and slammed the woodshed door wide open, slapping noisily against the exterior wall. It made her jump a little, then it banged again as the wind took hold of it. She'd not sleep tonight with the door banging about in the wind.

Once on the safety of the back porch, Hilda dropped the wood basket at her feet, preparing to head back across the garden to secure the woodshed door.

A prone figure waited in the snow for her.

It was camouflaged, except for its coal black eyes. She wouldn't have seen it had it been stood motionless. It had stopped as soon as she turned.

"What time is it, Mister Wolf?" asked a stray thought floating in her head.

It looked like a wolf, same shape, but longer, closer to the size of a fully-grown man. It appeared hairless, with alabaster skin corrugated and bumpy like that of an alligator. Its brow was bowed as it regarded her, apparently stalking her as a tiger would its prey. It looked like her baby, except fully grown and with protruding, jagged teeth that seemed far more deadly. They looked like carved wood that had been left to the elements for a decade or two.

'I suppose you want your baby, don't you?' Hilda asked as if she were talking to a pleasant neighbour. 'Well, you shouldn't have left him, should you? A good mother wouldn't do that. You're a beast, nothing more. But I'll let you have your son back.'

The great white beast remained motionless except for a blink of its soulless obsidian eyes, considering her, her words but daft sounds.

Taking trust in the creature's stance, Hilda turned and headed back inside. The fire had died down in her absence and her Baby had started to whimper, she guessed through hunger from the insistent tone it dealt out on her ears. Reluctantly she picked him up and carried him in the towel outside into the cold. His screams intensified once the cold enveloped him.

The white creature had moved forward a few paces. Its boldness, although troubling, did nothing to faze her approach.

'Here you go, be good to him,' Hilda said, placing down the bundle on the end of the snow-covered porch.

The creature hesitated, then it moved forward, sniffing the air with the curiosity of a dog that tasted hot sausages on the breeze. A couple more sniffs, then it moved forward slowly, bowing its head toward the otherworldly child. The creature moved its nose closer to the towel nest, its brow furrowed as if in disgust; it raised its paw to smash down upon the defenceless baby. Hilda, sensing the mother's distaste, picked up a log from the wood basket and smashed it down hard on the back of the creature's head as its claws were inches from slashing the child into sections.

The mother screamed, instead directing its anger towards Hilda, swiping out with its clawed paw. It caught her arm as she raised it defensively. The ragged talons cut through her coat, cardigan and flesh with shocking efficiency. Hilda didn't scream, instead she struck out with the log again, sweeping sideward, catching the brute across its jaw, sending stars and splinters into its brain. She kicked out against the wood basket, sending a cascade of logs over the top of the ungodly mother. Hilda grabbed the screaming bundle from the porch and fell back inside, locking the door behind her with rapid, one-handed efficiency.

Her arm felt cold, the pain had been momentarily bothersome but now shock had set in. Through the slash in her old coat she could see white bone of her wrist flooded over by the flow of pumping red blood. The Egg Baby screamed, the bad devil of a mother howled outside the door, scratching at the panel. Hilda collapsed into a chair, her legs shaking and mortally weak. Then she gave up and fell with a bump to the floor, finally resting her back against a table leg, facing the fire. Her arm started to spasm as if possessed, pain came in waves. Outside the mother that had abandoned her child screamed indignantly; inside, her child screamed through painful pangs of hunger.

Hilda raised her torn arm to the lipless hungry mouth of her adopted baby; it caught the scent and dashed out its tongue, willing the bloody limb closer, until it lapped happily at the gaping wound. The cry stopped instantly as it was appeased.

The mother continued her assault on the door.

It wouldn't be long before it was through, the beast had looked strong and wilful, it had fought its way from the torn earth, a simple door wouldn't be sufficient in holding her back.

Light-headedness flooded through Hilda, pleasant, almost an escape from the cold that she no longer really felt.

She smiled.

For Josephine.

For Derek.

For Lilly.

Not for John. He deserved everything. The rat poison especially.

All Hilda ever wanted was to be a good mother, to care, to love, to cherish a being that needed her. To sacrifice everything for something so useless and weak, it would take all her strength to help raise it. Parenthood was draining. She'd always expected that.

Darkness played on the edge of her senses, flooding in like a black tsunami in slow motion over and through her. She closed her eyes and sighed with utter contentment, a smile still fixed on her face, the Egg Baby still lapping at the red milk she gave.

DEVIL LET ME GO

Not That Way Home

Meredith Croft busied herself about the kitchen while she waited for her husband to return home, as she always did when he worked late on a Tuesday night. Nothing was out of order. The chicken was in the oven, thirty minutes from ready, the vegetables were chopped and prepped, awaiting their boiling bath. Her period was three days late, but she could blame that on a number of factors. Stress of her new job perhaps, maybe she was becoming in-synch with the girls in the office. She got on famously with all the ladies who worked in the accounts department of Fedler Furnishings, so why shouldn't she become moon sisters with them all?

Joe was usually back home by half seven, traffic pending. He'd discovered a short cut last month that shaved a good seven miles from his route, and brought him home that little bit earlier. It didn't seem like much, but add them up, it was maybe twenty minutes more at home a week, an hour and a bit a month and a good half a day over the course of the entire year. When you loved each other like they did, you didn't waste time getting home. For Joseph and Meredith Croft treasured every last second with each other. It paid to add up the minutes. In you could define love in a way; a snapshot of the Crofts would be a good example. They held an otherworldly bond over one another. One could tell what the other wanted when they ate out and what movie to rent. Often they sent text messages at the same time, often already detailing what the other was after. Some loveless cynics would say they knew one another too well. The Crofts thought otherwise; they called this connection, the *Psychic Rainbow*.

Meredith called up her sister, explaining the details of what jobs she was to do whilst she and Joe headed out on a mini break to celebrate their fifth wedding anniversary; a trip to a secluded cabin in the highlands of Scotland. Just him, her and the length and breadth of each other's bodies. Peace, quiet, good food and drink. Plus baby making practice.

Lots of.

Meredith had already raided the local Ann Summers in preparation for the mini-break. A nurse, a police woman and a French maid were all going on the trip with them. Joe didn't know that yet, she expected him to be happy when he found out, though she suspected he'd already read her mind regarding her collection of kink.

They'd put starting a family on hold whilst they concentrated on making a home for themselves, ensuring they had enough savings so they could live quite comfortable whilst the baby was an infant. They'd seen so many of their friends bankrupt themselves trying to provide for their children, grow dark eye bags from stress and lack of sleep and eventually divorce after the strain of family life became too much.

They both expected it to be a challenge, but the best they could do was to be prepared for the day a child would grace their happy little lives.

Sometimes Meredith wished she could send psychic messages to anyone she wished, then she needn't bother calling her sister at all.

Feed the cat.

Water the plants.

Record this show, record this one.

Pick up Mum on Thursday for her hospital appointment.

She was looking forward to it. A lie of course. Her sister didn't usually go out the way for anyone.

They said their goodbyes and her sister wished her a good time, even though, Meredith could tell she was jealous as hell, having four kids tying you down to eighteen years of holiday parks and zoo trips probably did that to a woman.

Her voice wasn't perfect, but she sang regardless, turning the radio up when the meandering melancholia of "*Ain't No Sunshine*" by Bill Withers began to pleasantly harp forth from the speakers, smiling and singing as she set the table. The benign routine of a dutiful wife continued

Then came the phone call, and a coldness ran through her skin, chilling every ounce of her being as a spear of sharpened ice punctured the warmth of her heart, letting in a terribly bleak sense of winter.

***

She'd told him that they were having roast chicken for tea, with vegetables and gravy infused with half a teaspoon of Marmite, his favourite. After they'd both finished the meal, he would remove the rest of the meat from the bones and store it in some Tupperware in the fridge to keep it fresh, then he'd boil up the carcass, sieve out the bones, skin and jellied meat, and prepare a stock to make a warming chicken and sweet corn soup for tomorrow's meal.

Waste not, want not, for tomorrow is another day, was his adage.

'At the roundabout, turn left.'

Joe Croft ignored the command and carried straight over the roundabout, tapping his fingers on the wheel to the repetitious bass drumming opening of '*9 to 5*' by Dolly Parton. He'd pick up the main drag a few junctions up. Heading left would only take him into traffic leaving the city and he'd unhappily spend an hour utilising the free parking on the motorway.

He had a dirty weekend with the wife planned for this weekend, which would more than make up for the red tape week he'd had. Wasn't that what wedding anniversaries were for? Cosy weekends of carnal commitment and fine food. He was now considering calling in sick tomorrow so they could set off earlier.

Trees lined either side of the road, diluting the pressure of the rain from the sky. Joe switched on his main beams and reduced the speed of the wipers to compensate.

High on the hill, he saw the house. Long and squat, every light on and set in exquisite grounds, featuring a manicured lawn and a cherub topped fountain that shone a dull grey in the dreary gloom. After passing this place more than a few times, he guessed at first it was a nursing home or perhaps a rehab clinic or hell, maybe even a day spa. However, the ten foot iron gate and barbed wire security fence suggested otherwise.

The house was stark and alone against the darkened sky. It looked wrong, out of place. It gave Joe Croft the creeps, yet he came this way diligently as he knew he'd make better time than taking the traditional route.

'Turn around when possible,' the brisk yet polite lady inside the sat-nav asked.

Joe ignored her.

'Make a U-turn,' she insisted, this time the voice over lady sounded a lot more commanding. She was paid to do that.

Jump in the shower and the blood starts pumpin', Dolly mused.

The rain came harder as the trees cleared a little and the road got rougher, the asphalt torn up from last winter's snow, now pock marked with jarring pot holes. He slowed a little, taking the road conditions into consideration, yet still telling himself that this way was quicker.

Well it had been when it was dry and a little lighter, but tonight he'd been delayed by a bullshit meeting with Jacobs about building proximity and task designation. The usual nonsense. Joe wanted to get home, was that too much to ask Mister Weatherman?

Joe Croft increased the speed of the wipers, and then braked as the bone white figure emerged from the green borders like a ghost train ghoul. Arms raised, mouth dumbly agape, eyes wide with fearful wonder.

With the diminished speed and weather conditions impeding his ride, Joe Croft had stopped right beside the naked man.

'Barely gettin' by, it's all takin', and no givin'.'

***

Blinking out the rain, Rixon was first and foremost, a survivor. He wouldn't be beaten.

Dad had beaten him, so had Mum. Uncles too.

Mum enjoyed putting cigarettes out on his bare skin. Dad liked to pinch. Often his legs, the back of his neck, his chest. Other places too.

Mum and Dad.

They didn't deserve such monikers as the pair had failed on so many levels of parenthood. In fact every level had been soured, spoiled and fractured by their deviant means. Birthdays, school, holidays, three square meals a day, bedtime stories. Everything else was missed out or neglected in some way. Mum liked her booze and Dad liked to play. Sometimes they swapped. Sometimes they watched each other. Sometimes it was both of them. As soon as he was sixteen, Rixon had paid for off road driving lessons with his wages from washing the pots in a local café. Despite being sixteen, you could have driving lessons away from the main roads; he took his on an abandoned airfield. His plan was to save up and buy a car after he had passed his test. He aimed to do this as soon as possible; he didn't just want to run away. He wanted to drive away from his problem family at 90 miles an hour. So he washed pots to pay for lessons, every bustling hour he could.

One- it got him closer to his escape dream.

Two- the more time he spent out of the house the better.

Whenever he was at home his parents regularly abused him further. They knew about the part time job and demanded payment from him. If he was earning he'd have to pay rent, even though the rent was paid for by the council. The driving lessons he kept secret. But one day, the beatings, the mental abuse and the strange will his parents held over him had to stop. Rixon never got the chance to pass his test, buy a decent old banger and escape the torturous life his parents had made for him.

On the morning of his seventeenth birthday, he'd taken a bread knife and a steak knife and plunged them both into the chests of his slumbering parents, both drowsy at dawn, still in the queasy flood of a drunken stupor. Then he carried on stabbing.

Their neighbours; the Jefferies, had a daughter called Lindsey, she was the same age as him, cute, though he never talked to her. Caged in by his impenetrable shyness which he wore like a suit of armour to deflect the mortal and emotional blows thrown by his not-so-darling parents, Rixon couldn't even summon the meagre amount of energy it took to even make eye contact with a beauty the likes of Lindsey Jefferies. Whatever mental elastic had snapped inside him that day, it wasn't courage that sent him knocking next door. It was something much darker that rages inside all of us. Rixon was still angry at the world, he needed to take this pent up force, all seventeen torturous years, and take it out on something. Something beautiful, maybe that would balance him out, destroy something beautiful and innocent to pay the dark debt off, alleviate the demonic pressures that had been bestowed upon him.

Lust is a fickle thing. It can carry us to the heights of love almighty or draw us deep into the depths of animalistic depravity.

He'd been watching Lindsey for a long time. Dreaming of a better life. Just him and her. She would accept him and all his familial scars. He just needed to convince her.

Her . . .

That was where Mr Jefferies found him. Inside Lindsey, in the house, the living room carpet to be precise. She'd being dead over an hour, yet Rixon had continued his assault with the knife still dripping with a medley of his parent's vodka and gin diluted DNA. Rixon had pinched Lindsey all over, digging his nails in sometimes, bringing out little bruises everywhere before she screamed too much and he'd ended his fun with the knife. Yet he let the fun continue.

Mr Jefferies had knocked out three of Rixon's teeth. By the time Rixon realised this, the police had arrived and had him in cuffs. Mr Jefferies' mind however, like Elvis, had left the building for good. Now, all these years later, his wife, spared the sight of what was left of her daughter, still looked after him, cut his food into tiny pieces, left 'Who wants to be a Millionaire' on the box through those long and silent afternoons, then into the night where his screams woke them up every single night. Variations of the same dream; The boy next door on top of his daughter, in the centre of a dark red puddle staining his living room carpet.

If Rixon had ceased his slaughter at his parents, the jury might have been more lenient in their sentencing, with the years of abuse from their hands on his shoulders, he could have got away with manslaughter, serve a few years and be out to enjoy the rest of life, free from the oppression of his parents bearing down on him. But for what he did to Lindsey Jefferies, the jury were disgusted by his actions; he'd taken it too far in their eyes.

It didn't matter to Mr Jefferies what had happened to his daughter. What mattered was that he had been there to witness it. If he, like his wife had been spared the horrific sight, maybe his mind might have been saved. But Rixon had done a thorough job of forever polluting his sleep and every waking thought.

Mr Jefferies would have killed himself long ago had he the cognitive ability, but nowadays he couldn't even tie his own shoelaces.

Rixon knew none of these facts, for he was ignorant of everything that had happened in the past twenty years of the outside world.

But now he was out.

His plan was to get as much done as possible before they brought him back here.

Well, there.

It was past tense now as he'd escaped his forced bondage.

He'd been amazed at how easy the human body came apart under pressure. We're just lumps of meat that pretend to care about one another in order to gain attention to ourselves.

As heavy as the rain poured, it still wouldn't wash out the ingrained blood from under his fingernails. His own and the orderly's. The rain however did make light work of his paper pyjamas, the heavy droplets pounded through the thin material like miniature meteors, shredding the fibre from its place on his body. By the time he reached the tree line, his shoulders and legs were fully exposed to the elements. Once beyond the safety of the tree line, into the bramble bushes, away from the crafted lawn, the suit had deteriorated to nothing more than paper rags that clung to him like a shedding skin. By the time he climbed over the barbed wire fence, cutting his arms and back to ribbons leaking crimson, and reached the road he was near nude except for a few straggling creases of wet pulp.

Rixon was a survivor. He survived. He didn't feel the pain, didn't want to, didn't need to.

His calm, predatory eyes spied a glare of headlights along the road, they were heading towards him.

Rixon stepped into the road. And waved.

***

Joe Croft offered a weary smile and shook the car out of gear as the hitchhiker opened the door and glared inside. He was naked, and this at first surprised Joe, but on closer inspection by the sparse interior light that had blinked on from the door being opened, Joe could see that the man wore rags for clothes. Something had torn them from his body, tearing his skin into thin red raw lines. From the zoned-out look on his face, the alabaster skin, the bruises and various injuries he sustained, Joe strangely reasoned that the guy had escaped a cellar or dungeon of some kind. He'd been held against his will and whipped every day of his life. Somehow he'd escaped. He'd heard about it in the papers, Mad Dads that kept unruly kids locked up beneath the house.

'But the boss won't seem to let me. I swear sometimes that man is out to get me.' Dolly sang. Joe Crofts' gaze shot over the naked stranger's shoulder and to the lights of the big house that stood illuminated through the trees. His gaze darted back to the man who was stood by his passenger door. Barely five seconds had passed when what happened next, again took Joe Croft by complete surprise.

The sentence that emerged in his head was "are you alright there mate?" But as the first open mouthed syllable began to form on his lips, the stranger pounced forward, clearing the passenger seat and landed practically on Joe Croft's lap. At first Joe thought the stranger was trying to cuddle him, maybe, just simply in need of human contact after years, maybe decades locked away from the light of day and basic mechanics of society.

An immediate heaviness built up in his throat, he protested in clicks and gurgles. The naked stranger's eyes trembled in front of his. They edged closer, free of menace or any emotion for that matter. Boredom perhaps? Apathy? Maybe he'd been possessed by aliens judging from his dislocated stare.

As the pressure spread up from his throat to his face, Joe grabbed hold of the stranger's rain slickened wrists, clamping hold, trying in vain to push him away, but couldn't gather any firm purchase as he was still locked in behind the safety of his seat belt. The battle for breath had begun, but this instinctive function was replaced by a bizarre sense of panic. *Was this a dream? Was this really happening to him? Was he being . . .?*

An intense compression built up in his skull, as if all the blood in his body was surging upwards into his brain, filling every artery and capillary with oxygen starved fluid. A roaring whistled through his ears. The mounting pressure made him feel like an erupting volcano, the worry bloomed that his blood, devoid of a continuous and clear passage throughout his person, might suddenly burst forth from his eyes, ears, nose and mouth in a gory geyser.

How did you get blood stains out?

Cold Water?

That was it.

I think.

A fading Joe Croft kicked out, his feet jammed on the accelerator and the brake at the same time in spasms of abandon. The engine roared, the car's red eyes glowed like coals in the slanting rain. He started to rock in effort to shake off his assailant, but it was useless, the safety belt held him back and to release himself would give the stranger further purchase upon his person.

He'd have to let go.

Joe released his grip, fumbled for the buckle release by his side, but his dexterity betrayed him, his fingers might have well been boiled worms for all the cognitive grip they offered. Instead his fingers glanced upon his phone which lay in the beverage holder. He pressed what he thought was CALL twice then dropped it back into the empty beverage holder.

A river rushed into his head, a crimson waterfall fell before his eyes as he fell into a dark tunnel, at the end of which the only light came reflected from the emotionless face of his gormless attacker.

A devastating crack exploded in his ears as he went over the waterfall, yet his nerves told him that the pain was in his throat. He tasted a mouthful of burning copper as he drowned in himself.

The river slowed.

The rush and flow abated.

A trickle.

The stranger smiled, and then pulled the manhole lid over the tunnel which he menaced so coldly, so calmly.

Somewhere, in reality, Dolly Parton wasn't getting the credit she deserved, or so she sang.

The river stopped, still wet, not dried up in drought, but the tributary that fed in to it was no longer a source of divine aqueous.

His last fading thoughts were of cold water washing the blood from his bones and of Meredith, reaching into the still waters, reaching out to what was left of him.

The house phone was picked up.

'Hello?'

***

Rixon let go. Blood rushed into his aching thumbs.

Two horn marks lay pressed into the driver's throat, angry red shadows, reminding him of where his tenacious grip had just been. The driver's eyes were open, staring left of the interior light behind Rixon. They looked like decorated marbles, nothing more. Pink spittle ran in a gruesome sheen escaping down the chin and spoiling the crispness of his white shirt.

Maybe he'd bitten his tongue, maybe he'd snapped his windpipe. Who cared? The country and western song he hadn't been paying attention to, ended. Rixon guided an aching index finger over to the radio and pressed power.

Silence, except for the beating drum of the rain.

He had a vehicle, transport, a way forward.

Momentum would carry him through.

Rixon looked at the controls of the car.

Could he remember how to drive?

He'd had a few lessons, but that was years ago.

It should be easy.

He could drive, but first he needed clothes.

Between the driver's legs, he reached under the seat and grasped the lever, pushing the seat back as far as it would go, then using the small circle of plastic on the hip of the seat, he turned it and reclined it as far as it would go.

He unclipped the belt, then climbing back he dragged, pushed and shoved the driver onto the back seat. He wasn't too heavy so all it took was time. The engine hummed idly and the rain drummed down on the bodywork. Then Rixon heard the little voice.

'Hello, Joe? Are you there?'

He stopped, pausing to locate the direction of the sound.

The voice was tinny, it spoke again, 'Joe, I can hear you you've called me by accident.'

A pleasant glow of plastic emerged from the cup holder. Rixon reached forward cautiously and picked up the device. A woman's face stared back at him; she was in another world, smiling, bathed in sunlight. A tight red top and a little black skirt that showed off her curves.

Rixon didn't know it, but he was smiling.

'Okay Joe, I'm hanging up now, you've clearly called me from your pocket,' the woman said without moving her lips. Rixon knew it was her. The voice matched her face. It had to. Above her was the title HOME.

Rixon held the phone closer, his panting breath caught in the aural catchments of the microphone for a second.

He liked the look and the sound of this woman. He guessed it was the driver's wife. He'd been a lucky man.

The pretty lady vanished, and was replaced by a picture of a sunset. Pretty, as it had been a while since he had seen one. But it still wasn't as pretty as her.

***

61

Meredith dropped the phone. It clattered noisily on the kitchen floor, the hardness of the tiles caused the battery cover to jump off and skitter beneath the kitchen table. The battery pack was dislodged but remained attached to the phone.

At first, after saying the traditional "hello", she had listened. She heard gasping noises; sometimes Joe accidentally called her from his pocket. He affectionately called these, "*bollock calls*".

Beneath the commotion she could make out a Dolly Parton tune that for the love of her she couldn't remember the title of.

The gasping had continued, as had the rapid shuffling. It sounded animalistic. The horrid thought hit her that Joe might be having sex with someone else, and what she was eavesdropping on was orgasmic gasps. But she could hear no pleasure in what she heard. The rapid and sudden shuffles sounded more like someone fighting.

A guttural crack silenced the commotion.

She listened intently. She could hear the engine idling, then more shuffling.

'Hello, Joe? Are you there?' she asked hopefully.

Silence, except for the uneasy hum of the patient engine.

'Joe I can hear you you've called me by accident.'

Again, nothing.

'Okay Joe, I'm hanging up now, you've clearly called me from your pocket,' Meredith waited a moment, expecting Joe to talk to her. Maybe Joe had stopped for fuel and the shuffling was simply the phone in his pocket rubbing against the lining? Maybe he was changing a tyre? Maybe. . .

'*Ahhhhhh.*'

The noise caught her off guard, it was subtle, yet noticeable, someone had breathed onto the phone. Somebody *was* listening to her.

Meredith Croft stared at the broken handset for a few minutes, a bubble of unease and wariness shielding her from whatever her mind could imagine had happened to her beloved Joe.

Meredith dropped to her knees and began to reassemble the phone with shaking fingers.

***

Rixon had the driver stripped down to his underwear. He was unsure of whether or not to take the boxer shorts as the driver's last act of defiance had been to piss his pants.

Rixon took his trousers, shoes, socks and shirt and put them on himself. They were a baggy fit on his bony frame, but he looked less conspicuous than he did ten minutes ago. He went through the man's wallet, finding money and credit cards. He took out the driver's license and discovered the driver's name.

Joseph William Croft.

Rixon knew his age and where he lived.

Where she lived.

How to find the place though? He had a town name, but not a clue of how to get there. He didn't fancy asking for directions or stopping to buy a map.

A second glow, this time from the dashboard caught Rixon's eye. It was a small screen built into the charcoal veneer, maybe four inches across and three high. A green arrow sat in the middle on the screen pointing straight ahead.

Rixon had never used a sat-nav, but he'd seen them on television and advertised in some of the magazines they allowed him.

Rixon looked down on Joseph William Croft as he now knew him.

He'd been going home. Joseph Croft had set the sat-nav for home. If he followed the route, more than likely it would take him straight to her.

This was too perfect. It was fate. He was to have her. It was his gift for escaping. Thank you Father.

Rixon picked up the piece of plastic and looked at it. It was a mobile phone; her picture had lit up the screen when she called. Rixon guessed that other pictures of her existed within it, yet he didn't have the technological finesse in which to operate it. He hoped that Mr Croft held nude snaps of his wife on this device. He could have a look at them before he got home. Get himself revved up.

Light swayed out from the building from where he'd just come from. Sweeping torch lights scoured the grounds. He had to move.

He looked into the rear view mirror, catching sight of his face for the first time in many a long year. He didn't recognize the creature that stared back. His skin was white and his eyes bulged unconventionally from their sockets whilst his cheeks appeared sunken and deflated. He didn't look like he imagined himself. They didn't allow mirrors in the home, once a week a barber came round and shaved their heads and their faces. Always with a guard on constant watch.

He wished he hadn't seen himself now.

Disappointed at how his appearance had changed over the years without him realising it, Rixon leant across and grasped the passenger door and closed it. The interior light went off, darkness prevailed.

Rixon climbed forward into the driver's seat depressed the clutch pushed the gear into first and set off slowly. It had been a while since he had driven. He'd only managed a few off-road lessons before he was sent away from the world. He didn't want to rush it. A crash was the last thing he needed. Be calm and you'll arrive safe. Then you can have your reward. Then you can let yourself go.

Rixon pushed the rear view mirror away from his eyes. He didn't want to see himself.

The fuel gauge read three-quarters.

Christ. Joseph Croft was a nice guy.

***

Meredith tried ringing Joe's mobile again.

It rang for seven rings, then switched to voicemail. She left a frantic message asking him to call her, if anything, to put her mind at ease from the terrible conclusion it was dead ending at.

She sent a text, then rang again to be sure.

No answer.

Meredith did what she thought was right and rang her sister, telling her of what she had heard. Her sister stated the obvious of what needed to be done next.

'Call the police you stupid cow!'

So she did

***

The deceased body of Joseph William Croft lay sprawled in the back seat, fading colder by the second, drained of life and further love. His corpse was all that remained of Joseph Croft. He still had the evidence of his existence; friends, family and possessions, but as for a soul, or a conscious mind, these had faded from his body and into the ether, where everything goes that we know not of.

***

Rixon had figured out the wipers; increasing their speed to dispense the wash of rain that crowded the windscreen. He tested the indicators and lights, reasoning that he should know how to operate the vehicle before he was let loose on the main roads. He pushed it up into fourth, instead hit second. The engine roared and grinded angrily, Rixon cursed, dropped the clutch and found the right gear on the second try.

The phone glowed again, her face appeared, joyfully and unaware of what was coming for her. Rixon ignored it. She kept ringing. He ignored it every time. He needed to concentrate on where he was heading. He followed the green arrow.

'Turn left at the next junction,' an oddly robotic female voice ordered from nowhere. Rixon jumped and braked so hard the tyres gave a protesting squeak against the slick road.

It was the sat-nav. He remembered that sometimes they talk to you.

Rixon approached the junction, marvelling at how technology had progressed since he'd been away. He turned left as instructed, and carried on down the road. Panic dropped in his stomach like a lead weight into a pool of mercury.

Ahead, swirling blue lights blazed towards him.

***

The police offered Meredith little help. A person needed to be gone twenty-four hours before they could be reported as a missing person. She explained about what she had heard on the phone, suspecting foul play. The emergency operator fobbed her off with the excuse that it wasn't proof, and if the matter was pursued further and turned out to be false, she could be charged with wasting police time.

Frustrated at being helpless, Meredith called her sister again, who was now frustrated in the process of getting the kids to bed.

'You want me to come over?' her sister replied wanly.

'If you don't mind. I'm worried.'

'I've got to get the kids to bed first. Jakes playing up, Sophie's got a temperature and Dan isn't back from work until ten. You're more than welcome to head over to ours, but be warned, I will give you a job to do.'

Meredith accepted her sister's excuse and hung up without saying goodbye. She began to pace the kitchen. She turned down the temperature on the oven and carried on pacing. She couldn't eat a scrap until Joe was home. Meredith assured herself that she was being silly. But that phone call from Joe's phone had left her caught in a whirlpool of unease. Something was wrong, that was the only right thing she could be sure of.

***

The ambulance with sirens wailing, blazed past like an apocalyptic disco, urgent to get somewhere. Rixon kept a close eye in the rear view mirror as it turned in where he'd come from.

The Home.

They must have called the emergency services.

They were quick, but he was quicker. He'd made it. He was beyond.

'Turn around when possible,' the lady sat-nav asked, her tone had grown deeper, as if her power had started to drain. Didn't the sat-nav run off the car battery? The last thing he needed was to run out of juice out here. The green arrow that glowed so helpfully began to rotate, suggesting he immediately turn around.

'Turn around.' The voice deeper still, dispensed with the pleasantries this time. A chill ran through him. The voice had him on an edge of unease. Was this how they behaved? Was this normal for a sat-nav?

Rixon pulled up and shuffled round in his seat. Joseph William Croft lay sprawled across the back seat. He had to twist in order to catch sight of his face.

65

His waxen, dead gaze focused on nothing. His body vibrated slowly with the gentle hum of the idling engine.

'You're dead.'

Croft didn't respond. This was good. Rixon depressed the clutch and stepped on the accelerator, he had a hot date waiting. In the corner of the screen, the sat-nav read in glowing text, 15 miles to Destination.

***

Meredith paced, running her fingers through her silken strands of dark hair, in a vain effort to undo the knots of stress that had formed within her head.

Something was wrong. An ominous cloud had formed upon her, pressing on her skin causing her to shiver and tingle all over.

The entire world felt wrong.

The kitchen was wrong, the sweet smell of hot chicken was wrong, even the floor tiles were wrong. As if the universe had been taken apart atom by atom and rearranged in a subtle way that the eye wouldn't notice. Everything was wrong with everything. She could taste it in her mouth.

Meredith cast her eyes to the comforting glowing light from the oven. The chicken inside that crisply bubbled away in its own succulent juices wasn't a meal any more. It was a dead thing, and it had died for her pleasure. A sense of loss gripped her, squeezing the effort from her legs, she collapsed to the floor. A terrible thing had happened, she had no proof, yet she knew that her world had somehow changed forever.

Impotent of doing anything, Meredith curled up into a tight foetal ball, letting the horrible spasms of weeping wash out of her. She needed to be bled of tears, fully before she could contemplate her next move. The worrying thoughts increased, paralysing her further. The feeling became apparent that this wasn't over yet. More horrible fits of anguish overtook her, gluing her body to the oh-so-wrong floor tiles.

***

Rixon never answered to his first name, because that was what his parents had named him. He didn't want to give them the satisfaction, even in death, that one of their decisions affected him. The surname he answered to. That was genetic. It couldn't be helped.

Whilst at a set of traffic lights, Rixon rifled through Joseph William Croft's wallet, wishing he had a collection of paper and plastic bound in leather to call his own. It's what defined a person; what they kept in their wallet.

Rixon found a picture of Croft's wife and began to daydream over the orange speckled picture of her in a bikini, reclining on a towel upon a tropical beach. The streetlight, diffused by drizzle illuminated the past scene, giving it a seedy quality. Rixon could make out the ample swell of her breasts, the tautness of her stomach and her thighs toned and tanned.

He hoped they hadn't had children. Rixon wanted her body like it was in the photo, a sagging belly and over fatted thighs would drive him into a rage. He'd have to cut his session short. He needed perfection. He needed to destroy perfection to ease the screaming burdens in his mind.

A horn piped in the queue that had formed behind him. Rixon tossed the picture on the passenger seat with the other scraps of paper and plastic which had made up the life of Joseph William Croft. In his other hand he had unwittingly being holding his under used penis, he'd been stroking the head with his thumb, teasing it back to life after incarceration from female wares.

Rixon had only been with a female once before, and it had been great. Tonight, he promised himself, would be even better. He knew what to do. He just had to put his fantasies into practice.

Rixon pushed the gears into first as the car behind blared its horn again. The deepening sat-nav voice told him turn left.

So he did.

***

Meredith thought about calling the police again. But she knew even if she did get the words out regarding her supernatural worry, why would they even begin to believe her?

What had overcome her?

Why had she become devastated over a silly phone call that was probably nothing?

Because it wasn't nothing.

Something had happened to Joseph Croft, her husband, lover and confidant. He knew all her secrets and she reckoned she knew all of his. Even the nudie mag he kept in his office desk draw. She even knew that he knew that she knew. But she'd let it pass. She wasn't the type of wife to blow up on her husband over something as pathetic as a nudie mag. An affair definitely, but Joe wasn't having an affair. She was assured of his faithfulness to her by female intuition. The way he looked at her first thing in the morning despite her tousled hair and morning breath, the way he held her when they made love, full forceful movements of the hips in perfect sync against hers. She'd never felt like this about anybody else in her life and she knew that she'd die for him if needs be.

It wasn't an affair.

Something worse had interfered with him on the way home and now it was coming for her. There was no logical explanation for it. It was just knowledge to her, a fact, like blue is the colour of a cloudless sky. Something supernatural had delivered this message to her, whether she wanted to know or not. Meredith hoped that somehow, despite how wrong everything felt, somehow it might right itself.

Not with palms together, but with them clasped tightly to her temples, Meredith rocked back and forth on the kitchen floor, praying to whatever god that was listening.

Meredith hadn't prayed since she was a little girl. Tonight she felt as helpless as an infant that had lost a parent, praying childishly that they could be reunited.

There was little else she felt she could do.

***

Even though the distance to go said 1.5 miles, the sat-nav had taken him down a country lane, the gradient increasing and dipping with each turn. He had to concentrate fully on what he was doing.

'Rixxxxx-on. Turn around when possible,' the sat-nav said in a deep baritone.

Rixon looked at the sat-nav, wondering how it knew his name. He understood that technology had come along in the time that he'd been away. But this was a little bit incredible, a little strange and unnerving at the same time.

The sat-nav was crazier than him.

'Turn around now. When possible. *Don't. Do. It,*' the voice continued, the sentence sounding like it had been cut and pasted from various phonic samples. Blocky and clumsy, yet still fully understandable.

'I know what you're thinking.'

Rixon stopped the car, applied the handbrake, then raised his newly shoed foot high and implanted it in the centre of the sat-nav screen. Three swift kicks and a buzz of electricity later, the screen colours died away, replaced by a dead blackness. A deadening white laced crack appeared across the screen where the oversized shoe had come into contact with the LCD display. It was dead.

Satisfied, Rixon put his leg back into the foot well and picked up Joseph William Croft's drivers license and looked at the address. He recognized the town name from a sign he had seen at the last junction. All he had to do was double back and trace his way to the town. Once there he could ask for directions and claim his prize of the dear Mrs Croft, soon to be Rixon's bride.

He didn't need the faulty sat-nav. He hadn't heard it say those things. His mind was playing tricks. Maybe he needed his meds after all. Maybe Dr Meadows had been right.

Rixon put the car in gear and begun to drive again. The road was narrow, dry stone walls lined both sides of the lane. He needed to find somewhere to turn round, either that or he'd have to reverse all the way back to the junction. Rixon didn't want to have to do that; surely he'd find a farm track at some point.

The road dipped into a descent, he fought to control the gears. The black rising shapes of rising hills erupted in the distance, monsters waking from their day of sleep. The reaching trees clawed at the side of car, rushing by, their grip never quite gaining purchase on the vehicle. Rixon tried the brake, too much was happening at once; he was going to get lost.

A tight left hand bend rushed up in front of him, Rixon struggled with the concept of gravity and what it was doing to the car, he gently tapped the brakes, but it wasn't enough to slow his descent.

'Turn right when possible,' the sat-nav said inexplicably, the deadly tones were calm and collected whilst the voice deep and in control. He thought that he'd smashed it in, that it was kaput, yet it was still talking to him, emitting useless directions.

'Turn around,' it said, then a deafening screech exploded from all of the speakers; Rixon grasped his hands to the sides of his head as his ear drums burst from the sonic impact, his legs outstretched in shock, jamming down on the accelerator, carrying the car faster forward as white noise filled his ears.

The car hit the turn at roughly fifty-seven miles an hour, not a great speed, but a thick dry stone wall stood between Rixon and the other side, and he hadn't been wearing his seatbelt.

The car crumpled and at the same time disintegrated the portion of wall it had collided with, carrying on through to the other side, and down a steeper embankment. Away from the relatively smooth glide of the tarmac, the route became bumpy and violent as the tyres bounced from soft contours of grass and over rough outcrops of rock.

The front wheels, revved off a low cliff edge, Rixon barely had chance to draw breath to scream when the car lurched forward impacting with the flat hardness of the valley floor; propulsion carried the car over, tipping suddenly until it landed on its roof, the struts crushed, giving way beneath velocity and gravity. Somewhere in the wreckage, Rixon's body was caught, trapped and twisted with the metal. The fuel tank began to bleed gushing vapour, the battery, swinging free from its housing touched the body work and a spark danced out into the night.

A fireball punched up into the night sky, not before a tinny male voice said pleasantly from the sat-nav's speakers, 'you have reached your destination.'

Rixon was still conscious when the flames took hold. Trapped, but conscious. They edged up around him whilst his paralysed mind screamed out in dire protest.

All my sins, I'm not surprised.

Whilst his body burned there, his soul burnt somewhere else. Somewhere deep and far away.

***

He was trapped in a darkened room, strapped down, he heard voices, dislocated from their owners, lost and mixed in with an eerie zephyr that also seemed to be made up of wandering and incomprehensible narration.

Fingers pinched at his skin, taking flesh away in sharp little pecks, each one shocking and surprising him. This continued, he screamed at every single nipping bite, snapping out with his teeth and trying to wriggle free away from his faceless oppressors.

They seemed to be able to take where he'd already had skin, muscle and sometimes bone pinched away.

It seemed he couldn't run out of flesh.

This could go on for a very long time.

***

A strange wave of euphoria swept over Meredith Croft. She felt relieved, but could offer no explanation as to why. She experienced loss, yet somehow having gained something at the same time. She didn't know what, but it was an understanding that everything was going to be okay. Different but okay.

She would survive, as Gloria Gaynor had always promised.

A bizarre acceptance overcame her that Joe wasn't coming home. He was with her, but she'd never kiss him nor lay with him again. This was sad, nerve shattering fact, but the pleasant memories of time with her husband remained.

Meredith didn't know whether to laugh or cry.

So she did both.

An urge to throw away the cooked chicken became a sudden obsession; get rid of the dead thing, live the life. No more dead things.

Meredith looked at the jar of Marmite on the worktop that she'd gotten out for the gravy, part of her secret recipe.

She wondered whether they had any peanut butter, because the inexplicable though delicious notion that Marmite and peanut butter would go well together on hot buttered toast. It was a strange craving, but she supposed she'd have to get used to them wouldn't she?

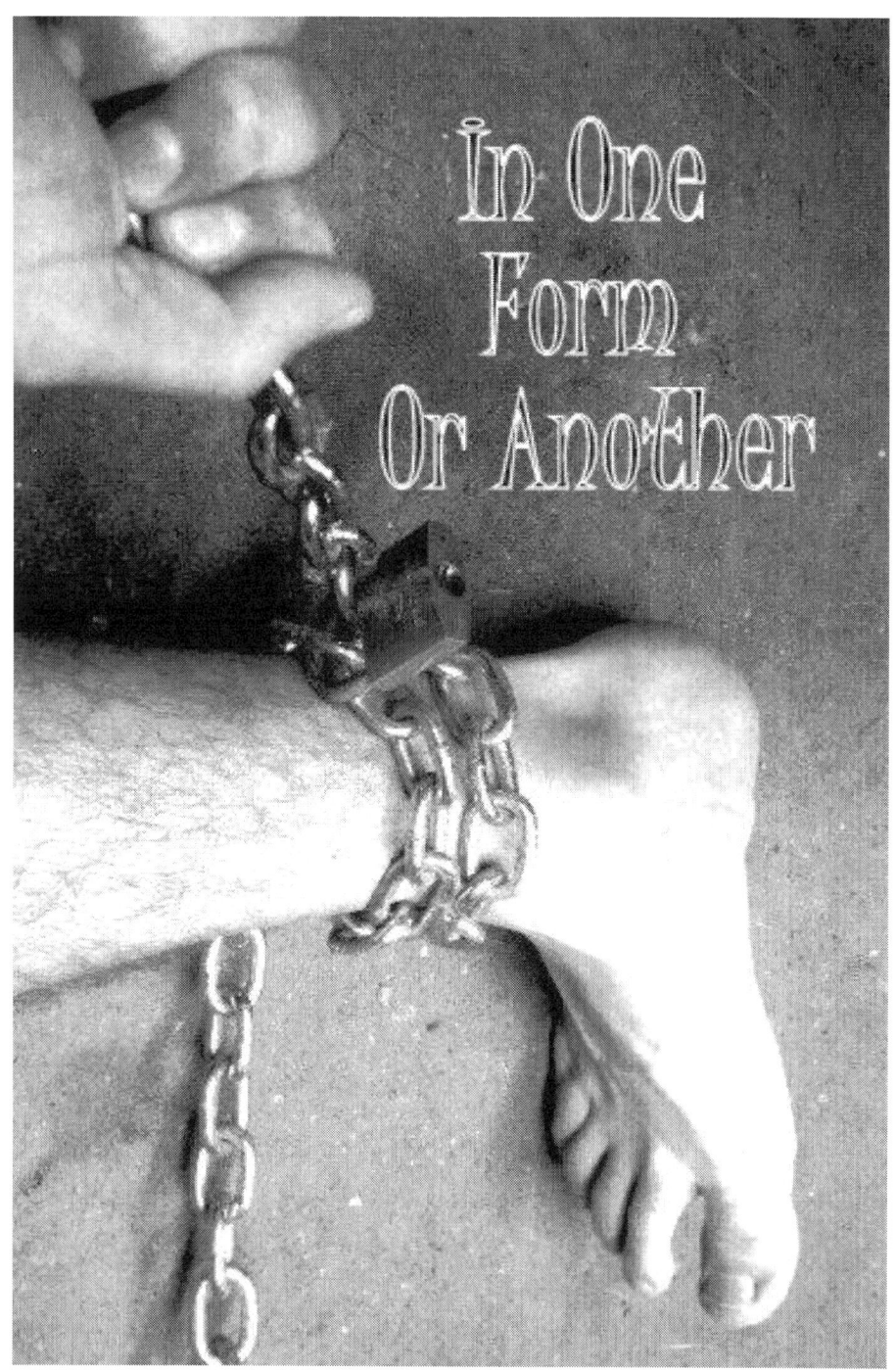

IN ONE FORM OR ANOTHER

I's wicked-I is. I's mighty wicked, anyhow. I can't help it
Harriet Beecher Stowe

It was the nicest house they could've imagined; grand, with enough floor space, nooks and crannies for epic games of hide and seek; yet quaint and modest, maintaining that countryside cottage feel throughout. High ceilings with real oak beams spanned the airy expanse of the living room. Pine cabinets lay empty ready to be filled with treasures, knick-knacks and family photographs. Each room was furnished to give the impression of age, though little in the house held on to the title of antique. Antiquated on purpose maybe, new objects built to look old and still be functional. Shabby chic drawers slid open on well oiled metal runners, the car sized fridge was hidden behind a wooden wall, almost undetectable if it wasn't for the ice dispenser. Everything old was new again.

They had over two acres of land surrounding Quiet Pines Farm, before the lawn garden gave way to neighbouring fields of corn, wheat and rapeseed, then to pine woods shaped like a horseshoe, acting as a crescent on three sides of the horizon. The former working farmhouse sat proud and alone on a small hillock, catching the very best of the summer light without interruption from wandering shadows. A narrow and stony private road led away from the house, trailing through the constant shade of a cosy oak filled copse, leading to the electronically controlled iron gate and then onto the roadside, where they could travel to the outside world. Should they so wish.

Edward Chapel had already stocked the house with tinned goods, fine wines and dry foods, in the spring he had hired gardeners to dig up a large portion of the back lawn, sacrificing the grass for simple rows of vegetable gardens containing all his wife's favourite foods and herbs. They had a small fruit orchard down one side of their spacious garden and an over abundance of bramble bushes exploding from inside one of their derelict buildings. It would be home-baked fruit pies and Devon ice cream all summer long.

All this was his gift to her, his love, his supposed soul mate.

Here in this marvellous, though lonely countryside retreat, he, Helen his wife and Jacob, their seven year old darling son would make a life for themselves through the coming summer days, possibly years if they could adapt to the country lifestyle.

The previous year, Edward had sold his engineering business for a seven-figure sum. Now, after years of 60-70 hour weeks, lonesome nights spent sleeping on the office floor and gut wrenching time away from his family, Edward Chapel was ready to enjoy his retirement. He was a month shy of forty and already a self-made millionaire several times over. It had taken twenty years, building his own business from scratch, but he'd done it to make Helen financially happy, but more importantly he hoped it would make Jacob happy. He was a sullen child, imaginative, but generally he languished in grey moods, or more often than not, lost in books. This would change. He and his son would be spending some much-deserved time together over the summer holidays. He'd do his best to bond the glue that had come unstuck over his years of hard work and neglect. Even though this was the end of his career, it was the beginning of his life to be.

The thought of never working again niggled at him. He longed to be challenged, tested. He hated to admit it, but he enjoyed the pressure too much. He'd neglected his family long enough. It was their time now; he'd had drinks with the boys too many times on Friday nights away from home, it was something he missed, but didn't need any more, or so he told himself. The prospect of returning to work as a part-time consultant had appealed to him. The board of investors had given him this option when they bought the company, as well as a handsome salary and generous amounts of time off. He'd think about it.

Let's get the summer over and done with before I make any more decisions, Edward promised to himself and his family. Though he hadn't revealed that plan to them just yet, he planned to get to Christmas and see how they all got on.

Now, he sat on his patio facing the dropping sun as it melted behind the teeth of pines, Helen was by his side, glass of red in hand, half emptied bottle on the table. The still warm summer breeze carried hints of heady rapeseed past their noses. Insects buzzed away, happily bouncing into each other. Jacob sat on the lawn, idly playing with diggers and dumper trucks that bore Edward's former company logo of the side; a present for his last birthday.

Edward smiled. Helen caught sight of his smirk.

'Why are you smiling?' she said, a little too severely for the situation.

'Why wouldn't I smile?'

She eyed him with mock distrust before leaning in for a kiss, her soft lips touched his and he gently touched hers back. She smelt his regular cologne, a smell she'd missed over the years. So much so she even bought a bottle that she kept around the house, spraying his wardrobe once a week to keep her sane and tell her that he was coming home. He *was* coming home.

'Aren't you happy?' he asked.

'Yes well, it feels strange, leaving the city behind. I'm not exactly a country girl at heart; I'm used to blaring horns and traffic. This calm, this nothing, it's unnerving. It's just us and no one else for miles.'

'Three point two exactly.'

'To what?' she asked.

'Our neighbours-The Jamesons. It's over four miles back to the village.'

'I don't think I've ever been this far from anybody in my life.'

'It's not far. I'm here. Jake's here.'

'It's just a little strange, all this space and we don't have to share it with anyone. It's weird.'

'That's the point, it's our space and we don't have to share it with anyone. We've earned it.' Edward smiled, all this was his doing, his accomplishment and still Helen wasn't entirely happy. 'I know you miss the city, we still have the townhouse, if you ever want to go back for a shopping trip or night out with the girls, it's still there, I don't mind if you miss it.'

Helen stroked his hand, she was warm.

'I do miss it. It'll take me time to get used to all this space,' she said with a floaty gesture of her hand to the garden, fields and woods beyond.

'Will cheese and crackers make you feel better?' he offered.

'Possibly, aside from the nightmares.'

'Cheese doesn't give you nightmares.'

'Strong cheese gives me nightmares, it's a fact, don't argue with me.'

Edward paused for a second, letting her think, 'Do you still want cheese and crackers?'

'Of course I do.' Helen smiled; they both knew cheese and crackers were part of the codeword for the rare act of lovemaking. It did actually involve eating cheese and crackers, but that was part of the fun, they couldn't exactly announce their intention to shag in front of little Jacob.

'Jacob, time for bed big man.' Edward called.

'Okay daddy,' he smiled, collected his toys and they all headed inside closing the patio doors behind them. The sun had now set; the pinewoods seemed to seep closer with the coming darkness, fingers of black ink trickled towards them, further diluting the darkening green of the corn.

***

Having had a busy day of moving house and relocating over two hundred miles from any friends or faces that he knew apart from his parents, surprisingly Jacob went to bed without protest. Once satisfied that their son was fast on in dreamland, Edward and Helen built up the fireplace to a crackling splendour and had a late supper of brie and crackers, opening another bottle of red to wash it down and lubricate the evening further. They slowly made love, finishing happy and slick with each other's sweat. Afterwards they dozed happily in each other's arms on the rug beside the living room fire. It made sense to commit their marital shenanigans downstairs. The living room rug didn't squeak noisily like the newly built bed they had upstairs.

They talked into the night, starting with the house. Even though most of the work was done, little jobs needed to be snagged to make this home perfect. The bottom fence needed repairing and painting, the wine cellar needed fixing with sturdy shelving to accommodate his vast collection of French and German wines that still resided back in their city home.

Their talk turned to Jacob, he'd be starting summer school tomorrow, give the lad a chance to make some new friends in a new town. It would be good for him and good for them. They'd get time alone during the day whilst Jacob gained some independence from them. Either way it would be good for them all. Time together, time apart. They'd started to patch together the desert that their marriage had become.

After letting the fire die down to the last crackling embers, they turned off the lights and made their drunken way to bed.

**

It was 3am when Edward awoke; firing bolt upright to a noise that he was sure had woken him. His back, shoulders and chest were slick with a fearful sheen, a feeling so damp his first thought was that he'd wet the bed. He continued sweating as the adrenalin coursing through his veins readied him for battle or flight or both.

'Did you hear that?' he stroked his wife's arm then gripped it as a tenacious fear took hold. Helen groaned as she opened her weary lids, moonlight filtering into the whites of her eyes. Sensing the serious nature of his tone, she became alert as well.

'What?' she whispered.

'A bang. Like a door slamming.'

'You mean someone's inside the house?' Rising fear crept steadily into her voice; her speech shook a little, a beautiful, nervous tremolo.

'I don't know…' Edward ceased his breathing as he adjusted his hearing, trying his best to make it more acute to the noises of the night.

Bombadabombadabombada . . .

His own heart.

Pheee ha. Pheee ha. Pheee ha. . . .

Helen's fearful breath through her nose.

Eeeeech. Ouwwwch. . .

The groan of the bed as he adjusted his leaning stance.

Hoooooommmmmmmmm . . .

The rushing hum of silence; an ominous hidden soundtrack of reality whistled a tinnitus tone in their alerted ears.

No creaking floorboards.

No calls of night animals.

No breath of wind.

But if he closed his eyes and really listened, developing his sense of hearing he could hear faraway music playing. Classical, but nothing he had ever heard. Like lilting poetry in foreign language, but no tongue he recognized. The sound seemed to move and progress more like a voice underwater than an instrument, but not operatic, more animalistic, a natural rush of a turbulent autumn gust pushing eerily through a tinkling wind chime.

'You hear that?' he whispered.

'I think so. What is it?'

A muffled voice came from somewhere, somebody talking to someone else.

'I think we have visitors.' Edward crept out of bed and towards his wardrobe, cursing the creaking old floorboards that strained beneath his feet.

'What are you doing?' Helen asked. She sat up from the bed, his movement making her more alert.

'I have a gun. I'm going to use it.' Edward reached into the wardrobe and retrieved a long mahogany box from the top shelf and placed it on the foot of the bed. Helen moved from her sitting position and shuffled towards Edward.

'You said the gun was just for show, you haven't even got a licence for it.'

Edward removed the double-barrelled twelve bore from its box and loaded two shells into the breach. It had been a gift from one of the investors; they'd taken him on a shooting trip to the highlands and let him keep his gun as a keepsake. An emblem of a stout and proud red deer was carved into the stock. *"Just don't go flashing it around"* they'd told him when the day was over, *"it's not registered… anywhere."*

'You said you'd keep it locked up and out of Jacob's way. You promised it was for show,' Helen pleaded.

'It was just for show. Now we need it for real.' Edward hissed. He clicked the barrel shut. It was heavier than he remembered, but he knew how to use it. Support foot in front of the other, the stock tucked snugly into the arc of the shoulder. The routine would come back to him; the investors had said he was a natural. He longed to have another go, head back to the wilds of Scotland to blast away at grouse and pheasant. That would have to wait.

'I'm going to see our visitor.' Edward wore only jogging bottoms; he was bare-chested and bare-footed, brandishing the shotgun proudly across his front.

'Check on Jacob, make sure he's safe.' He left the bedroom and crept as downstairs as quietly as the creaking floorboards would allow. Helen got up, pulled on a dressing gown and headed down the landing to Jacob's room with a hurried scamper.

Downstairs was untouched, the intruder hadn't moved or taken anything that he noticed, Edward moved towards the kitchen with slow, deliberate steps. A chill surfaced on his chest, back and feet. He shivered as he rounded the corner to discover the French doors were wide open, revealing the patio, eerily bathed in the glow of the high moon.

Edward paused and swallowed a dry lump. Fear was hard to keep down. He felt like his skeleton wanted to jump from his skin and back upstairs to bed. He steeled himself, willing his courage to balloon and carry him forward to investigate.

He waited a few seconds to see if an intruder would surface from the shadows. He heard Helen upstairs as she creaked into Jacob's room. His attention was divided as he listened to both his wife checking on their son and any potential scuff or creak that might reveal the whereabouts of their intruder.

He moved cautiously towards the patio doors. The keys were still in the lock on the inside, a quick inspection revealed that the door, frame and lock were free of damage. Whoever had opened this door had done it from the inside. He cursed himself for leaving the keys in the lock. The intruder had probably broken in through a window and left this way as it offered a quicker and safer route of escape.

He checked the kitchen table.

His wallet remained untouched, as did his mobile phone and the keys to the X-Trail.

Strange, they hadn't taken anything.

Maybe they got scared.

Edward stepped closer to the patio door. Edging closer, the sound of singing now seemed louder to his ears.

From upstairs, he heard Helen gasp and offer a stifled scream through the waking house.

He moved to turn back and head through the living room but she thundered down the stairs towards him. Her colour was pale, her mouth agape with shock.

'Jacob's gone, Jacob's gone!' she repeated in a panicked whisper, 'he's gone!'

Propping the gun into his shoulder he turned to Helen and said, 'I think he's gone outside, follow me and keep quiet,' Edward responded as quietly as his voice would travel. They stepped forward and headed through the doors and onto the moonlit patio, stepping softly; his bare feet winced on the night-cooled slabs. He peered into the dark. The soft voice that sang had died down, but unless his ears were playing wicked tricks he could still hear the low mournful sound carried along beneath the gentle breeze of the night.

'Wait!' Helen reversed back into the utility room, rummaged in a drawer then returned with a torch in hand. 'We might need this.' She didn't turn it on; instead she cuddled it to her chest for comfort.

Helen stuck close by him as they stepped off the patio and onto the lawn, the grass was wet with the dew that came with the dark. They stepped further into the garden, through the chewed up lines of the vegetable plots further from the safety of the house, closer to the strangeness of the corn fields and pine woods. Bushes and trees cast dark, infinite shadows that engulfed the bottom of the garden.

Ahead, small, evenly spaced footprints led away from them down the lawn. Edward was sure that the trail of disturbed wet grass was the desired line that his son had taken. He followed it until he found him. They stopped, breath paused in their lungs.

Jacob was at the bottom of the garden, stood by the broken fence, his back was facing them. He peered into the mass of corn that acted like a natural barrier at the foot of their property. The dilapidated fence resembled the busted mouth of a monster halfway through a fight with a much bigger beast.

Helen clicked on the torch, shining it on her son's back. She edged the beam along the stalks of corn in an effort to identify the source of the evening's weirdness.

The singing whispered past their ears again, seeming like it was coming from inside the cornfield itself. Jacob seemed to be transfixed by this. From this distance his parents could hear that he was talking to the stalks of corn. They couldn't make out his exact words, but they were certain that whispered sounds played past his lips.

Edward relaxed the shotgun, letting it hang down across loose his hips. Helen offered a sigh and a nervous little laugh as she lowered the torch. Their son was sleepwalking, that was all.

His parents moved closer, as they did, something stirred up and out of the corn, managing to leave every stalk unaffected by its presence. A dark shape that played from shadow to shadow, a mere ink blot on reality, yet monstrous, channelling the predatory stance of a bear or a wolf. It pounced, the soft song it had been singing ceased. A roar; primeval and hungry escaped its unseen mouth as it pinned the Chapel's young son to the wet grass. Jacob didn't even scream as the breath of the beast blew his hair about his face, freeing fresh tears from his eyes.

Edward fired into the air, not even a warning shot, an accident from the shock. It lit up the far corner of their garden; the creature vanishing with the influx of light, then returned. No features could be determined. It seemed to belong to the shadow of some great beast, yet pure black and impenetrable. No fur, no skin, just inky obsidian infinity stretching beyond their imagination.

Jacob's arm raised up as the monster took hold of it in its unseen jaw, then appearing from nothing, blood ran down Jacob's arm, he seemed to awake at this point screaming a high piercing shriek into the disturbing dead of night.

Helen screamed and frantically beat down on Edward's bare back for him to do something. Anything.

She pointed the torch at the otherworldly beast in an effort to illuminate the problem.

Edward levelled the shotgun at the black shape's back and fired. The buckshot carried on through the creature, decimating a circle of corn stalks behind it. Yet it bellowed with anger, a siren-shriek somewhere between a tyrannosaurus being eviscerated and a fairy tale giant stubbing his toe, a terrifying noise that neither of them had heard before. Then the black shadow turned to smoke, to fading grey dust, then nothing but the shade of night.

It was gone, but its roaring death knell still rattled in their ears.

Edward stood, struck dumb and shaking as his nerve endings threatened to burn out and every hair on his being tensed and stood to prickled attention.

They waited a second for it to reappear, but it didn't. Edward's next line of thought was to reload the shotgun; then he saw his son bleeding on the wet grass at the bottom of their garden. Even if the shadowy creature returned, Jacob was now the priority.

Handing the shotgun to Helen he rushed over to Jacob, his wife followed, clumsily dragging the empty shotgun by the barrel, the stock dragging through the wet grass. Edward grabbed the torch from his wife and shone it into the wound. Massive teeth marks had been sunk into Jacob's frail arm. His blood, almost black in the torch light, pumped out, covering and soaking half of the unconscious child. Edward dropped the torch onto his son's stomach and scooped him up into the cradle of his arms.

'We have to get him inside,' Helen reasoned.

'What was that? We didn't see that did we?' Edward replied dumbfounded, standing up with his injured son in his arms. Moving back towards the house, he cast a wary gaze back to the cornfield. All was quiet. The dark silence was an unnerving silk that hid things from their eyes not tuned to such natures.

'Are we dreaming Helen? Tell me that we're dreaming.'

'I saw it too Edward. I saw it too. We can't both be dreaming.'

'The black wolf sings in my dreams,' Jacob croaked.

'What was that honey?' Helen stroked her son's head.

'It sings a song we've all forgotten.'

'What's he saying?' Edward asked.

'I don't know.'

They reached the patio and stepped inside the kitchen, Helen relocked the door behind them, while Edward used his son's limp body to clear clutter from the table and placed his bloodied form on where they should be having breakfast in four hours time. The still lighted torch rolled from Jacob's belly and onto the floor. The bulb popped and the bright beam of light ceased. They both ignored it as it rolled under the table.

'He used to stalk beyond the fires. Too much fire for him now,' Jacob rambled, 'he was the last. He was telling me.'

Jacob sighed.

'What was that out there?' Edward asked again. He was still shaking. Helen was crying now, she flicked on the kitchen light so they could get a better look at the wound.

It wasn't as bad as they both thought, a lot of splatter, but no depth. The panic of the situation had caused them to think that it was a lot worse. Edward grabbed his son's arm holding it up to the light trying to identify the bite marks the strange creature had inflicted. He stretched out the blood-soaked skin with his fingers, searching for tooth shaped entry wounds.

He couldn't find any.

The wound had already healed.

***

Dawn came slow and warming, melting into what promised to be another summers day of clear skies and honey bees, yet it brought only brightening light, no happiness or joy enlightened this household. The Chapels were happy their son was safe and free from injury, but still, the events of the night had unnerved them. Knife-edges and tenterhooks, their raw nerves were on show to each other. Helen cried, as did Edward. But their son was alive. That was all that mattered.

Using a wet cloth, Helen had sponged off the remnants of blood that decorated Jacob's arm, with no visible injury they laid him to rest in his bed where he slept peacefully. She joined her husband back at the kitchen table. A few bloody smears cast maroon lines across the oak, dried and crusting darkening contours. It was strange to think that those rusted sweeps of crimson had once been wet puddles of blood.

Edward had dressed in a t-shirt and a baggy pair of shorts then he made coffees that now sat cooling on coasters amongst the bloodstains. He hadn't touched his.

'Do we call a doctor?' Helen asked, sitting down. 'Should we call a doctor?' she rephrased as she raised the coffee cup to her lips and blew roasted Columbian steam from the rim.

'For what?' He hasn't any injuries.'

'Do we take him to see the doctor?'

'Again, what do we show him? There's no bite mark, no evidence of whatever the fuck we saw out there. They'll think we're crazy. They'll lock us up. What would we tell them?'

'Maybe your right,' Helen breathed a sigh through her nose, looked through the kitchen window out towards the bottom of the garden, a frown was born, crinkling into life across her forehead as she remembered the events of last night. She hadn't slept an iota since then, yet it seemed like a strange, even false memory, as if it had been placed in her mind by individuals unknown. Just to upset and worry her. It wasn't a dream. The blood on the table was testament to that.

'How about the police?'

'The gun remember? The shotgun? I haven't a licence. They'll lock me up. We'd have to leave that part out. Even then, what do we tell them? Our son sleep walked outside in the middle of the night only to be attacked by some kind of fucked up shadow monster. Is that what we tell them Helen? That it attacked Jacob. That I shot at it and it disa-fucking-peered!' He slammed a palm down on the table. The coffee cups rattled, droplets of liquid jumped out and diluted the grainy streaks of their sleeping son's blood.

'There's no need to swear Edward. You're not at work now. You're at home, with your family. Relax.' Helen stood up and fetched a cloth from the sink then wiped up the coffee wetted blood.

'Relax how exactly?' His words were low and precise, almost cutting.

'I don't know. I don't know what to do. He seems fine, but I'm worried. Jacob was attacked by something. We both saw what happened didn't we. We've agreed that something attacked him. We just don't know what.' Helen returned to the sink and rinsed the cloth out and replaced it back from where she'd found it.

'Helen, what did you see?' Edward asked calm and slow.

She turned round, shrugged and offered a trying smile. 'I don't know.'

'What do you think you saw?'

'I don't know.'

'Try. Try to describe it best you can. I want to hear your version of what happened.'

'We found Jacob at the bottom of the garden. I heard the strange singing. Like opera, but different. It was like the wind. Calm and peaceful. Like a wind chime. I shone the torch on Jacob, then I shone it into the cornfield to try and see if anybody was in there, y'know hiding. Then it jumped out and bit our son. That monster. The Dark Monster. Like a shadow in the night.'

'What do you think it was a shadow of?'

'Some beast, I wouldn't like to think what. Nothing I've ever seen. I told you cheese gave me nightmares.' She smiled thin, with a little laugh of fear, showing teeth this time, trying to mean it for real. Edward got up and moved over to her, slipping his hands round her waist he kissed her on the cheek. She kissed him on the lips.

'Sorry for being such an arse.'

'It's okay. You're just worried about Jake.'

'I am. But I don't want to call the police for obvious reasons and I don't want to take him to the doctors for them to laugh at us. They'll probably blame the cheese.' Edward smiled this time, his face lighting up a little.

'So what do we do? What if he's got an infection?'

'I have a theory.'

'Oh go on.' she urged.

'We hallucinated, pure and simple. Maybe it was the cheese…and the wine. Maybe we both had internal fears of the dark, you said yourself it was weird being alone after all that time in the city. Maybe it was our subconscious reacting to that.'

'We both hallucinated?' she asked, her tone heavy with doubt, 'on cheese?'

'Yep.'

'At the same time?'

'Uh huh.'

'You expect me to buy that?' Incredulous, she tried to pull away. He held on to reason with her.

'It's the best I've got,' he replied with an open gesture of his palms.

'What about the blood?'

'Prop blood. Jake must have bought it and sprayed it on himself. Y'know, seeking attention and all that. Because I haven't been around,' he admitted with a shred of guilt. He tried to look sheepish, he failed.

'You think Jake is attention-seeking. You think all that happened last night was Jake's effort at getting our attention. Pure and simple?' she mocked.

'There was no wound! It must be a hallucination on our part. We imagined the beast, at first sight we saw the wound and assumed it was far worse than it actually was. Fake blood. We panicked, that's all.'

'And the singing, the strange singing? We both heard that.'

'Again, a group hallucination, a figment of our tired, drunk and cheese-infused minds.'

'The thing we saw last night was a figment of our imagination?'

'Yep, must have been. Nothing like we saw last night exists on this planet. Attenborough would have done a documentary on it by now.'

'And what if it's not from this planet.'

'You saying alien?' Edward furrowed his brow in doubt at the daft thought.

'Maybe, or perhaps it escaped from a lab? Like a super rat that can turn invisible or a being from another dimension?'

'You read too much Koontz and King.'

'You don't read enough.'

'We dreamt it okay. Final. I'll have a word with Jake when he wakes up about scaring his parents like that. It wasn't funny.'

'So we're not going to the doctors?' she pushed him away and turned round

'Or the police. We'll keep last night to ourselves. Families can keep secrets can't they?'

'And what if I don't want to keep it secret? What if I don't think we *imagined* it?' She gave imagined little bunny ear quotation marks to stress her point.

'You want to tell the world that we had a bad dream. You want me to go to prison for owning a gun without a license? This could turn into a clusterfuck.'

'My first concern is for Jacob. If he shows the first sign of a fever or rash or anything out of the ordinary I'm taking him to the clinic in the village and I'm going to tell them everything.'

'Even the gun?'

'Even the gun? I told you not to hang on to it. More fool you for hanging on to an illegal weapon.'

'Hey, if I didn't have that gun last night, if I didn't fire at that creature and make it vanish in a puff of smoke then last night might have been far worse. It might have attacked us as well.'

'I thought you said it was a figment of our imagination?' She had him there.

'Okay, if… and I mean a big if. If Jake gets ill in any way then we'll take him to the doctors, I promise.'

Helen turned to leave.

'Where are you going?'

'I'm going to check on our son. Make sure he's okay. Is that okay?' She looked slightly annoyed, not pissed off, just annoyed. He gave a little shrug as his response.

Then she left, leaving Edward alone in the kitchen with his cold cup of coffee.

***

Feeling the need to investigate last night further, Edward slipped on his shoes and a jacket and headed out through the patio door and into the morning sun. The night-time dew had started to evaporate with the intrusive glare of sunlight upon the grass. He made his way back down the garden taking the path he had followed last night and stopped when he got to the broken fence that bordered the cornfield. Edward dipped to his knees to get a closer look at where Jacob had been stood. A few splashes of dark blood had settled amongst the dewy blades.

Apart from that, nothing.

He considered venturing into the field and searching for the bottle of fake blood that Jacob had no doubt tossed into the corn stalks.

A shiver danced down his spine.

He didn't want to admit to himself that he had seen something, but if he let Helen have her way, doctors and police would be sniffing about the place by now. He had an illegal weapon on the premises; if the police caught him without a license there was the grim possibility that he could go to prison. Christ he didn't know how long for. He might get a caution, but it could just as easily be ten years. He didn't want to think about it. He'd decided. No police. They'd deal with this by themselves. If Jacob became too ill he'd take him to the clinic in the village. Helen would have to agree to that.

Edward leant over to investigate the broken fence. His gaze became entranced by one the slats that had made up the structure of the border fence.

Six scratch marks were etched into the wood. Fresh. Cutting through the old grey wood and exposing the yellow fibre beneath. A few stray pellets of buckshot had penetrated along the length, yet the structure had held fast. He bent down. On the other side of the fence a clear footprint was pressed into the mud bordering the cornfield. It looked like a dog print. Except it had six toes splayed out mightily.

It was about where the *thing* had jumped out and attacked Jacob.

Something had been here.

Unless Jacob had done this… but then how could he influence what they had seen?

He wouldn't tell Helen about this.

He had her half convinced that they had both imagined it.

Edward wanted to leave it that way.

He didn't want it to be anything other than a hallucination. The thought that if what they'd seen had been real, chilled him to his core. He touched the footprint with his fingers, expecting an electrical resonance to jump out and shock him. Nothing. He ploughed his fingers into the wet soil and mashed up the evidence, tossing and turning the churned up mud in his hands.

Edward got up, dusting the grains off with his other hand then wiping off the remnants on his shorts. He headed back to the house, the stalks of corn waving him goodbye.

***

He made strong coffee, he had to drink something. Maybe Irish it up a little? He resisted; instead made Helen a mug and headed upstairs. She was in Jacob's room, stroking his head. He was still asleep.

'How is he?' Edward asked.

'Seems fine, a little hot, just wants to sleep. Some nightmare huh?' she said soothingly.

Edward smiled and placed the steaming mug down gently on top of the bedside drawers.

'No shit.'

'Don't swear.'

'He's asleep.'

'He can still hear us.'

Edward took a sip, 'What are your plans for today?'

'What do you mean?'

'Well, what so you want to do today?'

'I want to look after our son, he's not well Edward.'

'He was probably up all night on his Play Station with the sound turned down, that's why he's knackered.'

'You reckon?' she turned round from soothing Jacob, eyebrows raised in disapproving disbelief.

'Well, yeah. He's a kid. It's what kids do.' Edward lifted a hand and stroked a spot on the back of his neck, it was sore to touch and ready to pop. It wasn't there yesterday.

'He hasn't set up his Play Station yet. It's still boxed up from the move,' she corrected, pointing to a collection of their son's things that took up one corner of his room. Various boxes and bags filled to the brim with clothes and toys spilled over each other. Edward shrugged.

From down stairs an irritating noise buzzed from the kitchen.

'The front gate,' the colour drained from his face in a wash. 'Someone's at the front gate.'

'Well who?'

'I don't know. That's what I'm about to find out. It's our first visitor.' He left the bedroom, leaving Helen alone to care for their sickly son.

***

The sun warmed Edward's face as he walked down the driveway to the front gate, he didn't rush. No need. Don't panic. Don't appear like anything is wrong. Be normal.

A police car sat parked across the driveway, a suited and booted policeman stood patiently on the other side of the gate. As Edward approached he noticed a policewoman sat in the driver's seat, she didn't take notice of him. She kept looking at the empty road ahead.

'Good morning,' the policeman grinned; it was a smoker's smile; slowly decaying yellow teeth grinned back. It held about as much charm as a corpse's grin. Cropped and receding grey hair topped his head, his uniform was crisp and black, detracting from the brightness of the day, whilst his skin had an odd scarred quality to it, as if he'd had his face washed in acid sometime during his youth.

'Morning officer, can I help you?'

'Actually it's Sergeant Porter,' he corrected. 'We've had a report of a gunshot coming from the vicinity of your house, would you happen to know anything about this?'

'When? Last night?' Edward feigned surprise, 'we didn't hear anything. I suppose we were knackered from all the unpacking we've being doing. Dead to the world last night,' Edward forced a tired half laugh.

Look like you been asleep.

Edward rubbed his eyes, ran a hand through his hair, and then yawned. To complete the illusion he leaned on the gatepost to support his tired form.

'Would you mind if we took a look around the property? Just to be safe…'

'I'd rather you didn't, we only arrived yesterday, and we're all tired. We still have a lot to unpack. My wife's head is a mess; she really doesn't want visitors today. It's bad enough that I'm in the way half the time.'

'I understand sir, but if a weapon was discharged we have to investigate fully…'

'I suggest you have a walk round the woods, probably poachers I should think. Besides if somebody did fire a shotgun I think my family would have heard something.'

Porter stopped speaking before he even started as if his mind had suddenly caught onto a new train of thought; he smiled in a knowing manner, becoming a shark in the blink of a wrinkled eyelid, 'I never mentioned it was a shotgun Mister...?'

'Chapel ... and shotgun was a guess, don't all farmers have shotguns. For pests. Is there another farm nearby? I mean I wouldn't expect Old Macdonald to be wielding a Kalashnikov, so I just assumed. An honest mistake.'

'There are no honest mistakes Mr Chapel. The Jameson's farm is closest to you. They called it in, said it came from your side of the woods.'

'Well sorry to tell you this Mister Porter...'

'Sergeant,' Porter corrected glumly, his face plain and hard now, tightening the cratered pockmarks that showed his age.

'Sorry sergeant, it's probably a misunderstanding or a strange coincidence.'

Porter's face crinkled into a suspicious, near condescending frown, 'I don't believe in coincidences Mister Chapel.'

'Neither do I sergeant, my mind is stuck firmly in reality. I'm not one for making up fairy tales.'

'Ahh, you'll not know about the woods then?'

'Well, no.'

'I'd stay clear of the woods if I were you, especially if you don't like fairy tales.'

'I'm not getting you officer.'

'Sergeant.' Porter corrected.

'Sorry, sergeant.'

'The Quiet Pines woods, behind your house. I take it you don't know the legends that come from there?'

'Well no, we've just moved here.'

'The Abcastle Witches, Mister Chapel?'

Edward shrugged. Nonplussed and no wiser to the policeman's ramblings.

'It wasn't called Quiet Pines a hundred years ago.'

'Why not?'

'They called it Gallows Woods. There's a swamp somewhere in the pines. The Abcastle Witches were convinced that the black water contained the blood of the devil, that's where they sacrificed the children. That's why your house is built on a hill. To keep it dry.'

'A quaint local legend I'm sure.'

'They never found the bodies of the children. Legend goes that the Witches held them under the swamp water to give their last breaths to their devil lord. They caught them afterwards. They found a corn dolly of a little girl nearby so that was enough evidence for the mob that came after them. They hung them from the pines. Ten of them so they say.'

'Why are you telling me this? You're a cop, why would you be telling me ghost stories?'

'Not many people live in this house for long Mister Chapel. I always warn them. They should raze it to the ground and leave it be.'

'Huh, then I'd be out of pocket. Why not warn them before?'

'That would be the estate agent's job. I don't believe in curses . . . but this place. Never liked it.' Porter looked up the driveway, a slight tremble on his bottom lip. He pulled a face as if someone had just spat in his mouth. 'I'll bid you good day.'

Edward watched as the police sergeant turned slowly and efficiently on his heels and climbed back into the car, the young police woman started the car, turned it round and took the grumpy, acid-faced Sergeant Porter back towards the village.

Edward breathed a guilty sigh of relief. He looked left, looked right down the now empty road that connected them to the outside world. He could have asked for help. Ask Porter to fetch a doctor, but no. That would have brought people onto his property. The gun would have been found and charges would be brought against him. He wasn't paranoid. That's what would happen. They'd take him away from his family that he's worked so hard to finally enjoy.

He had to get rid of the shotgun.

But after the events of last night, he felt a natural protective caution and reluctance to do so.

If that thing came back after he tossed the gun? Christ, it could kill them all.

Naturally, the events of last night had disturbed him. Tonight he'd be on guard.

Edward Chapel left the solitude that the front gate provided and walked steadily up the dirty gravel path back towards the house where his family waited for him. He wouldn't tell his wife about the mumbo jumbo about the witches. There was no need to fuel her already overactive imagination.

***

The rest of the day flowed along in a river of forced tranquillity. Edward tended the garden, plucking the occasional weed, shifting old pots broken and shattered by the cold of last winter and composting long dead flowers from last year. Helen unpacked ornaments and books, tending to Jacob in-between chores; making him soup, a sandwich, and serving him a plateful of chocolate biscuits. Every effort she concocted went untouched. Her fretting did however start to grate on Edward, who had been peacefully alone at the bottom of the garden nailing together the broken fence. He turned over the claw marked length of timber, nailing it the other way round, letting it face the woods, hiding the truth from his wife. Something had been here. The evidence was real in the bright light of day. There was no denying that.

'He's still burning up,' Helen informed him. At noon she brought him a glass of pink grapefruit juice with ice and lemonade. This did little to detract from what she had to say. 'We should still take him to the doctors.'

Edward took the cool glass from Helen and downed it in two gulps. 'Twenty-four hours, give me that. Let's see how tonight goes. He might be right as rain in the morning. If you take him to the doctors they'll probably give him an aspirin and send him back here. It'll be a waste of time. It's probably all a coincidence. Just keep him hydrated. The fever will break and come down eventually,' Edward gave the glass back to his wife and tried a smile. It did nothing to crack her demeanour. The wind caught up; tousling her hair, shaking the nearby apple tree, fragments of blown blossom caught up in her strands. He wanted to tell her she looked beautiful; but it wasn't right. She'd think he was trying to change the subject to slide away from her nagging.

'How can you be so sure?'

'Father knows best.'

'Again, how can you so sure? You're an engineer, not a doctor.'

'Trust me. Jake will get better; he'll be stronger because of it. All I can suggest is that we keep an eye on him and make sure he doesn't burn up or have a seizure or anything daft like that.'

'I'd rather get him to the hospital before that happens.'

'No hospital. That's final.'

Edward pulled the car keys from his pocket and threw them into the depths of the cornfield beyond their garden. They jingled as the silver caught at the sunlight, Helen watched them rise and fall into the natural spokes of corn. Although clenching at her palms, she still took a calm breath before speaking.

'Why final?' she asked coolly and calmly; his overreaction hadn't fazed her. She could find the keys easily. Besides they had a spare set, in a box somewhere.

'You know why?'

'The gun, you're risking your son's health for a stupid gun?'

'No, I just don't want to be taken away from my family.'

'And what if Jake is taken away from us?'

'Now you're just being pessimistic.'

'Edward, I'm being a realist and you're being a dick,' Helen turned and headed back to the house. Her urgent gait suggested that he'd pissed her off some. Didn't matter; all it meant was more time in the garden. In the sunshine. Sheer joy. Jacob would be fine. He'd taken his argument too far to turn back, and it would be a dent in his pride if he completed such a U-turn.

Jacob would be fine; he tried to convince nobody but himself.

***

'He's talking!'

Teatime had passed by without him hungering. Dusk arrived, bleaching the sky with fantastical burnt orange hues, bleeding into bruised purples. The country big sky was something to behold, a more divine canvas than the cluttered city skyline he'd become accustomed to. Edward was still pottering in the garden, shifting some old frost damaged bricks from behind the shed to an area that he had already paved over in his mind. Eight bricks at a time, he was well onto halfway through the spider occupied stack when Helen came bursting out of the house, tears nearly forming in her eyes.

'He's talking, Jacob's awake!'

'I heard you the first time,' Edward responded curtly, he dropped his last stack of bricks on the floor into the pile of rubble. Helen ran towards him.

'He's awake!'

'How is he? Does he want to eat?'

'I think you'd best come and see.'

Something in her eyes told Edward she wasn't entirely pleased he'd awoken.

***

His eyes were wide-open, dark circles sat like black bags beneath his dry eyeballs. He didn't blink. Edward and Helen stared at him from the doorway for over a minute and his lids didn't shift. Not once.

His chest rose and fell; only slightly, the breaths he was taking in were minimal, as if he were conserving his energy.

His lips moved, a word, a whisper. Naturally this intrigued his parents; they stepped into the room, moving closer to their sick son. They bent down on bended knees at his bedside.

'What do you want son? Would you like some water?' His father picked up the glass of tepid water held it close to his son's lips. He didn't partake in hydrating himself. The fluid ran in twin rivulets from his mouth and over his chin.

Another breathy word left his lips. Edward moved closer to his son's mouth to catch what was being said. Was he hungry, did he want juice instead of water? Maybe he should really take him to the doctors.

'*Annuvva…scelth…denom…matryji…ni…nu…noiob…sela…cap…sela…cap…pe …truin…net…fouer…*'

'He's talking gibberish,' Edward confirmed.

'Have you changed you mind about taking him to the hospital?' his wife raised her eyebrows, fully aware she was right and that her husband was wrong.

'*selluf…nana tubay…nana tuba…chrispo yalter nai nai nai…*'

Edward could see the dryness of his son's eyeballs. He hadn't blinked for a while, so now the surface had started to crinkle as the moisture had evaporated from the white of his eye, giving it the pallor of a drying mushroom.

'*fulluc anana…yabut opsirch… Rell! Rell! Rell!*' The strength in Jacob's voice grew in intensity, he became louder, but he still didn't blink, droplets of sweat had started to prickle forth on his pale forehead.

'Edward, where are the spare car keys?'

'Maybe we should call a doctor now?

89

'I said that in the beginning…'

'*Rell! Rell! Denom massaput sela luff! Bata mata shuboe kala!*'

'I think he may have a fever…' Edward laid his hand upon his son's head to gauge his rising temperature.

'*Bala non, caliba teo teo denom…*' the moment Edward's fingerprints touched Jacob's's forehead, the mindless chanting ceased. A second of silence drowned the room, reverberations of angered echoes passed through them. The bed creaked as Jacob sat up the heady wet stench of sweat and stale urine overcame their senses, the bed sheet beneath Jacob was soaked with both liquids. Jacob turned towards his parents; then lunged.

Edward was knocked over as his son crashed into him like a boy shaped bullet, both crashed onto the hard wood floor. Dumbfounded, Helen did nothing at first except offer a useless gasp, then she watched her son sink his teeth into his father's arm, then she reacted, grabbing Jacob by the back of his piss soaked pyjamas and pulled him off Edward, but the young boy wouldn't let go. He hung on by his teeth, incisors cutting down into the hard, bare bone.

An image of a serrated clamp tightening down upon dough exploded in his mind as Edward screamed and resisted the dire temptation to punch his son in the face, the more Helen pulled, the harder he bit down. Jacob's fingers worked their way up and towards his father's face, little scratchy nails clamoured and found purchase in Edward's mouth, his nostril and his eye sockets.

Enough.

Edward reared up, Jake still hanging on by his teeth as his father lifted him up and forced him against the wall, fighting off his little limbs with his unbitten arm.

'Jake let go sweetie!' Helen's pleas fell on deaf ears, the ravenous look in Jacob's eyes and the bloody foam that slobbered freely from his clenched mouth suggested that her son was now in another world. Jake's fingers worked into his father's eye socket, flapping at the lid, his sharp little nails scratching at the delicate white flesh that granted Edward Chapel vision.

'Hit him with something!' Edward pleaded as he became soaked in his own blood as he fought off his son's dual attempts to blind and eat him, 'Christ, knock him out…'

'You want me to hit our son?' Helen screamed, whilst looking round for an answer to Edward's question.

'I want you to stop him biting me. Christ! I don't care how you do it!' Edward pulled back from the wall then surged forward, hoping to knock the wind out of Jacob. After the third attempt and a boy shaped indentation in the stud wall, Helen grabbed the lava lamp from the chest of drawers and smashed it over her demented son's head. The water washed the majority of the blood away in a cool explosive instant, then still clinging on by his teeth, Jacob fell away, tearing off a strip of flesh like melted cheese. He sat slumped in the corner, dazed but still conscious.

'Get some packing tape,' Edward seethed grasping hold of the bloody wound on his arm to stem the crimson flow. His t-shirt was covered in his own blood and lava lamp water. He looked down at his son, his drenched head loped to and fro as he fought off the effects of the impact from the glass lamp. The lump of blue unheated wax sat clumped between them. Breathing heavy frightened breaths, Edward watched as his own blood leaked out from Jacob's mouth.

'Packing tape!' he barked at his wife, 'and bandages. Now!'

Helen ran off, her rapid, clomping footsteps vibrating down the stairs.

Jacob lunged again, going for his legs this time, bloodied milk teeth chomped easily around the succulent flesh that filled his calf. Edward screamed and kicked out with his other leg, catching Jacob in the ribs, lost his balance then fell on top of him. His leg popped free, so he used this to his advantage, pressing his weight down on the boy, Jacob let out an inhuman screech in protest, continuing with his strange mutterings now that his mouth was devoid of his father's flesh.

'...*telma ano pater semlin nurvisvelmar!*'

'Jacob...just calm down...it's okay...please relax.'

'*Seppa co no mar telba vah na telat a carvimar!*'

'Please son,' Edward pleaded during the struggle, 'please calm down!'

'*Quibe quibe na mar ghist selafelda miyt cha bach nar!*'

The sound of approaching footsteps brought his wife back into the bedroom. Edward pressed his knee hard into his son's back and felt something hard crack beneath his weight, not really caring at that point in time. This infuriated Jacob, who screamed so loud his eyes seem to bulge from their sockets and his lips drew back to reveal gnashing bloody little teeth.

'Tape his hands!' Edward shouted as he held tight onto his son's slim little wrists and jerked them round hard so they were behind his back, another crack, this time from the boy's shoulder. Helen winced as she lifted off the strip of packing tape and started to wrap it clumsily round her son's wrist. In the struggle Edward managed to shoot her a glaring look at her to hurry before their son attacked again. Judging from the detesting tears that escaped her lost looking eyes, she didn't want to be doing this. In an instant, Edward Chapel knew that his marriage was over, that was all it took, just one look from his wife to tell him it was all over. He'd never seen that look before; to be honest, it scared him. He didn't want to lose her again.

Edward grabbed the roll from his wife and carried on the motion of winding the brown packing tape round and round his son's wrist, the tape screamed as it peeled off the roll. Once satisfied he was secure, Edward span round and grabbed Jacob's legs. Helen didn't help, instead she watched, weeping and useless.

91

Edward stood up and regarded his son, who squirmed and rolled about the floor like a giant human worm, muttering to himself in his new made up language.

'...*tenbra moseleta cursa colie sambi scret vel vey nah tel...*'

'Helen...?' she had already turned and left before he could say anything else. Edward sighed, cursed the bites that his son had chomped out of him then followed his wife out of the room, leaving his demented son to struggle alone and chanting in his own new language.

***

Helen was in the kitchen, she was crying, glimmering floods fell away from her reddening eyes. He expected her to push him away, when he went in to embrace her, but she took him in. It was the right thing to do at the time.

'What's wrong with him?' she asked, her voice shaking with fear. Her arms limply held on to him. He felt no conviction in her.

'I don't know. It can't be a coincidence.'

'No shit Edward,' she pushed him away and moved to the other side of the kitchen, 'he's caught something, a disease, rabies or something like that.'

'Helen, you're being silly, he's most probably playing up now we've taken him away from his friends and...'

'It was that *thing!*'

Silence cut through the air like a sword through paper. Then after a second Edward took a heavy, yet hollow breath, the clock on the mantle ticked, the fridge hummed, all while his wife's eyes burnt into his. Upstairs, Jacob stopped his chanting, but neither of them noticed.

'It's not...'

'It's not what Edward? What I think it is? I saw it but I don't know what it was. What do you think it was, a werewolf, the bogeyman, what exactly is your theory on this? You're not still pushing the hallucination idea because that's absurd, so don't push it!'

'It's not rabies Helen. I don't know what it is, but it isn't rabies.'

'How can you be so sure?'

'I...I can't. I think rabies takes weeks to show symptoms. He wouldn't be sick this quick. It doesn't happen like this.'

'Then what is it?'

'I can't say, if we get a doctor in he'll take blood tests.'

'Will they want blood from us?'

'Maybe.'

Helen hesitated for a moment. She looked out the window then back at her husband. 'They'll find out he's not ours. That he's not adopted, but we bought him.'

'They can't prove that...'

'But they can prove he's not ours! We haven't got any papers, no certificate of adoption. Nothing!'

'Helen…please.'

'They'll take him away, we won't see him again.'

'Helen…'

Edward's words were cut short as the wind was knocked out of him. Jacob rushed in from the living room and rugby tackled him at full speed, knocking them both into the kitchen table. A sharp pang of pain tore across the back of Edward's skull as the corner of the wooden table ripped through skin and hair, drowning the back of his head in a sudden gory wetness. Jacob clambered upon his father, mouth agape, tongue wagging furious and far too suggestive for his age. His dark hair was damp with sweat and he still had scraps of packing tape stuck on his wrists and feet, but somehow he'd chewed through them. Edward caught on tight to his son's wrists before his clawed hands could scratch his eyes out. The boy screamed and began chanting again.

'…*meta phallus yeutla nema nema vouta ma ma maaa…*'

'For christsakes Hel…' Edward half screamed through seething teeth, '… open the . . . dammed . . . cellar door!'

Helen, still in a daze at the new terror she'd just witnessed, dutifully did as she was told.

Edward geared himself on top of Jacob, shifting his weight over until he dominated the boy. Getting to his feet, Edward dragged his demented son across the tiled floor whilst he kicked and chanted then flung him down through the open cellar door and down the stairs. He had the door shut before Jacob reached the bottom. Edward locked the door and ripped out the key; seconds later, footsteps thundered up the stairs and a rattling bang shook the door in its frame.

Bloodied, tired and confused, Edward collapsed in the doorway, letting the wood rattle against his back, he pulled his wife close, embracing her, wanting this to end, praying that it was a false memory that he could shake from his mind and get back to living the dream life he had planned for them. Paralysed and struck dumb, he held onto Helen whilst the moon moved as a silent beacon through the night sky, whilst the creature that used to be their son banged and rattled a relentless tattoo on the door through the night hours, screaming his chants, each vile unknown word meant for the pair of them.

***

The hours drew out to a blurring of eternity, until the relentless barrage became normality, a soundtrack to their lives. Neither of them slept. Helen cried throughout the long night, until dawn illuminated the kitchen with its ever warming glow, then their son ceased his all night screaming fit and continued assault on the door. Helen gripped her husband's arm when the chanting and shrieks ceased, they heard a shuffle then nothing.

'He's stopped,' Helen said as she wiped snot and tears from her face with her sleeve.

'I'm not surprised after nine hours of attacking a locked door,' Edward sighed. He sat up from his slumped position on the floor, cracked his back then headed over to the sink for a glass of water. Turning on the faucet and grabbing an unwashed glass, tinkling silver rushed into it. Edward downed it in one, the water washing through the desert tunnel his throat had become. A boiling pressure bubbled away within the confines of his bladder. He needed to piss like a thousand horses.

'Shall we check on him?' Helen asked, still curled up by the cellar door.

'Give it an hour.'

'But he's our son.'

Edward pointed at the door and the being beyond the frame, 'that thing is not our son....'

'He is.'

'...I mean he was, even if he wasn't ours to begin with, but now...I don't know what he is. It doesn't make sense. What do we do, this kind of thing isn't exactly in *Parent and Child Weekly* is it?'

'We should call a doctor.'

'Or Rentokil.'

'Don't say things like that Edward.'

Edward looked at the bite on his arm, it still stung and he still hadn't dressed it. An egg-sized chunk was cut deep into his forearm near the elbow. It hummed with a deep ache. Blood had coagulated in a dried puddle up his arm and over his t-shirt. With a tentative touch he gently patted the scrape on the back of his head with his fingers. It wasn't deep, as only the skin had been torn off, leaving a plasma sticky bald patch behind.

'He bit me Helen,' Edward said plain and calmly, holding up his arm to show off his wound.

'Stop thinking about you for once, our son is ill, I'm going to call the doctor.' Helen raised herself up from the doorway and headed for the phone on the wall.

'Helen, please don't call anybody. Think of the consequences. Think what will happen.'

'Think what will happen if we don't do anything. A dead son, that's the difference between doing what you think is right and what you know is right.'

'Aren't they the same thing?'

'I'm calling for an ambulance.'

Helen moved for the phone, Edward moved as well, grasping hold of the wire he wrapped it thrice around his hand and yanked the socket from the wall.

Helen said nothing. She turned and ran for upstairs. Edward followed. He found her in the bedroom, the cordless phone in her hand, she was dialling.

'Helen, don't do this…'

She held the phone to her ear, her face hard as stone, unflinching and set in determination. Edward reached down his side of the bed and gripped the cool, heavy tube of metal.

'Please Helen, for the family….'

'…if Jacob dies, our family will be over…'

'…don't make me do this…'

'Do what exac…?'

She didn't get to finish the question, as Edward raised the shotgun to his shoulder, and without hesitation or a blink; pulled the trigger and fired.

***

He didn't want to take the shotgun into the cellar; he felt it would be branching into overkill. He settled for a baseball bat, leaving the shotgun and the box of cartridges on the kitchen table. He found some chain in the shed. It was old and peppered with rust, but it was forged from heavy steel, so he hoped it would be strong enough for his cause. He wouldn't be able to chew through it. He hoped.

Before he had embarked any further, he bandaged the bite on his arm, soaking it with a healthy sting of surgical spirit, doing the same with the smaller bite mark on his leg and the graze on the back of his head.

He made himself a coffee, relieved himself of a long deserved piss, and then draped the ten-foot length of chain in heavy folded loops over his shoulder. From two of the outbuildings he borrowed two padlocks from their now unlocked doors. He placed the two ancient keys in his pocket, first checking that the locks fit snugly through the links in the chain. They did.

With his coffee finished, Edward unlocked the cellar door, turned the light on and descended the first two creaking steps within the grip of silent trepidation, cautiously locking the door behind him, he pocketed the key. At this point he wondered if he should have worn gloves. It wouldn't have mattered. If Jacob wanted to attack him, he could. Gloves would hinder the task at hand. It was his neck and face he should have been worried about.

At first he thought Jacob had escaped, as the cellar was empty except for the bitter stench of sweat and human waste. He found the boy in the corner, curled up, naked except for his fouled underwear. The rest of his blood and waste stained clothes lay in rags around the cellar, he'd torn them from his body, scratching his own skin in the process to denude himself from the fabric of humanity he seemed to find so disgusting.

'Jacob?' he asked of the boy, he didn't get or expect any response. The boy remained still as a fallen shop dummy. 'Jake? Son?'

Placing the baseball bat gingerly on the soiled floor, Edward set to work, wrapping one end of the chain round the iron drain pipe that carried waste from the upper floors to the sewage tank out back. He clicked the first padlock through the secure links and tugged it several times to ensure its strength and durability. It held.

With the other end of the chain he approached Jacob, moving as slow as he could, he gingerly picked up the boy's right leg and wrapped the end of chain around it, then pulled it back through underneath. He snapped the padlock on, tugged the chain once; Edward backed off, half expecting the boy to explode with gnashing fury.

He didn't.

Edward grabbed the bat, hurriedly retreated back up the stairs, unlocked the door and stepped back into the kitchen, locking the door behind him. He wasn't talking any chances. Not today.

Pocketing the padlock keys in the opposite pocket to where he kept the cellar door key, Edward stopped and stared blankly at the twin tubes laid on the table. The shotgun, what could he do with it?

Stash it back up stairs. Hide the cartridges somewhere else, just in case…

Taking the cartridges, Edward crept into the pantry and hid the box on the top shelf behind the peanut butter. Next he took both the shotgun, still with two spent cartridges in the breech and the baseball upstairs to the master bedroom. Helen was still on the bed, staring blankly into space, a ghostlike, lost expression on her face, somewhere between worlds of hate, her lips trembled in fear, tears bled clear trauma from raw red eyes which still stared impassively at the fragments of the cordless phone holster that her husband had blasted apart. Without the base, the phone was rendered useless.

'What have you done to our son?' Helen asked in a whisper.

Edward slid the shotgun onto the top of the wardrobe, out of the sight from prying eyes.

'He's not our son anymore, he's something else.'

'Okay…what have you done with my son, you haven't hurt him have you?'

'He's safe; hopefully he won't harm himself now. He tore his own clothes off, scratched himself up.'

Helen slowly moved her gaze up from the scattered remains of the cordless phone and bedside table her husband had shot at, decimating them into fragments of wood and plastic. Her eyes now resembled raw wounds instead of visual organs from all of her tear shedding. Strangely, Edward felt nothing. He thought that he should want to, but he didn't, not at all.

'Will you let me see him?' You won't try and stop me?' Helen held her breath after she finished, her gaze glistening over.

'Knock yourself out. The only person he can hurt now is himself. Unless you let him.'

Helen got to her feet and motioned towards the door.

'Wait,' Edward said, he removed the cellar door keys and passed them with slight unease to his wife, she took them without word and left.

'Just make sure you lock it back up after!' he called after her as she thundered eagerly down the stairs.

She didn't respond.

He didn't care.

He did care about his own aroma though. The last few days he'd gone without a proper wash, or even brushing his teeth. Now a clingy film had grown over his incisors, creating distaste and a sense of loathing. A heady masculine perfume emitted from his pits; he'd started to offend himself.

Edward stripped off, placing the keys to the padlocks in the back of his sock drawer. He stepped into the cubicle, letting the thrust of shower blast off the grime of the move, the sex with Helen and the whole horrific madness regarding Jacob. The stress started melting away with the force of water, knots untied themselves, niggles calmed and any significant worry was drowned out by the refreshing blast of hot water. Blood, sweat and dirt swept in cyclical gurgle down the drain.

Whilst drying off, in between the bubbling murmur of the hairy plug and the last drips from the showerhead, Edward heard singing from down stairs.

Seeking answers, he pulled on shorts, a loose shirt and trainers and stomped downstairs, which he found empty.

Voices came from the basement, so he followed his ears.

She'd made a ham sandwich, which sat on plate, which sat on a tray beside a tall glass of milk and an unopened bag of cheese and onion crisps. Helen sat on the floor beside Jacob. She had a damp rag and a bucket of soapy water, and was happily singing lullabies to herself whilst wiping the muck and blood from her unconscious son.

Her sweet voice stopped as soon as she heard Edward creak the third step down.

'Please don't say anything Edward. I have to do something. If you won't let me phone for an ambulance please let me care for him.'

'Your singing was nice, you haven't sung like that in ages.'

'Edward…please.'

'I won't say anything sweetie. Just don't let him bite you. He's stronger than he looks.'

'I know, I saw,' she stopped, dropped the soiled rag back in the water and looked up at him. Her eyes looked a little better, content now that she was helping. It hadn't taken much for her to look a little better.

'I just want to look after him. I want him to be okay, I want us to be a family again, like we wanted. Like we always wanted.'

'I know.'

'Could you fetch me some clean towels and blankets please, I want him to be comfortable if he's staying down here until he's better.'

Edward nodded wordlessly and retreated from the cellar to complete his task. Helen squeezed out the rag and carried on sponging down the thin naked form of her comatose son.

***

With little coaxing, Edward even helped wrap Jacob up in the blanket, laying him on the towels so at least he was comfortable. At first he was weary as to whether or not Jacob would attack him again, to be on the safe side he held his legs as they shifted him over onto the towel. They left him the food nearby and headed back upstairs.

Pouncing on her husband's guilt regarding the matter, Helen persuaded Edward to keep the cellar door unlocked. He compromised, agreeing that the door would stay shut and the chains remained secured to his ankle. Every ten minutes to half hour, Helen checked on Jacob. Each time returning disappointed that he hadn't awoken or touched his food.

The day continued in partial silence. Edward persuaded his wife to get showered and refreshed whilst he made them a lunch of baked potatoes and salad. She returned and both of them played idly with their food, mashing it around the plate until it no longer resembled the original dish, but a green-veined alien life form.

'You don't have to eat,' Edward said, 'but eat something, even if it's to keep your energy up.'

'Not hungry, don't feel like food,' she said listlessly, 'how can I with our son down there like that? It's not right.'

Edward sighed, considered his words, then, 'You prefer the alternative, you'd like me to go to prison.'

Helen didn't even hold her pause, her eyes lit up slightly, as if she'd seen light at the end of the tunnel after time in the dark, 'If that's what it takes, then so be it. Anything to get my son better…'

Edward roared, surging up and out of his chair, it fell back with a clatter to the quarry stone floor. His hand swept the plate of half eaten food against the wall, the porcelain shattering into jagged shrapnel, cheesy lumps of potato starch splattered messily against the far wall.

Helen looked at her husband plaintively; she didn't flinch nor change her expression from the grief-wracked mask of melancholy that she'd worn all day. She'd become used to this monster, before she was glad when he'd worked all the time, and dreaded the day when he announced his retirement. These outbursts seemed to be never remembered, sure he'd turn up with flowers and that puppy dog expression he worked so well, but he soon swept his emotions back under the rug once she'd forgiven him… again and again.

Edward bore down on her, his face tense and morphing into something that wasn't the man she married and once loved, she didn't recognize this stranger, this odd man who had somehow wormed his way into her life, sucking all the goodness from her, casting her into a shadow. Sure he'd provided, but was this tyranny worth it? This wasn't a marriage; it was a performance they'd both kept up for Jacob's sake. Now, with Jacob's life hanging by a bizarre thread, the curtain was slipping and both of their acts and judgement was coming under doubt.

'He's not our son!' Edward seethed, 'we bought him … remember? He was a week old, and we bought him from that poor woman. She's gone and pretty soon he'll be gone, and you'll go back to being a dried up old maid with a desert for a womb and I'll divorce you. If that's what it takes Helen, if that's what it takes.'

'Why are you threatening me?' she replied coolly.

'It's not a threat, it's a promise…'

Edward was a moment away from hitting her. They both could feel it as a possibility. He took a deep breath then managed to reel in his anger. He jutted his jaw out like a primeval ape then swept towards the backdoor, his footsteps crunching across the gravel, fading; then he was gone. Only when she couldn't hear his footsteps anymore did she begin to cry, soft, weeps that she did her best to clench behind already raw eyes, then when she felt she'd couldn't hold it anymore, she collapsed to the floor in a weak pile and let out terrifying roars of screams that echoed throughout the rest of the empty, desolate rooms. Not even his mother's screams could wake Jacob from his induced slumber.

***

Eastern Europe; a rough little town in the midst of a big forest. They weren't even sure what country they were in when they met the old woman. Edward had decided to take six months off work to take Helen travelling around Europe. No plan, no itinerary, just drive and drive through wonderful vistas, isolated orchards of paradise and quaint fishing villages mostly untouched by western tourism. They'd come back with more than they had left with.

A hellish rain bore down on them one afternoon, forcing them to stop and pull the canvas roof up on their rented convertible. A little further down the road, the bent shape of an old lady shuffled along the muddy road, a screaming bundle in her arms. Helen had said pull over. He did, though reluctantly, as they had no room for luggage let alone a third passenger. Helen being the generous soul she was wanted to help anyway.

As they pulled up next to her, Helen asked the old woman if she wanted a lift anyplace, remembering that thankful smile as the rain traversed down the wrinkled gulleys of her craggy face, immediately she offered the bundle to Helen, urging her take it. In broken English they managed the briefest of conversations.

'Mama gone. Dead. Birth.'

Helen and Edward listened solemnly as the old woman pleaded and repeated herself. She held out the bundle to Helen, letting the clutch of dirty blankets rest on the edge of her cold, trembling fingers. Helen remembered thinking that she was worried about her dropping the child.

'Mama gone. Dead. Birth. You buy!'

They didn't have a chance to even discuss it. Helen had tried for a baby since she and Edward had been married to no avail. They'd tried fertility treatments and consulted various doctors and experts on the matter, but deep down after all the frustration she'd felt, Helen knew she couldn't bear a child. This awkward twist of fate, this strange meeting that presented opportunity to her romantic side. Here she was, offered a fast track chance to motherhood. How could she not take it up?

Rummaging in her purse, she grabbed a wad of various currencies and handed them over. Upon seeing the wad of cash, the crone dropped the baby through the window on to Helen's lap, snatched the money with gnarly bony fingers and then vanished into the maze of trees.

That was how they got Jacob. They were his parents; it was as simple and as mysterious as that. She was sure that people other people had stranger upbringings.

Back home they registered him as their own, telling friends that Helen had been unknowingly pregnant before the trip and had delivered 'Jacob' in a little village during a thunderstorm to add drama. They got a birth certificate once home, stating that they'd lost Jacob's original one during their travels. The years passed and the lie held true. Everybody believed their little made up story. Nobody questioned their make believe little world.

Life and success had continued quite uneventful until the day they moved into Quiet Pines.

***

Helen sat slumped in the streaming blaze of the afternoon sun, all her tears burnt away by grief. She didn't feel like she could cry anymore, her grief was spent. Her marriage was over, she'd decided that much. When Edward returned she'd ask for the key to the padlocks holding her son prisoner, call a taxi and head back to the city, then to her mother's house, taking Jacob with her. This was her plan.

Done with feeling sorry for herself, she got to her feet and checked on Jacob; he was fine, sound asleep, with a constant assurance of little snores that told her he was still breathing.

Knowing that Edward could return at any moment, she decided to be ready for him when he came back through the door.

Helen washed her face with cool water from the kitchen faucet, refreshing her tear stained skin, then went up stairs and started to pack bags for Jacob and herself.

***

Edward traipsed.

Hard footed on the forest track, kicking stones into the undergrowth.

Smashing through bracken, smacking shins into falling limbs, cracking dead wood into breathable soft splinters of dust; Edward rampaged.

Green enveloped him, stagnant air sought his lungs as he broke and stamped into swampland devoid of any footprint bar his own, staining black water soaked into his trainers, oddly cool on his toes.

He stopped and looked round, trying to place the sun where it had been before he left the track only seconds ago. The way he had come had returned to what it was before, the long grass and rushes swayed as they always had, revealing no trace of his trail, keeping that secret to themselves.

Edward cursed the maze of nature.

He was lost.

He had only meant to head out for a little walk to cool off before he did something to Helen that she'd regret. He didn't want to hit her, but he had felt the desire of a red tide rising inside him, bubbling away as a seething pan of hateful, boiling liquid.

The tall rising pines looked down on him, judging him as he sunk further into the cool, black mud. Which way had he come? North, South? He had hoped cutting through the forest would take him back to the house, cut straight through the trail and back home.

He'd been wrong so far.

He planned to be gone an hour or so, yet the afternoon had dragged on without him, letting him saunter around mindlessly. He'd been gone nearer three hours. He could have been miles from home or just a few metres.

He looked at his feet, the stagnant, over saturated soil resembled mashed cake. In places, calm pools of oily blackness reflected the monochrome sky and forest surround.

Looking up into the bough and branches, a slight shiver befell him as he thought of hanging witches with blackening, wrung necks and purple faces, adorning the pines like rotting human fruit, their grey tongues poking out like burst pips. He shook his head, trying to shake Porter's tale from his mind.

Edward trudged on, stopping when the swamp abruptly sloped down into a pit. The sides gave way where the earth itself swallowed the ground. Even the nearby pines leant inwards like spiny teeth towards the collapsed pit. One was leant across the expanse of the pit as if gravity sucked down hungrily on the roots, clinging on to the soil before the pit swallowed it whole.

Black water trickled from the land and flowed towards the boggy pit, filling the air with a tinkling as the land drained into the sinkhole.

Slightly in awe of this strange sight he estimated that the hole was at least fifty feet in diameter; he had no idea of the depth. He had the urge to get closer and take a look inside, but the boggy ground filled him with the fear of getting stuck. He waited a moment for something to happen. If something was to happen, it would be jumping out from this freaky, ominous pit in the middle of the woods and tearing him to shreds.

Edward admitted to himself that he was lost in this strange back yard. He did some calculations in his head. Three/four miles an hour for three hours. He could be at most twelve miles from home, but he knew he couldn't be that far. He'd been heading in circles for the past ninety minutes, unwilling to admit to himself that he was lost.

He wanted to punch something, a tree, the soggy ground, anything.

Without asking himself why, Edward slapped himself once on each cheek, hard. Then with a sucking sound that stole his left trainer from his dampened foot, he carried on his trudge through the mud, this time keeping the sun on his back, away from his eyes. He turned round twice as he left the edge of the swamp hole, the fearful thought emerging that it might suddenly open up wider and swallow him as he trudged his feet back through the mud.

The sinkhole didn't gape wider after him. Even though the pit was deep, it was empty.

***

Whilst her husband trudged and trudged, Helen packed her clothes into a suitcase and Jacob's into a sports bag, she carried both of these to the front door, leaving them to wait beneath where they would have hung their winter coats. It was never to be.

The afternoon drew on; the sun sinking a steady glide into the western sky. She wondered once where Edward had gotten to, but tried not to concern herself too much. He'd gone to blow off steam; that was all. The worry had gotten too much and he needed some air. That was all. He'd made her choose between her son and him. Why not just get rid of the gun, it was simple. It's not like he'd used it to rob a bank or anything. He couldn't make her choose.

She had considered walking into town and finding the doctors that way, but the thought of leaving Jacob alone upset her even more. He needed her, but she had to do something.

With a sigh, Helen shuffled to the cellar to check on Jacob, as she had routinely being doing since his incarceration in chains. She flicked the cellar light on and instantly something struck her as different about the scene.

She stopped halfway down the stairs and ventured no further through fear and suspicion.

The food had been moved. The glass of milk had spilt, spreading and taking on its own desire lines in an alabaster Rorschach puddle. The bag of crisps had been torn open, crushed fragments of potato shrapnel littered the floor around Jacob. The two slices of buttered bread that made up the sandwich had been pulled apart and cast aside, grains of dirt and fluff stuck to the ruined buttered slivers. As Helen tentatively approached, she noticed that the slice of ham was gone.

Although she didn't jump, it did take her by surprise and she gasped a little. Jacob was slumped on the floor, his head resting on his arms half hiding his face. He'd wrapped the covers around himself and lay as a chrysalis on the concrete floor. From a gap in the covers, Helen could see that he had one eye open, peeking out upon the scene. It watched her as she descended the stairs, dark and brooding. Helen warned herself to check her distance, although Jacob was her son, he had already proved himself dangerous, so whatever infection, disease or syndrome that failed his being and possessed him, turning him into this *monster*, distance was the key. Even if she did love him, she had to stay safe.

'I see you ate the ham, but not the sandwich?'

The cover remained motionless, that dark eye concentrated on her like a sniper sight; unmoving, unblinking, but deadly all the same.

'How about the milk? Usually you love a glass of milk with your sandwich. Not today?'

A small grunt escaped Jacob's mouth. Not a response; it might have even been involuntary. But it was progress.

'So you like meat do you? Just meat? If that's what you want…'

Helen forced herself to smile as she opened the kitchen fridge and took out the plastic package. They were supposed to be for a barbeque Edward had planned for yesterday. They were still in date so it was okay. She returned to the cellar, punctured a finger into the taut skin of plastic and tossed one of the cool slabs of prime steak onto the cellar floor. Just to see if she was right.

Slow and with the cautious patience of a striking cobra, Jacob's hand stretched out from his fabric cave and across the floor over to the piece of beef. His fingers locked onto it, dragging it through the milk puddle, making little scratching noises as the twenty pound a kilo of raw flesh rolled over granules of grit and dead dust. Jacob pulled the fistful of meat to his mouth and began to eat as quickly as his jaw could chew.

The evening brought with it a clinging heat. Even in the cellar the warmth of the day offered its embers.

Despite this, Helen shivered.

***

Circles, Edward Chapel was convinced of twisted circles. In his head, in his mind and in reality, he must be walking in warped circles. He hadn't noticed the sunlight bleed away behind him. He'd been trudging through the undergrowth in such a fugue state that he didn't realise he'd lost daylight until he saw the moon wink at him from behind a cloud. The sun had gone for the day, abandoned him to this side of the world alone and careless. Rain heavy clouds soon robbed the moon from him, stealing the skies from the bright day, billowing and spreading like ink in water, filling the purple coloured sky with all their unwanted grey murk.

Edward stopped, listened and waited.

He felt like he was being followed. He had no evidence of this, hadn't heard twigs cracking or heavy breathing from behind the trees. Just a presence bearing down on him, or maybe it was the change in air pressure from the coming storm. Maybe it was nothing.

He was bursting for a piss, but daren't reveal himself for the fear whatever now stalked him suddenly pounced and ripped his skin from his skeleton.

The wind whispered wordless verse past his ears. The cool breeze made him shiver, he felt a spot of rain dash against his cheek, a low ominous rumble of thunder rolled over far fields, getting close, vibrating the primeval caverns of his soul.

A whisper again, more familiar this time, not from the air around him but from the hiding fern fronds at his feet and beyond. Eerie and hard to pinpoint, Edward formed words in his mind's ear.

...tenbra moseleta cursa colie sambi scret vel vey nah tel...

The wind couldn't speak. The dead don't lie and there was no such thing as bad luck, only the superstitious got bad luck. He wasn't inclined to the supernatural, but this was freaking him out. The devil's poetry.

...denom massaput sela luff. Bata mata shuboe kala...

Edward tensed, expecting the bogeyman to jump out and snatch him and suck his eyeballs out, he expected kids to jump out and say BOO! Then laugh, it was all a joke mister...

It's wasn't the forest that was talking to him... talking about him... hell he didn't know. He wanted to burn the trees, take out whatever ancient and evil lurked in wait. He tensed his fists into tight balls, digging his nails into palm. A pinch, wake me from this nightmare. His knees melted into jellied hinges, knocking back and forth threatening to be toppled by the wind.

More whispers, words he couldn't understand or even begin to pronounce. He so wanted something to happen, just to stop the torture. End it now.

Either tear me apart or let me go!

It was a good thing he had stopped; for this moment, the wind helpfully breezed up against a branch carrying it skyward in a bend and revealed the twinkling porch light of Quiet Pines Farm. Edward smiled and started to run with a straining bladder, losing the other trainer in the process. He hit a wire fence and fell over it into a field of fragrant rapeseed. The threat of wetting himself became too much and he pulled himself free of his shorts and began to piss while walking backwards; facing the forest he'd escaped. The whispers left him with the wind and the forceful sloshing of his wastewater amongst the summer baked mud and rapeseed stems. A sigh escaped him, he was out of the woods and almost home. He hadn't wet himself since he'd been a child. The voices that spoke from the woods reminded him of being young and scared, of fearing the closet monsters and the shark behind the grill at the swimming baths. His parents warned him of sweet giving strangers; this was a similar feeling, the terror before the unknown. It was just the sheer imagination of a world gone wrong, where evil escaped its normal domain and dips a gnarled toe into the real world; a caustic smile creasing its lips.

Tonight, Edward Chapel was sure he'd tasted evil. And evil had tasted him.

***

Helen sat at the table; she'd removed her wedding ring and placed it in front of her. With the emerging moon, Jacob had fully awoken and now gave out little sighs and whines, his mournful tune reminiscent of a lonely puppy that wanted to explore the big wide world. The gourmet steak she'd given had lasted about twenty seconds, the second one even less, the third likewise. Next she fed him some uncooked pork and leek sausages, he even spat out the tiny green flecks of leek. Then a pack of apple wood smoked bacon; still half frozen, his teeth crunched through the rashers as if they were chunks of tough fudge. She'd thrown the meat down from her seat on the stairs and Jacob's thin arm would reach out from beneath the cover and retrieve the offered lump.

Her son; correction, her adopted son, was now a dedicated carnivore, to the point where he preferred his meat as raw as possible.

Helen watched as halfway through the pack of apple wood smoked bacon, which he stuffed into his mouth three rashers at once, a mouse scurried from a crack beneath the skirting board enticed by the abandoned bread. Jacob spied this little creature and pounced out from the duvet with the bacon still grasped in his hands, the length of chain rattling and scraping on the hard concrete floor. Leaping from above, he pounded the mouse with his bacon clenched fist, stuffing the twitching, broken sack of furry remains into his mouth. With a stringy tail sucked into the corner of his mouth, Jacob returned to his comforting safety beneath the cover to carry on with the bacon feast.

He just kept eating.

It wasn't this that disturbed her the most.

It was his eyes. All the while he ate; he looked at her hungrily from his sheltered abode, almost a perverted, twisted lust. His bulging eyes stared at her, ever unblinking, ever hungry. She knew the first chance he got he would tear his teeth into her. The fact that she had fed and clothed him all these years, raised him as if he were her own didn't matter anymore. He would tear into her like a pack of wolves would a broken legged lamb.

His greying skin was smeared with squirts of dark mouse blood that he licked off with vile glee. He attempted to smile as he tongued between his fingers. When he was finished he looked at her for more, the look told her to even offer herself to him if that's what it took to satisfy his animal hunger.

No, no more. After watching him kill and eat the mouse, she left. That was when she took off her wedding ring.

Helen Chapel wanted out.

***

Edward burst through the patio door, breathless and filthy. Helen had expected something like this. She had to check herself when the dutiful housewife within her piped up to chide Edward for muddying the floor. It didn't matter, she was leaving. With or without Jacob. She decided this after that look he gave her. It wearied her.

'I'm leaving Edward. I can't do any more for Jacob. He's beyond help now. He needs a doctor…'

Edward wore black trousers of stagnant dirt. His shirt was ripped; the cuts carrying on the bramble tears up and along each arm, sweat dampened his brow, urine the front of his shorts.

'…you look like shit,' Helen pointed out.

'I feel like shit. I've had time to think, you're right. We should get him to the doctors. It'll be for the best. I'm willing to face the consequences. No matter what.'

'It's too late darling,' Helen gloated sarcastically, 'Jacob's gone away with the evil fairies. He's not in anymore, please leave a message after the beep.'

'What you trying to say?'

'It's not Jacob down there,' Helen pointed with a furious finger down at the cellar and got up from the table, seething. 'It's something else. At this point I would *love* to see you try and get him up and dressed for a trip to the doctors. *I would love it!*' This time the sarcasm unnerved Edward a little.

'What happened?' Edward looked around at the mess from lunch. She hadn't bothered to clear it up, he didn't blame her. He'd been a dick. He realised this now.

'He's a monster; he only eats meat, nothing more. That's it, that's all he wants!'

On cue, Jacob howled a sorrowful melody up the stairs.

'Whatever bit him, and don't deny it!' Helen continued with a justified and poised finger aimed his way, 'whatever bit him is now inside him. He's turning into something, something inhuman. Something we've never seen before.'

'You thinking werewolf?'

'I don't know what to think anymore.'

Helen moved to one side, Edward now noticed the bottle of scotch on the floor beside her chair.

'You're drunk,' he said cool and calm.

'You're a fuckin' idiot.'

'I'm not going to hit you, I know you want me to so you can tell all your friends that you're a battered wife, but I'm not gonna give you the satisfaction.'

'It's the only satisfaction you can give me,' she retorted, her lips curling in a cruel smile.

'Helen you're drunk, get to bed.'

'No! I want this sorting now. We have to fix Jacob before he turns into a Wereboy! Or a Dracula or Damien . . . *forfucksake*!'

'Please, Helen, calm down, let me think.'

'No, you've had plenty of time…'

A brisk thunderous knock at the door interrupted their argument, bringing welcome pause to the slanging match. Edward thought it was the storm, waiting a few seconds only to hear a second knock. Harder this time, more urgent. Helen wasn't even sure she had heard it.

'Who's that?'

'How should I know?' she snapped and reached down for the scotch. Edward should have grabbed it from her and poured it down the sink, but didn't. They had more bottles and she'd only get another one of them to replace it.

'I'll go see, somehow I think they won't go away,' Edward said and left Helen swigging back a generous glug.

When he opened the door, his heart sank and his bowels turned to foul water that gurgled about inside him, threatening to leak out and make his day worse.

It was Porter. The policeman. Had she rung him? It didn't matter, he was here.

He smiled with those yellow teeth of his, but his fakery evaporated as soon as he clapped eyes on the dishevelled Edward.

'Mister Chapel, you look like you've been ten rounds with King fucking Kong. Is everything okay?'

'Just… trouble. We've got vermin. I've being trying to set traps all day. We're infested.'

'Oh Mister Chapel that does sound terrible, may I come in.' Porter stepped through the threshold as he asked. His eyes glanced around hawk-like, drinking details of the scene like an old pro. He was every bit a stereotypical detective. He did himself no favours.

'I've been talking to your neighbours Mister Chapel. It appears they heard another gunshot last night. They all say it seems to come from your home. They all agreed.'

Edward remained silent. Don't answer, admit nothing, and deny everything.

'I've checked up on you Mister Chapel. You're rich and I know the type. You could probably afford a lawyer to get you out of a little muddle like this. I say we avoid all of that. I know you haven't got a license, but I know you've got a shotgun, maybe even a few.' Porter looked Edward up and down, wrinkling his nose at the filth before him.

'Maybe you've been shooting rats instead of setting traps. I really don't care. This is a quiet little village and I don't want any trouble. I only want what's best for everybody. Including you. So just hand over the weapon and I'll be on my way. It'll be as simple as that.' Porter sniffed, taking in the aromas that poured off Chapel. A slight look of detest filled his craggy features.

Edward considered the offer. He liked it. In another world he would've liked Porter, in other circumstances he could see Porter and himself sat in *The White Swan*, supping *Speckled Hen* and discussing cricket. That would've been nice. Pleasant even. But they weren't in that world. That world was far away, more of a gruesome fantasy than the world he'd found himself in.

'Well Chapel?' Porter asked, his tone gruff and demanding.

Jacob howled, louder than before, an otherworldly shriek that echoed through the house.

'What the…'

'I can explain, really I can. I'll have to show you.'

'Chapel what was that?'

'I have to show you, it's my son he's not well.'

'Lead the way man!' Porter barked and pushed Edward with a gentle shove towards the kitchen.

Jacob screamed again, this time it petered off into a maniacal half laugh, part hyena, and part demented clown.

Porter wrinkled his nose at the sight of Helen who sat half slumped at the table, clearly drunk. He wanted to ask a hundred questions at once, but he was getting carried away in the situation, following his nose.

With a nervous hand, Edward opened the cellar down and pointed into the darkness.

'Down there…my son, he's not well.'

'Well call a doctor then! What's up with him? Have you got a light in the cellar?' Porter's gaze burned into Edward's with pure, unadulterated concern. It shifted into the waiting dark of the cellar, where the howls came from.

Edward flicked on the light, 'You'd best see for yourself. I don't think a doctor can help.'

Porter took two steps onto the creaking stairs whilst Edward slid behind him cautiously, the anguish draining from his face. Whatever took control of Edward Chapel's actions it wasn't him. He hadn't planned this, how could he have?'

Edward flicked off the light.

'Christ Chapel! I can't see put the light back on for…'

Edward placed his bare muddy foot on the top of Porter's shoulder blades and kicked out, pushing the inquisitive cop down the creaking stairs. Then he slammed the door, backing up to it in case he tried to make it back up. Porter let out an exasperated grunt; this was followed by three thumps, another heaving grunt, and then a twisted half yelp.

The last thump as Porter reached the base of the stairs was followed by a delighted shriek from Jacob. Helen half came to her senses and screamed; then came the eating sounds that silenced her.

They didn't open the door for a long while.

***

They didn't talk.

They drank further into oblivion, drowning and dampening their tortured spirits with liquid spirits.

Edward turned the radio up as loud as he could and they both drank through the night. Brain jarring dance music blared in their ears, anything to drown out the noise of the feast beneath their feet, the booze to soothe the itch of sin. Helen cried and shook her head at her soon to be ex-husband. Edward clenched his fists into tight, bony balls; necked whisky straight from the bottle, vomited in the sink and carried on drinking to wash away the taste of bile.

Outside the storm had started. Thunder rolled through dark tumultuous skies, rain belted down against the kitchen window. Edward watched nature's tears die against the night cooled glass.

Helen passed out before midnight, slumped in the corner of the kitchen; the trails of dry tear tracks gently marked the grime on her face. Every so often her legs would shudder in a spasm of terror. Edward didn't notice this. He was in his own little world by the sink, gazing into the night, expecting demon red eyes to peer in an ominous glow through the darkness. Predatory eyes hungry for him. He wanted to get the gun, thought about it a lot. Kill Helen, kill his self. End of. Game over.

The whisky bottle kept him there, frozen by the sink gazing dumb and drunk at the nothing that wasn't there. Nothing was coming for him and nothing did. The whispers in the woods; must have been his imagination, nothing more.

A peeking dawn blazed across his sleepy cheeks, he looked up from the sink where he had slumped in his drunken daze; considered the last dregs in the bottle of whisky, winced at the still wet vomit that clogged the plug hole and replaced the cap on the whisky. He reared up and tossed the bottle at the wall above Helen's head, not too far from where the plate had smashed yesterday. He was weak, the bottle didn't smash upon impact; instead it bounced off the wall and clattered with a violent tinkle on the tiled floor. Helen awoke with red eyes slanted and angry.

'What we gonna do?' Edward asked, spitting into the sink, adding to the mess.

Helen tried to part her lips but they'd become glued by evaporated secretions of saliva. She fought through the barricade, splitting the corners of her lips in the process. She winced. A devil of a hangover pulsed in her dehydrated brain. All she wanted was water. Lots of water.

'Hey! I'm talking to you…'

'I know,' Helen gulped, her throat felt like hot sand grating on dry leather, the sun was too bright, Edward's voice too loud, the reality of the situation far too real for her to want to cope. The evening before came back to her. Her husband had pushed the policeman down the stairs. She vaguely remembered his face as he wandered through the kitchen turning his nose up at her, a gnarled and worn pockmarked face with a set of stained yellow teeth, his lips bared back into a condescending sneer.

'You pushed him, you're doing the time. We can't cover this up. People will come looking for him Edward. You can't hide this, you can't hide the body.'

Despite his behemoth of a hangover, Edward smiled, squinting in the all too bright sunlight.

'What if there's no body, then what?' he hurried over to the cellar door and whipped it open, flicked on the light and stomped down the stairs.

Helen heard him laugh. It sounded hollow, not a tempered echo like she expected. Like he was suppressing it somehow.

Down in the cellar, Edward retched.

Helen didn't want to move, she wanted the hangover to go away and reset her aching brain. She wanted her son back the way he was, a shy little man who was happy playing by himself or reading a book quietly, a dream child, no fuss, who could be cheeky when he wanted to and could tug at her heartstrings simply by asking for a hug when he didn't feel too well.

Just bring my Jacob back…

Edward retched again, this time she heard liquid splash against the wood grain of the stairs.

She didn't want to look at the mess Jacob had made and her dumb prat of a husband had caused.

Helen pushed herself up from off the floor, drew herself a glass of water from the sink and sank it in three…four gulps. She gasped heartily as the water filled her, replaced the glass on the counter, grabbed the knife they'd used to carve cheese from the block those distant nights ago, stashing it in her waistband and moved over to the cellar entrance.

Edward was stood on a step above a puddle of dark drying blood on the concrete slab. A muddied and bloodied handprint swept through half the puddle, this must have been as far as Jacob could reach.

From where she was stood she could see no sign of the policeman or Jacob.

Edward looked round eyes agape, startled, shocked, sickened. His white face explained it all.

'Even the bones,' a nervous wan smile tried to break free from Edward's mouth, but the shock wouldn't let it fully emerge. 'Even the bones. He even ate the bones, there's nothing left!'

'What do you mean nothing left? There has to be something!'

'Scraps of clothing, come and have a look. Jacob's asleep.'

Helen crept down the stairs wary of each straining creak, though she knew that Jacob slept during the day. He only awoke when the sun went down. She knew this now. It was his pattern. He was nocturnal. He had joined the ranks of bats, moths and vampires.

Sure enough Jacob was laid in the corner, hidden by the blanket, the blanket stained with a grim wash of blood and faeces, the stench overpowering and inhuman. Helen shivered. He was an animal. A creature. She still loved him, but how could she love him. He had killed a man.

No, Edward had killed a man. Jacob was merely the weapon used, an innocent implement. How could he even conceive what he was doing in his state?

Little circles of bloodied silver lay scatter around Jacob. Coins, things he couldn't or didn't want to eat. She spied other items. A bent belt buckle, a chewed and broken mobile phone leaking yellow battery acid, a wedding ring ruined and misshapen by gnawing teeth.

'I say we take him to the doctors,' Edward said with a face of condemned seriousness.

'Now you want to take him to the doctors?'

'It's the right the thing to do,' he nodded earnestly.

'It was the right thing to do two days ago.

'But it's proper, it's serious now.'

'Like I said, it was serious *two days* ago!'

'Do you want to take him or not?'

'Of course, but what about the car keys?'

'I have a spare set. Chucking them was for show.'

'The keys to the chain?'

'Upstairs. I'll get the shotgun as well, y'know in case he wakes up…'

'He sleeps during the day. You should know that by now.'

'But what if he's… pretending.'

'He comes round late afternoon. He should be sleepy after… well eating so well.'

'If he comes round I'm blaming you.'

'If he comes round whilst he's off the chain they'll be nobody left to blame. Literally.'

'So we've got a few hours.'

'Just get the keys Edward.'

Edward headed back upstairs and did as he was told, bringing the padlock keys hanging off his finger. In his hands he held the shotgun, loading fresh shells into the breech.

'So if he wakes up, you're going to shoot him?' Helen queried.

'If he wakes up and attacks me I'll shoot him. You saw what he did to the cop, Porter.' Edward corrected himself the guy had a name. And it was him or us he reasoned.

'Undo Jacob.'

Edward eyed his wife cautiously for a second, propped the loaded shotgun against the wall closest him so he had both hands free, bent low and unlocked the padlock that secured the chain to his son's dirt smeared ankle.

Edward held his breath, all but expecting Jacob to lunge for him and tear his throat out from its happy and content place in his neck.

The boy remained still though.

Helen however, did not.

Edward would have never guessed in a thousand lifetimes that his beautiful wife, who he had fed, clothed and given whatever her fashion conscious heart desired would ever turn on him. She moved calm and casual. She didn't mutter a demented scream, call him names or offer any other sound than the push of breath from her lungs.

The knife they'd used to slice strong cheddar, soft Brie and fine pungent Camembert, plunged just as easily into Edward's shoulder blade. So easy in fact, when she twisted the handle to remove the knife, the blade snapped off inside him.

Edward yelped, thinking she'd only punched him. Pain diluted through him in a pounding wave as the alien thing throbbed and glowed hot in his back. He dropped the keys amongst the mess that shrouded his son, he fell forward, the sticky stinky mess staining his already soiled clothes.

'What the…'

Helen dropped the redundant handle and grabbed the shotgun, cocked it and pointed at her soon to be ex-husband.

'What the…?' Edward repeated, shuffling in abject terror from off of the sleeping monster that his son had become. 'Helen?'

Edward gripped at the wound on his shoulder, wincing as the blade continued to bend inside him with the movement of his body.

'Helen? Please…why?'

'It's too late for Jacob, have you not realised that. He's gone. Doctors can't save him…'

'But we've got to try, please darling, we can't kill him, it's not our choice!'

'Who said anything about killing him… put the chain around your ankle and lock it. Tight.'

'What?'

'As you did so well to Jacob, chain yourself.'

'You going to kill me are you?'

'No, I want you safe.' Helen moved the stock up to her shoulder and pointed at Edward's head,' either I shoot you and I do it, or you do it quietly.'

Edward gently took the chain where it lay near Jacob's leg, still ever cautious not to wake him and wrapped it once around his ankle, then took the padlock and secured it through the chains and locked it. Seeking a way out, he searched for the keys. Helen spied them first, bent down and picked them up, hanging them off her little finger.

'Do you want the car keys if you're taking him to the doctors?'

'I'm not taking him to the doctors Edward, I've told you. It's too late. I'm leaving Jacob here; with you.'

Edward looked at Jacob, the chain and his ankle, then at Helen.

'You fucking bitch! Tell me you're joking?'

'No.'

Edward motioned towards her.

She fired above him. The explosion in these close quarters deafened them both. A dusty chunk of the wall behind Edward evaporated into rubble.

'Jesus Christ! Are you crazy?' He couldn't even hear his own words from the tinnitus ring in his ears.

'Stupid question. Make another move like that and I'll turn your face to pâté!' Helen started to back out of the basement, all the time keeping the shotgun trained on her husband's weary face, ready to carry out her promise.

'Please Helen, you can't leave me here,' Edward hissed whilst pointing at the comatose monster child, 'he'll wake up and I'll be stuck here!'

'That's the point,' Helen responded, her voice cold, sending a direct chill down Edward's spine.

Edward screamed, not caring whether Jacob awoke right then or slept forever.

'Helen please!' he beseeched, his voice taking on a higher shrieking tone of a condemned man at the foot of the gallows. He pulled in vain at his shackles, willing the padlock to burst open. 'You can't leave me here, he'll tear me apart!'

'Like I said, that's kind of the point,' Helen smiled as she reached the stairs, she lowered the gun, safe in the knowledge that Edward couldn't reach this far.

Edward surged after her, dragging the heavy chain behind him. It rattled against Jacob's sleeping form beneath the cover but did little to rouse him. He was a creature of the moon now. Full and qualified.

'Please, how can I change your mind?' he begged at the foot of the stairs, hands clasped tightly in prayer. He didn't want to be left alone in the devil's basement with shadow monsters and witch spawn. Edward felt his guts hollow out as he started to fully comprehend this true nightmare.

'We're a couple, a married couple; we're supposed to listen to each other. When I said we should take him to the doctors, you said no, you should have said yes. That's the only thing that would have changed my mind.'

'Helen darling, wait!'

Helen carried on to the top of the stairs, turned off the cellar lights and left the door slightly ajar, not only to let a little light in, but to ensure that Jacob could safely get out once he'd woken up.

***

113

What was once Jacob, dreamed.

Evil dreams as good dreams. Conquering opposites, making what isn't theirs, theirs. Putting what wasn't right, right.

Butterflies and birds fly, fish and frogs swim. What Jacob was becoming had existed long before they'd took to the seas or the skies. Biological, though still mystical, they had evolved from slime as others, though favouring the still dark rather than the burn of day, a primeval force, existing in the shadows, deep in the throat of the night.

They ate.

The lost and the missing, the weaker and the fatefully weary fell to be absorbed by their dark light.

Protein is protein.

Meat is meat.

Energy is energy.

It keeps every motion moving forward.

Over the aeons, many had become feast to their cause. Undiscovered and unknown, merely speculated to as the bogeyman, the creep in the night, the thing around the corner, the dark that man dreams, imagining and fantasising the worst that could ever happen.

What lay inside Jacob had fled to his depths when confronted by light, where it waited and spread its shadow throughout his form. It could only be safe if it took him to be a vehicle, then it could escape this prison and return to the dark below.

Night would soon arrive. Meat was nearby, from beneath the blanket, the dark would emerge, teeth proud and smiling.

***

Even at the bottom of the garden, she could still hear Edward's pleading screams.

She kicked off her shoes and clambered over the bottom fence and into the field of gradually yellowing corn. Here, with the cool and calming susurration of the gentle morning breeze through the proud stalks, her husband plea's fell on to no more concerned ears, fading to be but a bad memory from times gone past.

She knew Jacob was gone. She didn't know how, she didn't particularly want to know why, as to even to begin to understand would be a road to madness. But he was gone, his soul had passed onto another place whilst his body had been hijacked by a netherworld being, the origin of she couldn't explain. It hurt to think, she turned her mind to remembering good times past.

She'd raised him the best she could and when you're a parent the number one concern over you own health, wealth and general well being is the happiness of your own child. Whatever Jacob was, she could only speculate, it wasn't of this world she knew, though it was now. It was still Jacob though and she wanted him to be happy whether he was her son or not. She wanted him to be free, not cooped up like a deranged animal, she owed him that much at least.

He'd been her son for a while at least, even if the connection was only in her mind and spirit. Not body.

Tonight she planned nothing but a slow and aimless wandering of the vast woods beneath the stars, waiting for him to return to her. He would find her, he'd soon return to his beloved mother.

In one form or another.

DEVIL LET ME GO

IF YOU EVER MEET A GIRL NAMED MAISIE MAE...

MISSbuttereyes99;) writes- hav u eva seen that film?

MRKNOWITALL writes- nt yt.

MISSbuttereyes99:) writes- wnt 2 c it? My mates say it's 2 scary n ive no1 2 go wiv now!

MRKNOWITALL writes- my dad got it on pirate but wud mucho rather c it in 3D.

MISSbuttereyes99:) writes- me 2! 3D rocks. checkd times show at 7.30 if ya fancy it?

MRKNOWITALL writes- Yeah defo, shud b gud. Cnt wate!!

MISSbuttereyes99:) writes- ok. C u there! Cnt wate 2 meet u finally.

MRKNOWITALL writes- likewise. Be there about 7ish so that we can get a good seat.

MISSbuttereyes99:) writes- got to go 4 t now c ya later shane!!!

MRKNOWITALL writes- bye bye buttereyes.

PRIVATE CHAT ENDED

LOG OFF

YES/NO

***

Lupo drummed his hairy digits on the dash. She was late. He hated being made to wait. The incessant rain beat down on the roof of the car; the waterfall of pattered white noise increased his frustration further.

He said seven.

It was now twenty past.

How did she ever in her tiny mind expect to make the show arriving so late?

Typical female. Probably still at home doing her makeup like a dammed whore.

He cracked his knuckles, cracked his neck, and then stretched his legs, pushing his heavy form back into the straining leather of the driver's seat.

The collecting droplets of rain blurred the windscreen, marring his view of the neon rich, cinema entrance. He tapped the wiper switch and the blades dispensed the moisture in a single swoop.

And there she was, walking towards him now as a delicate silhouette against the stark neon.

He hurriedly started the engine and pulled the car forward so he was now up next to her, winding the electric window down as they drew level with each other. Lupo forged a friendly smile, baring his teeth.

'Miss Butter Eyes I presume?'

She stopped in her tracks, turning to his call and bringing her head closer to the window. She didn't even think to carry an umbrella, the silly little girl, just a backpack. Even in the orange glow of the streetlight he could see how beautiful she was.

And how young.

'Yeah, maybe, why?' she answered coolly, pulling the electric pink hooded top closed tighter around the Fallout Boy t-shirt she had on beneath. He knew she was a big fan of Fallout Boy, this was her. He guessed her eyes to be baby blue.

'I'm Shane's Dad, Mr Terry. I came to tell you that he can't make it tonight, he's a bit ill.'

'Oh. That's a bit of a bummer, is he okay?'

'Yeah just a stomach bug, he tried ringing but couldn't get through, kept going to voicemail he said.'

'Yeah my battery is dead; I'm always forgetting to charge it. I'm such a dumbass sometimes!' she admitted with a goofy smile.

'I'm sure you're not. Anyway listen, Shane's got the film on DVD, I have a friend who works here, gets me all the latest films, so the wife and me don't ever have to leave the house and spend our hard earned cash. If you want you're more than welcome to come back get dry and watch the film in the back room with Shane. He's ever so sorry he couldn't make it. I blame the wife's cooking, she could burn water!'

Miss Butter Eyes smiled at this. A gap showed on her front two teeth. Christ it was cute. He quivered a little, hoping he didn't let it show.

'I can drop you back off home later if you want, save you getting drenched. I don't mind at all.'

'Hmmm, okay. But I do really want to meet Shane.'

'Jump in then, before you get any wetter.'

Miss Butter Eyes opened the door and tossed in her backpack as he flicked the switch for the window, its drone cancelling out the rush of the rain outside. Once she was safety inside the car the doors locked automatically.

'You want to phone your Mum and Dad, tell them what's happening? You can borrow my phone if you want.'

'Mum and Dad are dead. I live with foster parents now."

Lupo handed over his mobile to her.

'All the same, ring them and let them know you're safe.'

She took the phone and said with a weak little smile, 'thank you.'

He watched the screen light up and she began to dial before putting the phone to her ear. No signal. She tried the number again.

Lupo smiled patiently. He had switched the phone to flight mode before she got into the car, no incoming or outgoing calls without turning it off and back on again, then entering the four digit pass code.

'No signal?' he queried innocently.

'It looks that way.'

'Probably the weather. Never mind, you can use the house phone when we get back. It's only a ten-minute drive. There's a bottle of Diet Coke in the foot well that Shane bought earlier, you're welcome to have a drink if you're thirsty.'

'Thank you.' The young girl reached around blindly into the dark of the foot well, her fingers found the bottle. She twisted off the cap and brought it to her lips, supping back the sugary fluid.

Too easy.

He pushed his eyes to the side, away from the dangers of the slick road to watch her neck move, gulp and pull the liquid down her delicate, pale throat.

'So you got a name Miss Butter Eyes? Or do me and the missus call you Butter?'

The girl removed the bottle from her little lips with a smile, "Maisie Mae."

'Maisie Mae?' he repeated it a few more times in his head, somehow, from somewhere in the distant corners of his mind, a sing song nursery rhyme entered his head.

"If you ever meet a girl named Maisie Mae..."

He smiled again, for his own pleasure this time. Unconsciously tonguing an ulcer on the side of his mouth brought him a tingle of pain. He bit into it, nibbling away at the wet, ulcerous flesh, bringing the taste of copper blood into his mouth. His thick fingers gripped the wheel in frustration as he turned onto a straight, leaving the lights of town behind. The safe lights.

God he was ready for this.

'We live a little ways out of town. Not far now.'

She smiled once dreamily then turned back to looking out the rain-splattered window. He kept on watching her, only for a moment, didn't want to scare her too soon. Back home, everything was ready. It would be perfect, a most excellent night of succulent delights, he had already decided that he would take his time with this beauty, not rush it; savour it.

It hadn't taken long this one. The quickest by far. She seemed quite eager to meet Shane, the distraction had held.

'Just round this next corner,' he assured her.

She offered a tired grunt, barely moving her head from off the cool plane of the window. The Coke ploy had worked. It had really knocked her out quick. He hadn't long.

He upped his speed and arrived home faster then he thought possible. The empty farmhouse greeted him with a single lighted eye from the bedroom; kept on with the radio at half blast to deter any would be intruders.

A nervous sense of anticipation overtook him as he rushed round to her door and helped her to her feet and out of the car.

'Looks like Shane's up in his room, you go straight up if you want.'

Through glazed eyes she tried to focus, she wanted to reply but the drug had its grip on her. Good. Not a struggler this time. At first he preferred them to lay back and be quiet while he got on with the job; they could scream all they wanted later. He checked over his shoulder to make sure they weren't followed as he led her towards the house.

With his giant hands, Lupo fumbled the key in the lock, tried it twice. It wouldn't turn. Cursed then turned it the other way, kicking it open and pushing her inside. Nervous excitement was getting the better of him.

'SHANE! SHANE, SHE'S HERE!' he shouted theatrically up the stairs.

Miss Butter Eyes smiled; a spider silk thin line of dribble hung from her young pink mouth that sent him wild inside with expectant animal lust. The hungry and baying beast inside him salaciously suggested that he lean in and lick it off her burning hot teen lips, taste her essence, while a throb swelling up in his pants told him to readjust his self .

Now he had her in artificial light he could see she wasn't older than thirteen, fourteen at a push. Electric pink streaks through her jaunty, punk rocker black hair cut confirmed her childishness, she had on one of them studded black leather belts with a skull and crossbones buckle, that would look good as a leash, pulled tight around her slender neck while he…

Enough, he thought cutting off his fantasy mid flow, he had to get her downstairs first, where it was safe.

'You okay?' he asked, her eyes didn't catch on to his, and instead she stared vaguely at the floorboards at her feet.

'Tired,' she whispered, almost a guilty confession.

'You should lie down. I have somewhere for you to sit, rest your tired feet. I'll help you then I'll go get Shane.'

'Sounds good to us but…' she swayed on her feet, lurching towards the wall. Sensing that she was about to cause herself harm, Lupo thrust forward in a parry, catching her under the arms.

'WOAH! You nearly hurt yourself there Missy Butter Eyes. C'mon I'll show you something cool in the basement.'

Without any effort or unnecessary noise, Lupo lifted her over his shoulder and carried her towards the open doorway under the stairs. With a tug of a grimy, yellowed and well-used piece of string, the worn smooth wooden stairs became duly illuminated. Lupo took the first two steps and turned, careful to not bang Maisie Mae's head on the bare brick wall. He locked the door, as he always did, leaving the key in the tumbler, as per routine. His lizard brain told him to leave it there in case of a power cut. He'd always held the fear of fumbling around in the dark of the basement hunting for the key he couldn't find.

He turned and started his descent only to feel the girl stretch, slightly slowing his descent. He turned back to see her fingers weakly grasping the door handle to the outside world.

'Phone…' she managed to say, an effort that seemed to sap at her energies.

'The phones' down stairs,' he assured her with a wicked laugh that echoed into nothing; He jolted forward, pulling her free from her last handhold.

The basement he kept clean. No spider webs, no dust and certainly no DNA, he wiped everything down with bleach after each "trip", including the dentist chair.

Years ago he spied it at an auction and simply had to have it.

Lot 27, he remembered with nostalgic fondness.

It held a power over him in an instant, the steel framework, the patches of torn leather; it commanded something, not an evil, not a respect, no not demanding in any way.

A pull, yes a pull. It wanted to be used. It had a purpose. And the second Lupo decided that he would place the highest bid for that worn out dentist chair, he knew what its purpose would be.

He got it cheaper than he would have paid for it, dragged it home like a prize kill and cleaned it down with bleach to remove the remnants of its previous purpose, covering the torn parts with shiny black duct tape and installing it lovingly in the centre of his basement, surrounded by five hi-definition digital video cameras attached to the exposed ceiling joists.

Aside from the dentist chair covered in a fresh, thin clear sheet of polythene, was a large wooden wardrobe for his "things" and a desk with a glowing laptop awaiting his command. This was all he needed to document the evening's proceedings.

In the corner beneath the wooden basement steps sat an antique Belfast sink for cleaning himself up afterwards before he headed back upstairs to the real world.

Lupo removed her backpack and slung it into the corner for later. Afterwards he'd have a rummage and maybe acquire a trophy or two. He laid the prize of Maisie Mae in the dentist chair and pulled off her pink hooded top over the top of her head like flayed skin. The t-shirt clung tight to her lithe teenage body, a slight promise of tiny breasts hid beneath the Fallout Boy logo, something stirred happily at the promise of her soft pink peaks. He liked them small, not flat, not an ironing board. Just a hint of womanhood was all he needed to get his kicks. He ran a hand over the fabric above, pausing deliberately and teasing himself. He smiled and moved on to her face, stroking away the pink and black strands of hair that had become glued by a nervous sweat to her forehead. One eye was closed; the other struggled in a losing battle to stay open.

Give in, he willed himself.

'It'll be easier on you in the long run. If you're nice to me, I mean really, really nice, I might give you another shot in an hour or two so you don't wake up halfway through like that last silly bitch. Ruined my flow. Mmmm, maybe I will, Maybe I won't. We'll see how rambunctious you get eh?'

'Phone…' Maisie repeated the last thing she said.

'No phone home Eee Tee.'

Lupo loved to tease. He'd been like this at school when he'd tear through girls' bags, eviscerating the contents, spilling their secrets on the corridor floor. One time he found a pack of sanitary towels amongst the spillage, so held the girl down and stuck them all over her face. His friends laughed, egging him on. He took it further, reaching under her dress and pulling out the one she was wearing. She screamed and he'd felt half disgusted half turned on by the sight of that thick smear of dark maroon blood. The girl screamed louder, managing to wriggle free she launched a kick to his crotch. Fuming, Lupo mashed the tainted towel into her face, polluting her shy look with her own pungent mess. She cried and ran home with a stagger, a week later dying of embarrassment by downing three bottles of aspirin and sinking one of daddy's bottles of Jack Daniels after he spread rumours that she'd slept with him and his mates.

Bending down he picked up his latest roll of duct tape and pulled out a piece the full length of his arm span, wrapping it tight around the wrist above her clenched fist, fixing her solid to the dentist chair, so she became an extension of its being. He repeated this for the other wrist, although this fist seemed a lot more relaxed. He put it down to the sleepy cocktail reacting with different sides of the brain. He left her legs free as he needed to get in there later.

Lupo headed over to the computer and started his program. Each of the five cameras flickered to life. All his own design; God, he was some sort of a genius. The cameras were now rolling, one in front, one behind, one left, one right and one directly above Maisie Mae's face to capture *every last moment* of detail.

Each of the five angles had now opened up in different windows on his laptop in nipple sharp high definition. Every second recorded straight onto his hard drive forever and ever with the other hours of footage he had collected over the years. He and the others of the Blossom Society traded films over the net. Sometimes watching somebody else do it was just as exciting. Some even paid for the privilege. Paid well indeed. Often these were the ones afraid of taking the next step into becoming fully fledged members of the Blossom Club.

In the face on angle, Maisie Mae opened her eyes fully and stared straight at him through the screen.

Lupo whipped his head round almost jarring his neck in the process. Her head lolled lazily to one side, she had dribbled again. He turned back to the screen to where it still proved true.

Maybe his eyes had played tricks?

With the program compiling the images megabyte by megabyte and the cameras witness to everything, Lupo wandered back into shot. He stroked Maisie Mae's forehead again, wiping the sweat onto his fingers, he brought the moisture to his lips and licked the absorption off his guilty fingerprints.

She tasted different from the rest, and not good different. It wasn't salty in any way. Not the sweet pungency of youth that he would happily drink up all day from every crevice and orifice. Not poison. Not even distasteful, just wrong.

He spat what was in his mouth onto the floor.

This taste unsettled him.

So much so he headed over to the sturdy Belfast sink and washed his hands and dried them softly on the towel. Then he squirted washing up liquid on them and cleansed himself once again. He filled his mouth with cold water and swilled out his bitter mouth, repeatedly spitting to flush out the acrid taste that had settled on his numbing tongue. Then he swallowed to wet his whistle. The clinging taste of diseased and stagnant water still remained in his throat somehow.

He went back over to Maisie, this time taking the towel with him, dabbing away the offensive seepages from her brow.

Time to get on with it.

He kissed her; the bad taste had gone now, it made him happier to forget the image that had formed in his mind.

'You may notice that I haven't taped your mouth shut. The reason for this is I really don't mind you screaming. The walls and ceilings are acoustically insulated and the nearest neighbours are half a mile away. I'm not expecting visitors any time soon, so please, scream all you want. In fact, I encourage it.'

She murmured.

'Now, I'm going to get a beer, and then we'll get started, okay?'

She groaned this time.

'Want anything?'

Lupo lumbered back up the stairs to the doorway and reached in the dimness for the key in the lock. His fat searching fingers felt smooth brass and no protrusion; an empty key-shaped hole remained. The key had gone, must have fallen out when he closed the door, keys do that sometimes. At least the power hadn't gone out.

He tried the door anyway.

Locked, as he expected, but not hoped.

Lupo span on the spot and headed back down the steps to the basement.

Miss Butter Eyes was wide awake.

She stared straight at him.

The second thing he noticed was her free hand raised in front of her face, a sticky bangle of torn tape stuck to her wrist and a shiny brass key in her fingers.

Maisie Mae smiled, and then dropped the key into her mouth and down her once delicate throat.

Lupo surged forward as if rushing for a train, his thick arms poised to grab her. With a single swipe she knocked him off balance and down to the concrete floor, scraping his arms and elbows across the harsh surface as he skidded.

Im-fucking-possible.

The second band of tape ripped just as easily as the little girl raised her arm with no effort at all. On his back, Lupo scurried towards the wardrobe, he had tools in there. Tools he could use as weapons.

Maisie lifted her top and tossed it to the floor, revealing a tight pink bra.

'*I'm not expecting any visitors, so please, scream all you want,*' he heard himself say, but his lips hadn't moved. Maisie's had, she had imitated his voice far too perfectly.

'*In fact, I encourage it.*'

Lupo let out a terrified little shriek as she advanced in a slow and deliberate strut. With frantic, probing fingers he reached inside the bottom drawer of the wardrobe and yanked out the battery powered angle grinder. The sight of this did nothing to deter her, though it brought a measure of comfort to Lupo as he started it up, the blade whirled deafeningly to life.

'I'll…I'll cut you…' he promised with a trembling shout.

Undeterred, Maisie Mae smiled; the once innocent baby blue had flushed from her eyes, now replaced with a complete yellow ball, no pupil, just pus yellow. Rotten butter yellow.

Miss Butter Eyes.

Now he got that one.

Her smile had changed too; her mouth had somehow got bigger to accommodate her arsenal of perfect and pointed teeth.

Like frightened prey, he struck out with the grinder, Maisie snatched it by the blade, mangling her fingers then tossing it behind her where it skittered around noisily on the floor before losing power and turning itself off.

From the wound where her hand used to be, a new one emerged, fingers thicker than his arm impossibly sprouted forth, clean talons like forged Samurai blades.

Inside her, Lupo could hear bones cracking, stretching and reforming. Her face and jaw seemed to bubble beneath the skin, all trace of youthful beauty dissipated.

Lupo had definitely lost his mojo now. If anything, it shrivelled inwards to his gut. The sight becoming too much for him, Lupo pushed himself to his feet and ran. The thing that was once a little girl didn't even reach for him, not even an eyelid batted. When he rushed up the stairs and battered on the door, he knew why.

No escape.

He had reinforced this door himself. It could be burning on one side for six hours and it would still hold strong. The only things that would get through the heavy barrier would be a few sticks of dynamite or a chainsaw.

Remembering the grinder at the bottom of the stairs, Lupo started to descend in order to retrieve his only means of escape when the Maisie Mae *thing* rounded the corner to block his passage.

Her shoulders had broadened in the brief time she'd been behind him, popping off her pink bra with the ongoing strain of new muscle. Her mouth had doubled yet again and every tooth glinted yellow and splinter sharp. Her head seemed too big for her body, the black and pink hair now sporadic across the back of her big head. Her jeans and shoes had ripped away, revealing tree trunk like legs covered in coarse black hair.

She advanced, lurking up the stairs towards the useless drum of his heartbeat and drinking in every moment of his fear.

Lupo cried and fell back against the door; his pitiful legs kicking out like a petulant child. The Maisie Mae thing grabbed at his legs with her thick fingers, pushing them together (he had no choice for her strength was incomparable) and started greedily feeding his feet into her gaping maw. Lupo bucked and struggled in vain to free himself, screaming louder and louder, hoping by some chance that the neighbours would somehow hear him and save him from this monster. Prison would be a dream in comparison.

With an unsatisfying crunch, Lupo watched as the ungodly thing that was once Maisie Mae bit off both his feet. He clenched his ghost toes in anticipation of a scurrying run out of there.

Lupo shrieked so loud he tore something in his throat. Something warm and coppery slid down into his gullet. He screamed no more as his lower leg dropped off and disappeared down into her oesophagus. He could manage to utter nothing but a slurping and breathy gasp. He raised a fist, or at least in his mind he did.

The thick dark tongue flicked suggestively over the stumps as she swallowed, drinking him in.

She continued her munching, feeding him in, inch by inch. Each time licking the wound with that dark eel-like tongue so he didn't bleed out. He felt the pain still even though numbness overtook him, paralysing his fight.

Her consciousness entered him and he saw what she was, what she did for a living.

He was the latest of many and certainly not the last. She had been around longer than he. All of her previous meals passed by in a flash, every face locked into a hideous death throe. He was to join them.

She wasn't born; she was created, put here for a purpose by the old gods. She checked on mankind. Kept the bad ones at bay. An overseer.

She had reached his crotch now and it was here she paused. He looked into her old milk yellow eyes and she into his. She was waiting for him to die.

And she would.

She wanted him to feel every last excruciating moment. Something in her saliva kept him going, stopped him from bleeding to death yet kept the nerve endings brutally alive and awake, buzzing with agonising activity.

It took hours.

Then sometime before dawn, his heart gave in and stopped. Maisie continued her feast.

Below him, hell beckoned.

***

Once she had regurgitated the splinters of chewed bones, hair and anything else she couldn't digest into a bin liner, including the basement key that she easily fished out from the mess as it was the last thing on the pile of steaming waste. Maisie returned to her unnatural form and stripped off the rags that her clothes had become and washed off the blood in the cold water that the Belfast sink provided. She dried off with the towel and changed into a fresh set of clothes that she kept in her back pack. With a cheap pink tooth brush she scrubbed the meaty bits of Mr Lupo from her teeth and combed her hair into her preferred punk rocker Joan Jett style, although she longed to head into a more Blondie-esque territory for her next guise. She dumped the toothbrush in the bin bag full of Mr Lupo.

Once she felt vaguely human again, Maisie Mae logged onto Mr Lupo's computer and checked his contacts list for the Blossom Society in the hope of securing herself a fresh meal for the next night.

DEVIL LET ME GO

Eat your Heart out Lorena

EAT YOUR HEART OUT LORENA

It was Brant's wife flushing the toilet that woke him up from his sauced up slumber. His fat stupid wife who can't even use a treadmill without pulling that dumb flustered expression like a hippo having an asthma attack.

Even though he loved her to pieces, he still found the time to take the piss out of her.

Her...

Beth, Big Beth, Beth the Behemoth, Bethemoth.

Huh, he liked that one, said his whisky soaked brain, what else can we call her? The sea cow? Mount Beth. Ha! She wasn't that fat, but his jibes weren't helping her weight loss regime, neither was his cheating. He was sure she knew. Little side-glances she gave him every time he said he was heading out was evidence of her knowing. Her glare, that chubby cheeked, swollen stare, a gaze so guilt inducing that he had to go out and bang something, just to take his mind off of her.

Last night was no exception. Head out, meet the boys at the bar, chat to that nice blonde bar maid, then end up settling for that gawky young student with the mild case of acne, against the bins in a furious three-minute thrusting fumble of hello/goodbye animalistic pumping. She and all women loved fucking him, he was blessed in the trouser department, so used his gift from the lord every chance he got. In the showers after football his mates nicknamed him two-tins, as downstairs he looked like two tins of coke welded together. He knew it was his personality that grated women, not that he cared; he wasn't with them for sparkling conversation. He was with them to satisfy a carnal need, nothing more. He fucked fast and hard, he wasn't bothered whether the girl he was with came or not, he didn't care much for the female orgasm. The cave man inside told him that women were good for one thing; Well three if you count cooking and cleaning.

Beth had been up when he got in, slumped like beached whale on the sofa, remnants of popcorn remained in a metal bowl, she played with an elastic band in her hand, she smiled as he stumbled in, tripping over the cat, which shrieked and bolted for the kitchen. She made him a drink, another whisky that half lurched his stomach, and then told him to head up to bed where she would join him shortly. She winked and gave her lips a slight lick; giddily he downed the JD and thundered his way upstairs with the promise of a blowjob from his fatty fat wife. In his experience they always appeared more grateful.

Brant had passed out on top of the covers, not knowing whether Beth serviced him or not. It had been a while since they had done anything in the bedroom, since her mother died she'd been up for nothing, but he still had needs, that's what led him to cheat, her selfishness. If she'd only got over the death of her mother that happened well over a year ago, then they could get on with their lives and start a family. That was one sure thing he loved about Beth, he knew that she'd be a good mother. She had the whole attitude; good with other people's kids, a great cook, it was the bedroom department she lacked confidence in.

Brant wanted sons, three of them; he wasn't too fussed about girls. He couldn't watch a little girl grow up only to bring home some nerd or sex pest sweating as they asked for permission to marry his daughter. His mind would be too obsessed on what she was doing to him behind closed doors. He couldn't handle that. That's why he wanted boys to conquer the world. He'd already researched hormone treatment on the Internet to favour male foetuses; all he had to do was get Beth to agree to the injections. Expensive, but worth it for the peace of mind.

Downstairs he could hear Beth giggling at something, probably *Only Fools and Horses* on the telly, she was always watching the repeats, he was sure she fancied Rodney. From this disturbance, Brant cracked open a sleep sealed eye, the first grey hum of dawn slipped dull light around the edges of the curtain and into the bedroom. A glass of water stood on the bedside table on Beth's side of the bed, next to this was a travel sewing kit and a packet of what looked like painkillers. Why would Beth bring a sewing kit to bed? Maybe she'd put a few stitches either side of her mouth to stop her eating as much. Outside birds tweeted their morning song as the bin lorry pulled up outside, he heard a rolling dirge of wheels on concrete before their bin was lifted and emptied in the back with a mechanical whine.

 His mouth felt like he'd been gargling grit, dry and with the distinct taste of vomit. Had he been sick? He couldn't remember for shit. Although a further nauseating vapour from the carpet next to the bed raised his suspicions further. Beth hadn't cleaned it up, so he suspected that she'd be mad with him for the mess.

His thighs felt semi-wet as he shifted his weight. Christ, had he pissed himself again? He sent down a searching hand to investigate, a sticky, crumby crust greeted him. Nah, he'd shit himself, a less frequent but messier episode. He offered a heaving sigh in response to his predicament. Beth definitely wouldn't be happy. That was why she wasn't in bed with him, she'd probably slept on the sofa, Beth was good like that. Still, she'd have to change the sheets; Brant was useless at such domestic drudge, which was more than a good reason to find a doting wife.

With a drunken reluctance, he opened his eyes. The bedroom was empty except for him. He lifted his now crusty hand up to his face, his digits covered in a dark viscous mess; it pleased him that the shit didn't smell as bad as he feared. Knowing that the entire bed would need to be changed, Brant wiped his fingers to and fro on top of the duvet, and then sniffed them. Copper, not shit.

A brief, all too sudden alarm, emptiness resided somewhere. Brant shoved his hand down into his crotch and dropped into a drowning vat of panic.

It was missing, his penis was missing. His cock, his dick, his Wang, Man Cannon, his plonker was gone.

Absent.

Vanished.

Vamoosed.

He pushed frantically searching fingers of both hands round to his arse, in case he'd sat on it during the night, but all he found was more crustiness, and no balls, just an empty scrotal sack, they had vanished as well. He felt the wound, soft, pliable and encrusted with a thin layer of tenderness. Brant's breathing became rapid, his first thought was to get out of bed and start to look for his missing member. He did this, shooting up from the bed with rapid fervour and caught sight of his naked, blood crusted eunuch body in the mirror. The bile elevator rose up his throat and deposited its load down his bare chest. Brant slapped himself, smacking and smearing vomit across his cheek in effort to wake up from every man's nightmare. Fixing his gaze on what wasn't there anymore; Brant nipped the skin on his forearm between index and thumb and pinched until he bled. Nothing could wake him up from this reality. The rising scream cleared the remainder of stomach lining and digestive juices from his throat, sending horrendous spittle decorations of acid yellow and soft specks of carrot orange onto his mirror image.

'Morning darling, I heard you were up. Would you like a coffee?'

'YOU BITCH!' Brant hollered as he span, 'What have done with MY COCK?' Bubbles of yellow red spit hung freely from his bottom lip, he had started to cry. Beth stood in the doorway, smiling with a splashed bloodstain down the front her Snoopy nightie.

'I need to call an ambulance, and then you can tell me where it is.'

'There won't be any need to call an ambulance, I fixed you up good an' proper, I've left you an urethra so you can still pee; sitting down of course. I stopped the bleeding straight away. Not that there was much blood, the elastic bands helped there; I cut off the blood supply first so you wouldn't be so drowsy with blood loss. I crushed up a good few Co-codamol in some water to numb the pain, but I wouldn't do any physical activity for a few weeks and...'

'A few weeks? You're talking like a doctor; you're a fucking vet's assistant, not a brain surgeon! How could you do this to me?'

'It was quite simple really...'

'I don't mean your fucking method! I mean HOW COULD YOU DO THIS... TO ME?' Brant pointed at his empty ball bag that hung pathetically from his crotch like a small, worn out leather purse.

'I did it for us. I was ready to leave you. I didn't want that. I followed you last night, I saw you with that girl. I saw after closing what you did to her behind the bins, on top of that beer barrel. I don't want you doing that. I want you to love me for who I am. We're supposed to be together and I can't have you sniffing round other women.'

Brant looked at Beth with a melting gaze, he felt faint, he'd had a massive trauma; he should be in hospital, not bleeding and covered in his own vomit discussing his relationship with this mad bitch.

'I thought you wanted children? How could you? Where is it?'

'I gave you a wink last night didn't I?' Beth gave that cheeky smile that he fell in love with, once. 'You don't need to be awake to be satisfied darling. I serviced you good and proper, then I spat it into a syringe then serviced myself, I checked my dates, my cycle is at the right place and I've been off the pill a while now, so there's an eighty-percent chance that I'm pregnant right now!'

The look of glee and her jubilant smile defied the situation. Brant was now fully submerged in disbelief, the how, why, and when had been answered, he knew Beth's motives, he understood why she did it, he'd been a fucker to her, yes, he could live with that.

All that needed answering now, was the what.

What had she done with his cock and balls and could they be reattached? Doctors could do amazing things in surgery nowadays. He cast his mind back to the bin lorry that had just pulled away from their house. Jesus, had she tossed his cock in the wheelie bin? He could find it, he'd chase after them and they'd have to stop. They'd see what she did to him and they would have to help him sort through the rubbish to get his member back. He'd get it reattached then he'd sue and divorce Beth, get her in court, sent to prison for a few years should teach her a lesson, then he'd sell his story to the papers and never get married again, that was a given. Women are far too crazy when it comes to relationships. The wrong sort of crazy.

'Where is it? What have you done with me?' Brant asked, his voice as hoarse as sandpaper on concrete, but he kept his calm, but beneath, he seethed and hissed like a cauldron full of vinegar. She smiled, walked forward and stroked his face regardless of the sick.

'We'll get you cleaned up, and back into a clean bed.' Beth's eyes had taken on a defiant glaze, as if the true meaning of her mutilation meant nothing to her, not even on the level of a shaving cut or a banged funny bone, all the concern of a wife pushed too far, he'd pushed so far there wasn't a way of bringing her back, not on this plane of sanity.

'I'll phone work, tell them that you can't make it in today, so don't worry, I'll look after you if nobody else will. I can't see any other women wanting you now.'

Despite that truth he asked, feigning quiet and calm, 'where is it?' his voice low and of complete artificial peace, he had to know the truth.

'Well, Brant my darling, you're such Big Boy, it took a good few flushes to get rid of the damned thing...'

DEVIL LET ME GO

BANANA BOXES

"Will you walk into my parlour?" said the Spider to the Fly
Mary Howitt

With arms fully laden, Jeff Danes left the chilling winter winds behind to gush and swirl the first flurries of snow on the cold side of the front door, which he kicked closed, then stamped loose the snow from his shoes.

Inside their top floor flat, the last on a row of red bricked terraces, his wife, Tobi had the heating full blast, the electric fire was on and yet she was dressed in hot pants and a tiny pink vest. Three tea lights flickered along the mantle piece. He'd told her a thousand times, if she was cold, put a jumper on, get a few layers on your skin. It was starting to snow outside so he thought that he'd leave it for now. He didn't want to seem like a miser so close to Christmas.

He stepped in front of the makeover show she was so engrossed in and with a stretch of a smile he dropped the five cardboard structures at his new bride's feet.

'What the hell are they for?' He noted a callous tone in Tobi's voice, but he ignored it, keen to get this over with.

'They're banana boxes. I expect you to pack your crap. I've done mine, now it's your turn.'

Tobi flexed her hands out with a knowing grace, then her toes, admiring her glittered pink handiwork.

'But I've just this minute done my nails, it'll take a while for them to dry, you'll have to wait *Jeffy*.'

He hated *Jeffy*. It made him sound like a toilet cleaner. Anything but *Jeffy*. Jeffo, Jeffa, Jeffman to his malarkey friends, only Tobi, his beautiful blonde bride of three weeks called him *Jeffy*. But he didn't have the heart to tell her, he felt that if he told her not to do something, she'd shatter like glass; she had that kind of brittle demeanour. He had to take things slowly with her, think about his reasoning before he urged her towards doing something. Christ, it took six months before she slept with him. But she was beautiful, and she was worth the wait. Well that's what he told himself.

'Listen darling, we have to move out by tomorrow morning, the landlord says that the lease is up and we have to go. The new couple are moving in and we can't share a bedroom with them now can we?'

'Don't be condensation *Jeffy!*'

She pouted in that ever-moodily glamorous, not a hair out of place way of hers, she had one of them faces that when she tried a bad attitude he didn't know whether he wanted to kiss her hard on the lips or slap her harshly across the face. He knew for a fact, having seen her G.S.C.E results that she probably didn't know what condensation meant, she probably meant condescending.

'Fill these boxes with your make-up and all your other crap and then we can take them to my mother's.' He stepped up his tone to harsher level, not too high though, if you push her too far too early she won't do a dammed thing.

'I don't want to go to your mother's, it smells of old.'

'She's only fifty, and she has very kindly let us have the use of the spare room for a few weeks while we sort ourselves a new place out. Now please my little pumpkin pie, please, please get packed so we can go.'

'Don't call me pumpkin pie; it makes me think that you think of me as orange and crusty.'

'It's a term of endearment darling. Do you want me to help you or do you want to do it yourself.'

'I'll do it myself, but you'll have to take the boxes to the bedroom for me. My nails aren't dry yet.'

Jeff sighed, giving in to his wife's pleading.

'Of course I will, but we need it all packed up tonight, my brother is coming round tomorrow at nine AM sharp, so we have to be ready.'

'Whatever, I'll do it in a minute.'

'I know you will. Right I'll get the kitchen stuff sorted. You can tackle your mass of products. Did you pack your clothes in the suitcases I brought?'

Tobi pulled back her glossed lips to reveal hissing white teeth.

'Err, not quite, it won't take me long.'

'For Christ sake Tobes! It took you four days to decide what bikinis to take on honeymoon; you've got more shoes than Topshop and more handbags than the bargain bin at T K Maxx. Please get it sorted.'

The perpetually huffing Tobi flared her nostrils and jumped up off the comfort of the sofa, a pillow in her hand and red in her cheeks.

'Fine, but if I ruin my nails, don't blame me if I get pink stardust all over my new knickers!'

Tobi slammed the pillow back towards the sofa, missing it by a good few feet, hitting the side table with a muffled clatter instead. She picked up the first two banana boxes and stormed off towards the bedroom.

Jeff smiled at his minor victory, knowing that this battle was merely a nosebleed in comparison to the war that their relationship had become.

His victor's grin soon melted when he looked down at the luminous splash of Pink Stardust nail polish that had made itself a new home over the thrown cushion and the cream carpet at his feet.

'That'll be coming out of the bond then.'

He rushed to the kitchen with a sigh, grabbing absorbent towels, fairy liquid and a damp cloth then returned to the living room where he positioned himself on his hands and knees and began to soak up the excess spillage with the towels.

'I paid the bond, this'll be coming out of my bond,' he grumbled quietly to himself, 'she barely pays the rent as it is.'

After mopping the excess Pink Stardust, he began tracing a green line of Fairy liquid to lift the stain up from the cheap looking, though now expensive carpet.

***

The vague scent of a female being had moved him from his poise, her trail masked by an unnatural, though extraordinarily familiar aroma that reminded him of the primeval forest into which he should be venturing. This exotic perfume tickled his senses, strange, yet a degree of intrigue made him want to investigate this alien land further.

A simmering heat warmed his brief drop of blood.
With an unfolding of his legs, he hatched.

***

Tobi had dumped the boxes next to the warming radiator and began slinging her various make-ups and potions into the cardboard with a selfish jangle of glass and plastic.

Before Jeff had arrived back home, she'd been soaking herself in the bath, soaping her curves with that tropical fruit bath scrub, knowing he adored the smell, even doing her nails nice and pretty. She hoped that he'd pounce on her as soon as he got through the door; instead he was intent on moving them on. The landlord had only raised the rent by a small amount, something about matching the rate of inflation. Jeff being a stickler for a good deal, immediately handed over their tenancy notice, his reasoning being that the rent was too high for them to afford. Now they had to up sticks and find somewhere new and at about the same price they were paying now, an effort she doubted could never be accomplished in their price range.

Knickers stuffed with bitterness into the bottom sports bags.

Delicate dresses thrown with rage on top of one another into a battered suitcase. Socks stuffed into trainers to save space.

Tobi continued her maelstrom of packing away her bitter pills and wares.

***

Jeff finished clearing up Tobi's mess, binning the soiled cloths he used to soak up the mess and placing the half emptied bottle of polish back on the coffee table next to her collection of nail files, scissors and nail varnish remover.

With all of his stuff already packed, he could either help Tobi out with her efforts or get started on packing the pots, pans, bottles and jars in the kitchen.

With a sigh he grabbed the last cold beer from the fridge and started on the utensils.

* * *

With all his legs free and the unnatural heat quickly warming his minute bodily fluids, he emerged fully from his speck of an egg. Light burned into his many eyes; this brightness took him a minute to adjust. But he adjusted. A stranger loomed.

***

Tobi's scream bit and bounced into the walls of their tiny flat, echoing all at once, causing Jeff to swing round too fast, knocking his beer off the worktop with a jutting elbow. He dozily reached out to catch it, but he was out of time. The bottle exploded with foamy pop on the tiled floor, sending wet shards in every direction.

'Shit!' he cursed then remembered Tobi's scream, he briefly considered mopping up the second spillage of the night, but Tobi screamed again.

Jeff burst into the bedroom, wild eyed with wonder. Tobi stood barefoot on the centre of the bed, hands clasped to her face, frightened eyes gazed from behind a prison of white fingers, the tips decorated with smeared glittery pink.

'What's up? You screamed my love?'

Tobi took in a few rapid breaths and removed her hands from her face and pointed at the half filled banana boxes upon the floor.

'A spider, or something, it moved, it came from behind the boxes.'

'You sure? A spider?' Jeff felt his face crumple under concern. 'You screamed because of a spider?'

'You know I don't like spiders Jeff! This one was different. It wasn't one of ours.'

'We don't have any spiders. Because . . . you don't like them...'

'I don't mean like that dumbass! I mean it's not from this country, it looked tropical, different colours, not just black.'

Jeff narrowed his eyes at her, then at the stack of banana boxes; pondering. A stowaway from the banana plantation, he once read somewhere that farmers in the tropics encourage spiders on their crops as they keep down the number of fruit flies that attack crops. He turned back to his wife, holding out a supporting hand to help her off the bed.

'I'm not coming down until you kill it!'

'Can't I just catch it, maybe a specialist would like to identify it?'

'Jeff, the only thing I'd like that spider to identify with is the bottom of your shoe as you squash it into the carpet.'

'I don't want to kill it. I want to have a look at it first.'

139

He bent down, onto to his hands and knees, and edged his way over to the boxes.

'Where did it go?'

'Don't mess with me Jeff, I'm not kidding, I will divorce you if you mess with me.'

'Where did you see it?'

'It was on the side of the box then it ran on top and into the clothes.'

Jeff reached in and delicately picked up the first item of clothing, a bright yellow top that he had only seen Tobi wear once. She looked on with a wide glare, her alert pupils taking in his every movement. Deliberately and with a degree of caution he raised the garment up to his face, slowly twirling it to get full 360, he couldn't see any sign of any spiders, time to have some fun…

Before he had time to think he had thrown the yellow top at Tobi, just to scare her, teach her a lesson for her laziness. As soon as it left his fingers, a pang of regret burst inside of him. He knew that she'd scream, and that she'd probably punch him in the arm. Although it happened fast, he still saw it in slow motion. A flashing object broke away from the garment, tiny and colourful, at first, his brain assumed it was a button, come loose and now spinning away, chopping through the light, causing reflected twinkles.

But buttons don't have legs.

Or change colour.

His eyes caught Tobi's, she had seen it too. Her mouth gaped into a scream as the spider and the yellow top harmlessly slammed into her at the same time. With hardly any acceleration she bounced from the bed and disappeared through the doorway. The devilish smile had melted from Jeff's face. He'd pay for this one.

***

The brief loss of gravity had alarmed him, causing his defence mechanism to instigate, vessels on his back rapidly expanded and contracted, causing a flashing effect, in place to dazzle and confuse predator and prey alike. He dug in, finding solace in a patch of darkness beneath the yellow. Tensing his eight limbs, he knew that he was being hunted. Oxygen flowed into his extremities, inflating through every pore and sphincter, gaining in size. Within a half a human minute, he had doubled his presence.

***

'I'm sorry darling, I didn't mean to. I didn't know.' Jeff rattled the bathroom door, yet it remained locked.

'I don't care! You still chucked a spider at me. And that *mister*, is unforgivable. What if it's poisonous? Then what?'

140

'I'm sorry, pumpkin, I mean, do you want me to kill it.' A metallic click and Tobi pulled the door back; she'd laid a rolled up towel along the bottom of the door, obviously to prevent the imminent spider invasion that she was expecting. Tears hid behind her shimmering eyes, her soft pink lips parted, and she spoke softly, a whisper so her nemesis wouldn't hear her plan.

'Kill it and dump it in the outside bin. I don't even want to see it. Just get rid of it before I divorce you. And I'm not joking. I will.'

Jeff leaned in for a kiss, but by then the door had shut in his face and the lock re-engaged.

Disheartened, he headed for the kitchen, stepping over his smashed beer bottle; he picked up one of Tobi's celebrity gossip magazines from the accumulated pile on the worktop and a pint glass that he had packed earlier. He didn't plan on squashing Mr Spider, as he got sentimental and squeamish over killing God's creatures outright. He'd catch it and drop it out the front door. The bitter cold outside would take care of it. He just didn't want to see it die in front of him. He thought back to the hypnotising flashes that the spider had displayed. Clearly it wasn't evolved for this country; this was an alien species, stowed away in the folds of a banana box. But hell, it had lived this long.

Jeff entered the bedroom armed with the magazine under his arm and the pint glass in hand. He eyed the bed with caution. The yellow top remained discarded on the bed, half covering the imprints of Tobi's footfall, and most probably the infamous Mr Spider.

He crept forward, reaching out he whipped the top up and into the air, jumping back, poised ready with the glass. Nothing moved but the crumpled bedclothes settling back down.

His spidey sense tingled, if he could call it that. Jeff ducked low and peered into the shaded expanse beneath the bed. A tiny object waited. Even from here he could make out a brief twinkle of light. Was that the same spider as before? It seemed bigger, wider, and longer.

It advanced.

The illuminations he had seen before glowed brighter with the shade of darkness instead of the glary dilution of bulb above.

Red.

Green.

Blue.

So rapid were the undulations that they seemed to pool into an entirely new colour. He broke free from being transfixed and raised the glass ready, judging in his mind the arachnid's approach. This was strange, as usually spiders would cower from humans, seeking solace along skirting boards and beneath sofas and cupboards. Not this one.

Mr Spider emerged from the shade of the bed and into the light, immediately the flashes dulled yet remained visible.

Jeff glanced the pint glass down in a confident, fluid motion, smiling as his trap seemed to work, then giving a childish little squeak he'd never heard come from him before as Mr Spider jumped back then up and over the upturned base of the awaiting glass and scurried onto the fleshly white expanse of his hand.

Jeff shrieked again.

Then came the nip.

***

Tobi heard Jeff's yelp. He sounded like a girl. He acted like an old woman and he sounded like a little girl. What a man she'd picked. Her mother had told her that she found Jeff too weak and wet to look after a girl like her. No backbone. Not exactly a go-getter, happy in his shitty little job, shitty little flat and shitty little meagre income. As a couple they were going nowhere slow. Nevertheless she persevered with her love for him and pressed her ear to the bathroom door.

'You okay Jeff?' she called through what now felt like a flimsy wooden door.

He didn't answer.

Tobi shivered.

'Jeff, don't piss about, what happened?'

Again, nobody answered.

Then a light moan, a hiss or a gasp of pain perhaps.

Tobi kicked out the wedged in towel, unlocked and yanked the door open, bolting for the bedroom.

Jeff sat slumped against the wall, his right wrist clasped in his left hand. His face looked sticky white, droplets of sweat beaded out from his alabaster skin. He turned to her as she crouched beside him and said coolly, but with a hint of a tremor.

'He bit me, he actually bit me.'

'Where did he go?'

I…I…I don't know, he jumped over me; I think he headed out of the door. He bit me. He's something new…'

Tobi looked down at his cradled hand, on the fat of skin between his thumb and index finger a penny sized welt had appeared with two tiny red dots in the centre.

'It bit you?'

'Yeah, my bones hurt, I guess it went deep.'

'We need a doctor darling. My phone's in the kitchen, I'll phone for an ambulance.'

Tobi got up and stepped back into the hallway, she flexed her toes and felt very naked and vulnerable in bare feet. Having pretty toes was useless when a deadly spider was gallivanting around your home. She spied Jeff's smelly running trainers dumped in the hallway and moved towards them, if she was gonna do some spider stamping, she'd need armour for her delicate soles. With toes an inch from the tongue of the old trainer she stopped.

A premonition; a shiver from the future, call it what you will, but something danced up and down her spine. The dark crevice of the awaiting trainer had turned into a mouth full of hidden teeth, eager to snap her foot clean off to a neat, bleeding stump. With ease of caution, Tobi pulled her foot back. If she was a spider, that's where she would hide, in the dark, dry sweat safety of a trainer. She continued her mission to the kitchen, gaining speed, fearful that the spider had pounced out from his trap and was now in pursuit.

Tobi reached the kitchen with speed, spying her phone straight away she stretched out for it.

Friction gave way as her feet slid effortlessly over the chilled patch of spilt beer and broken glass that her darling husband had carelessly left on the cold tiled floor. This became warm as an eruption of blood, fresh from the new slices on her feet mingled with the spillage of beer. Even with her toned and sculptured legs, she struggled for purchase and went akimbo over the shallow lake of beer. She reached out and grabbed the worktop to steady her descent, her grip fixed hard.

Tobi hissed, cursed and forgot about the phone; dropping to the floor she tended to her cut feet by grabbing a kitchen towel from the hanger to staunch the flow of blood.

***

Mr Spider, using his needle like fangs, had delivered a defensive blow to his adversary. Crippling paralysis would soon follow, then terrifying hallucinations, eventually followed by a more than welcome death. Having delivered the tiny bite and injecting a quantum particle of venom, he jumped over his wincing enemy, and landed in the mess of his hair, so far his presence hadn't been detected. He waited. Poised and prone.

***

He felt like his stomach had shrunk, twisted and knotted itself around inside him as if he'd swallowed a bag of hot, shrinking snakes. A sickly cold sweat perspired out from his skin; he shivered within his own slickness. His hand hurt the most; even the bones beneath seemed to flame up with a relentless pressure.

The tiny fang marks on his hand pulsed, making him want to suck and bite at the miniscule wound.

I want rid of the poison, please dear God, don't let me die. Not yet, not here, not like this. I wanted kids . . .

Jeff tried to move his legs, they were frozen solid like cut timber, he tried to lift his hand to shift his legs along, they wouldn't move. He tried to cry, but the tears wouldn't come no matter how hard he pushed. A mumbled scream tried to free itself from his lips, amassing to nothing more than a garbling of foamy spit. A portion of his spine still responded to the message of movement he sent. It twitched seven times; he slumped and fell over to the carpet.

***

Sat wincing on the kitchen floor, Tobi mopped up the blood the best she could. Through the influx of her pain, she had forgotten all about Jeff. Hearing his whimper from the bedroom created a sense of urgency within. She grabbed her phone and hobbled back to the bedroom, dialling through for the emergency services. Behind her she left a sticky trail of crimson prints.

Jeff was on his side, bright red spit flowing freely from his mouth, he'd bit into his own tongue in frustration. Tobi dropped to her knees and cradled his drooped head in her hands.

'Oh Christ! Oh darling, I'll get you an ambulance, don't you worry.'

'Emergency. What service?' The new male voice in her ear made her jump, taking her a second to get the words out.

'My husband, he's been bitten.'

Tobi didn't hear the operator's response; her own scream drowned his words. From her husband's hair to her own, a beastie stirred, eight legs rolled and stretched towards her, she jumped up dropping the phone beside Jeff, from the corner of her eye she saw it moving effortlessly along her silky dyed strands. She screamed down the hallway, she screamed into the living room. Here, she started slapping at her own head in effort to dislodge the creepy crawly that adorned her brow. A speck of flashing, indescribable colours raced up towards her eye. She felt a multitude of miniscule legs on her eyelid, tickling her prickled skin.

Fangs met the white flesh of her eye.

A vicious slap to the forehead and the demented spider fell to the floor. With one eye now blinded, Tobi began to stamp with naked feet in the general direction of the scurrying arachnid. With venom leaking from her eye and reduced depth perception, she missed every time.

***

Mr Spider danced his way across the fur of the carpet; every time he sought shelter a stomping foot blocked the way. The rapid changes in direction caused his heart to race, why must they single him out, two against one wasn't justified. All he did was protect his self. All he ever wanted was a nice place to call his own…

A poison worse than his own engulfed his being, burning his eyes, blinding him. It flowed into his mouth drowning out his function to breath. It soddened his young limbs, the vile liquid burrowing into joints rendering them immobile. The excruciating pain got worse. When Mr Spider, who thought he knew the worst agony he'd ever experience in his little life, felt everything he ever knew burst into the hottest light imaginable. A pain so intense he could see it before the last of his burning eyes.

***

Half a bottle of nail varnish remover tipped on top and the gentle lick of a tea light flame had done the job. Sure the carpet was ruined, but the spider was dead.

Tobi breathed a sigh of relief at the half sight of the dead, now incinerated to nothing but a crumbling black husk. All evidence of him ever existing now just a bite on her eye and a nip on her husband's hand. Her eye and lid had swollen up in the briefest of moments. She'd best speak to a doctor before any real damage is done. Without any sense of urgency, she returned to the bedroom and picked up the phone. Jeff's flickering tongue lolled about his mouth as he tried to pronounce words that didn't even exist. A faraway gaze adorned his rolling eyes.

'Hello, I'm back!' Tobi announced, her voice induced by a tremor, 'sorry, I've been bitten as well.'

'Okay, what bit you?' thankfully the operator had the gumption to stay on the line.

'A spider, a spider bit my husband and me. He bit me in my eye and my husband on the hand. We think it came in a banana box we were using to move some things.'

'Okay in order for the doctors to prescribe the correct anti-venom, we either need a photo of the spider, or we need you to catch it for us. Can you do that for me…?'

DEVIL LET ME GO

BRIAN OF THE NIGHT

He was just sitting there. Like all good patient predators

The Father had gone into the bedroom as soon as he heard his baby girls' cries in the night, motioning through the familiar route bathed in darkness, a path that he could have easily conquered blindfolded. Having completed it up to ten times a night for the past three months since she had been in her own room, he was now rather adept at jumping up in the pitch black and tending to his young daughter's needs.

He let his wife sleep; the pregnancy and birth had been hard enough on her as it was. Postnatal depression sunk in, clouding her world with darkness. She'd said that her daughter never smiled at her, only screaming incessantly whenever she came near or held her. She said that her baby didn't love her. This was a tragic shame. Now, even nine months after his baby girl had arrived in the world, she still needed her eight hours of sleep every night. The Father was happy to provide this; being a Father was something he always wanted and he revelled in doting after his first-born baby girl since she popped out into his world. He was the first one she smiled at, that day his heart exploded with joy. With each passing day he looked ever forward to her first independent steps and whatever her first full word might be. Secretly he hoped it was Daddy, or to a lesser extent, Dada.

Any day now.

She was a smart bright thing, smiling and giggling with him, such a happy baby.

Stepping into the lily pink bedroom he had decorated while his daughter was baking in his wife's belly, he noticed nothing different. Routine as ever, he headed over to his daughter's wooden crib, reached in and through some kind of parental night vision magnetism, his searching fingers instantly found her dummy and gently pushed it back between her tiny pink lips. Her urgent chuntering ceased and the house was calm yet again.

The Father turned, and half dreamily noticed the dark character sitting slumped down in the nursing chair that usually sat empty in the corner of his daughter's bedroom. He took a hazy double take before fully concentrating on the still, silent figure. Shivers of fear prickled his skin.

The figure was vaguely illuminated by the soft blue glow of the night-light, but the Father couldn't determine any features in this paltry luminosity. What he was wearing betrayed his eyes, was it a leather suit or was it his skin? It was so well fitting that the nature of the material couldn't be determined.

His face was down; his distorted features half hidden by the angle and darkness. His mouth seemed full. Bulging lips played out away from his face, he was bald, a smooth scalp without a freckle nor mole, no imperfections whatsoever. Smooth, like an alabaster plain, almost like a landscape then a human head.

He couldn't be human.

He moved slowly, looking up with thickened eyelids closed as if in prayer, he heaved a sigh through his piggy nostrils.

Something told the Father to run back to his bedroom and fetch the wooden baseball bat that he kept in the wardrobe for such an occasion; an intruder in his house. Strike out and kill this thing before it did anything. He hadn't heard any windows breaking, all the doors were locked, he was sure that he'd set the alarm. How did he get in? Life seemed to drain from him; his chest became heavy, lead lungs that weighed his breath down. His heart boomed, deafening in the silence.

Fetch it, he told himself. Fetch the bat now.

He tried to move, but his legs betrayed his order, some power held him back; he couldn't leave his little girl, not with this pale freak.

'The bat would be useless my friend, I assure you,' the intruder spoke, his voice a semi-Bela Lugosi rasp. Cultured yet tinged with potential malevolence, a tone that sounded both young and old. It promised of danger, but at the same time soothed and transfixed him, like the hypnotising gaze of a poised cobra.

'How…how…how?'

'Ask no questions my friend, you won't get any answers I'm afraid,' the intruder opened his eyes, marvellous white orbs that defied the darkness revealed themselves from behind the thick, fleshy lids. Staring yet without any visible or definition of pupils, the Father was somehow grimly assured that he could still see him; perhaps better than he could see the imposing intruder.

'All I need from you is an answer, and then I'll go. I promise, with no harm coming to you or your baby.' Something unnerved the Father about the way the intruder said or, like it was an option.

Left or right?

Ketchup or mustard?

Up or down?

Do or die?

Behind him, he heard the door to his daughters room creak as if under immense pressure, like an old ship straining against the immeasurable pounding of the ocean waves. He knew that he if span and tried to pull the handle open, it would be in vain. Some otherworldly supernatural force held it closed; fleeing at this point was not an option. He concentrated back on the stranger's eyes. The size of grapefruits, bulging out of his skull they didn't look comfortable at all, full pressured and ready to pop like overgrown cists.

'My name is,' he paused as if pondering an alias, then said, 'Brian,' the Intruder announced with a untrustworthy smile that revealed fifty or so needle like fine teeth, shaped perfectly inwards in that uncomfortable mouth, but somehow looking as strong as ivory.

A word, an image, stark and all too real flashed through his thought processes at this point.

Whale Bone Comb.

That's what his teeth looked like.

'…and I'm a Baby Eater,' Brian continued. His smile faded like dead morning mist.

'No, do not panic, I'm not going to eat your daughter, she is far too beautiful for a creature such as myself,' that smile came back, briefly. Brian looked at the cot then back at her terrified Father.

'I've looked into her. Deeply. Her future, her very being in fact. She comes from good stock, if I may congratulate you on that at least.'

'Th…Th…Thank you.' Why was he thanking him? Smash him in the face with something, grab the baby and jump out the window. That would be better than this fate. He imagined punching him seeing his arm sucked into the needle sharp mouth all the way to the hilt of the shoulder, then snap, crunch as the fine teeth closed around his arm. Brian furrowed his white brow, disappointment rained down his stony face.

Stop thinking anything. He is reading everything you think. He will see it coming before you do. Besides, you'd never be a match for this ungodly monster.

Seemingly pleased that the Father was now dissuaded with launching an offence against him, Brian continued.

'As I was saying, I've seen her future, and she will be very happy, she'll have three beautiful children, triplets may I add. All as gorgeous as she is now. I shall come back for one of them when the time is right. Such a delightful feast will be worth the wait!' Brian chuckled to himself; the Father didn't see the funny side. At the back of his mind he discreetly searched for something to hit this "Brian" creature with. He didn't care whether he heard the thoughts; he wanted him to know that he was detested. From the vile stink of his breath, he guessed that "Brian" already knew he wasn't exactly welcome in this world.

'This is where you come in, you get a choice,' Brian continued, he stood up from the nursing chair, all dark eight feet of him. Towering above the Father, he made a sweeping gesture with his black spindly arm over the top of his head. His entire reach nearly constituted half of the width of the room; the Father watched the thin, razor-like nails as they seemingly swished over his scalp, cutting through air and atoms. A shiver that would have delighted "Brian" fell down the rickety staircase that was now his spine.

'The choice is you for your daughter. Are you game?'

Now that his eyes had adjusted to the light a little better and Brian was now stood closer, the Father could make out tiny black pinpricks of pupils in the centre of his eyes. He could feel himself aging as he looked into them. He averted his gaze and turned back to his daughter, although still reluctant to turn his attention away from Brian, he found a spot in between them both where he could fix his gaze.

'Why me?' The Father managed to utter.

'Well I adore eating children to put it bluntly, babies more so. But sometimes I like it when someone gives their self up onto me. Self-sacrifice, if you like. It makes the meal far more enjoyable if your dinner *wants* to be eaten. I cherish it. I revel in screams and pleadings. Besides, I can come back and claim your daughter's children at a more appropriate date. Time is of no consequence to me. At all. I cannot say that your death will be pleasant, not in the slightest. I will have to eat you alive to gather any enjoyment or nourishment from it. I will want you to willingly scream your lungs off. All you have to do is take my hand, that is all and the deal is done.' Brian held out his sharpened claw. Offering it as a deadly way out.

'How can you promise that you won't come back for my daughter, I know that I would be powerless against you anyway, but how would I know?'

'You wouldn't.' Brian smiled that deathly grin, but then, 'I'm only joking, do you think that if I wasn't a man of my word I would have eaten her already?'

'I suppose...'

'Don't you think that I, a being that no living creature has ever lived to see more than once couldn't devour the pitiful human contents of your world in a lazy afternoon?' He asked as if it was an actual question that could be answered by a mere mortal.

'Well I could, and I have done in the past and I probably will again. If I ever get that angry again, maybe? The point is I choose not to destroy you all in one mouthful. You're stock and I like to toy. I like to play and imagine sick little games like the one that you find yourself playing now. What's the point in eating all of your food at once?'

'It's not really a game though is it? You know that a decent human being with love in his heart and a soul would not and could not stand by while some otherworldly creature ate his first-born child. Good people do not do that. You are a monster nothing more. Are you the Devil?'

'Oh you do amuse me you simple little creatures. With your talk of souls, love, and bullshit. You're base animals designed to eat, drink and rut and get sleepy when you have done all that. That is all. Anything else is filler.'

'Are you the Devil?' The Father repeated.

'I have nothing to do with that old queen, we fell out a long time ago; all he does is mope about idly torturing the dead and the dammed. Now where's the joy in that I ask you? Let's torture the innocent and the living, that's where the real fun lies.'

'What would it take for you to leave us alone? Just go? Fuck off and get out of my sight and remove yourself from out plane of reality?'

Brian's eyes went wide.

'Well I do love your attitude, most parents are willing and take my hand straight away and off I whisk them to my realm where we enjoy a nice meal together. However, not you Daddy. You do have balls. I like that. I like that a lot. I like balls. Nobody ever tells me to "Fuck off". Usually they cry, weep and shudder. Nobody ever tells me to take their child. This is different. It's a change.'

'You're joking right?'

'No, you see I promise myself with this deal, to make it interesting I wouldn't falter. I need a decision. If you're not willing to come to one. Where does that leave me? Hungry. That's where.'

'So you'll go? Just leave?' The Father asked, a light of hope started to burn within his soul.

'Oh yes, I'll go. However, I will be back, I'll ask your wife what she thinks. And I'll be back every night until one of you gives in.'

With his final words stinking the night with a sense of doom and rot, "Brian" folded, shrivelled and melted into the darkness as mysteriously as he'd arrived, leaving the Father shaking in a river of his own scared sweat, basking in the dull glow of the welcome, yet shadow hiding night light.

Now free from the grip of the insane situation, the Father sighed then leant forward and stroked the soft hair upon his daughter's head. Even in the near darkness he noticed that his hand was shaking, smearing his fearful sweat upon her brow. He smiled dreamily, everything was okay, and he'd had a waking nightmare that was all, some parental psychosis that probably affects one in ten new parents. Just a nightmare, that was all…

'Only kidding,' clawed hands raised up from the shadows beneath the crib, death cold fingers clasped tight over his mouth whilst the other gripped fang like nails into his ankle. With the briefest of tugs he was pulled from his world and down into another, filled with stinking depths of endless black, where he now belonged.

The Skeleton Tree

THE SKELETON TREE

'How do ya' suppose he got up there?' Kelly asked, scratching at his sweat drenched crotch, pulling away the clinging fabric of his shorts from beneath his ball sack.

'Well he sure as shit didn't climb up there,' Clark answered, crushing his second can of warm beer since they set up camp. He tossed the can on the ground; Kelly narrowed his eyes at Clark in disdain, but didn't say anything. He looked at the can, then back at the tree.

'Maybe he fell out a plane, or he's a parachutist or something,' Ramsey added, squinting his eyes at the fading sun that they all faced, soon hidden behind the next hill, darkness would fall across the land.

'Do you see a parachute?' Clark turned to Ramsey, his mocking tone whining in the near twilight.

'Could've blown away,' Ramsey theorised.

'Nah, it would have been tangled up in the branches and shit. They'd be scraps at least,' Clark reasoned, nodding, almost convincing himself.

'How about he fell out of a plane, could've happened. What you reckon?' Ramsey put forward again.

'Nah, the branches wouldn't have broken his fall that well. Besides, none of the branches above him are broken. He had to have come from below.' Kelly nodded this time, 99% sure he was right.

'What makes you think it's a bloke?' Ramsey asked, his brow furrowing.

'Because he's got a boner,' Clark said with a smirk, the other two laughed as well. Clark removed his camera from the pocket of his cargo shorts and snapped a few pictures of the form ten feet up above, trapped snugly between two dissecting limbs of the Larch.

'You're taking pictures?' Ramsey chided.

'Who'd believe us back home?'

Ramsey didn't answer; he shrugged and looked back up at the skeleton. The bones didn't look as white as they all would've imagined. They appeared grey, weather worn, almost like sun bleached driftwood. They wouldn't have noticed the body unless Kelly hadn't cracked his back like he did whenever they stopped to remove their rucksacks.

They all stopped for the day, set up camp beside a stream then childishly ran up the hill towards the towering larch tree that oversaw the valley. Kelly won. Once there he swung his arms left and right in an aerobic fashion before arching his back and looking up at the dwindling blue sky. Two soulless sockets stared back at him. He didn't scream or whimper as he'd thought he would. Instead he simply said. 'Hey fellas, check this out.' Then they all looked up.

Kelly checked his mobile phone for signal. None of course. Why would he out here in the Canadian wilderness. Their last point of civilisation was the town where they'd left their rented Jeep, and that was fifteen miles away. Half a day's walk at least. It's what they all wanted from this trip. Complete isolation from the outside world. No internet, no papers, no television. No nothing.

'Well, we can't phone it in. Even up on this hill, I've got no signal.'

'So what do we do?' Ramsey asked.

'Could we carry him back?' Kelly suggested.

'Fuck that!' Clark screwed his face up and blew a raspberry as he tucked his camera back into his cargo shorts. 'I ain't carrying shit, he's dead.'

'Or, we could just mark it on the map and show it to the police when we get back. We can show them the pictures so they'll definitely believe us. It's too late to head back now. Besides, we've made camp.'

'It's a bit creepy don't cha think?' Ramsey asked, 'Y'know sleeping near a dead body. I'd rather head back. What if he's a murder victim?'

'It's not murder Rams,' Clark teased, 'Who murders someone by putting them in a tree? Besides it's not like he's going anywhere.'

'Yeah I think the murderer's long gone as well Rams.' Kelly grinned knowingly at Clark, who smiled back at his friend's naïveté. Kelly walked round the tree, casting his gaze up and down the trunk. He smiled and his eyes went wide.

'Ahh, mystery solved. I know how he got up there.'

Ramsey and Clark followed Kelly round to the far side of the tree. All three of them looked up the tree trunk, their eyes following the line of climbing rope that had been cast up and tied round a branch, now it hung loose, tinged green with mould and frayed by the weather, brushing softly against the crumbly bark of the tree.

'See Rams, it wasn't murder.' Clark playfully arm punched his friend.

All three of them paused for a second before Ramsey spoke.

'So he climbed up there and died?'

'Maybe he was gonna commit suicide and was distracted by the view. Or forgot. Bonehead,' Clark said, laughing at his own joke. Nobody else did.

They stood in silent contemplation for a while, strangely enamoured with the skeleton.

'Weird,' Ramsey said beneath his breath.

By now the sun had sank beneath the far off ridge behind the darkening lake. The three friends silently tracked back down the small hill to the three tents that they would call home for the night.

***

Kelly gathered firewood, tying up the kindling in a spare belt to make it easier to collect and transport. Dipping a net bag in the trailing and gurgling stream Ramsey cooled the four remaining beers and the 78% proof Russian vodka they bought from a liquor store before they had begun their hike, a dwindling cigarette hung from his lower lip as he enjoyed the expanse of the epic dark purple sky framing the jagged teeth of mountains in the distance. Clark was left at camp, having emptied four tins of beef stew into a pan and buttered a plateful of crackers; he now tended to a camping gas stove that now furiously bubbled the stew above a searing blue flame.

Kelly returned and dropped the belt full of kindling next to the fire they had already started.

'That should keep us going for a few hours,' Kelly said with a satisfied smile, 'Dinner ready yet?'

'Yup, just waiting on Rambo,' Clark replied.

Upon hearing his name, Ramsey docked the cigarette out into the stream and fetched three nature cooled beers up to accompany their evening meal.

The blind eye of the moon watched over them as they ate the hot stew. The clear night sky cast a million more eyes upon them, each tiny mighty eye unfathomable generations away, but still watching them all the same.

The three friends talked into the night, each had taken a gap year after they'd finished college to take this trip. Ramsey planned to work for his Father's construction firm once he was back home, eager not for an office job, but as a foreman. An inside job would kill him he admitted, he needed the elements to prove his mettle.

Clark, having his way with words, hoped to get into journalism. He'd already written several pieces for his local paper and was hoping to return there once he had finished university.

Kelly, however, had no plans. He hadn't thought past the trip. He'd gotten half decent grades, so had his pick of what to go into next. His parents pushed him towards medicine, his heart however meandered elsewhere.

'I met a girl,' he told his friends during a lull in the conversation, 'I got her pregnant.'

Ramsey and Clark gawped back at him.

'Really?' they both asked in unison.

'Yeah, she got rid of it. Well said she was going to. I wanted to keep it. Settle down, get a normal boring 9-5 job and support her. She didn't. Said she wanted to live her life first. I loved her. She only *liked* me.'

'So she didn't like you enough to have your kid?' Clark asked, it sounded like a joke, but Clark actually meant it.

'Nah, that takes love. It takes love to raise a kid,' Kelly replied.

'That's a shitter,' Ramsey added, draining the last of his beer.

'Yeah I know. That's why I was so keen on coming on this trip with you fellas. To get away from her.'

'Do we know her?' Clark asked, leaning in. He wanted to know whether or not he had bedded her already.

'Nah, she was from my course. She wasn't your sort. She had standards Clarky.'

'Any woman can lower her standards for me,' Clark smiled grimly, theatrically raising his eyebrows up and down.

'I know. I've seen your Facebook pictures,' Ramsey added, his grin carrying wider.

'I wanted to tell you guys now, because I wanted you to know. I didn't even tell my parents that she was going to get rid of it. Well, he, she, whatever it was,' Kelly choked down a hard swallow exposing a glint of tear, 'I had to tell someone. But I didn't want the trip to be about getting over her,' Kelly finally admitted.

'Hey it wasn't!' Clark half shouted, 'Remember that night in that logging bar, with all the shit country and western. By the end of the night you were slurping shots from that barmaid's belly button.'

'Yeah that was a good night.'

'How about when Clark nearly killed us on that road through Dove Pass, remember?' Ramsey added.

'Hey the brakes were shot, that wasn't me. Besides it was icy out. It wasn't my fault,' Clark defended.

'Clark, you were doing about a hundred miles an hour on a frozen road,' said Ramsey, 'what did you expect?'

'I didn't expect you to shit your pants at a hundred miles an hour!' Clark replied.

Ramsey stood up and pointed one of his thick fingers down at Clark. 'Hey I didn't shit myself! Don't be telling people when we get home that I shit myself!'

'Okay, you didn't shit yourself. It only smelt like you shit yourself and you had to change your pants afterwards. I'll tell people that.'

Clark scowled a beam of concentrated venom at Ramsey.

'Tell them nothing okay,' Ramsey pleaded.

Clark smiled and turned back to Kelly.

'So what happened next, did she get rid of the kid?'

Kelly sighed, cracked his knuckles and his neck. He looked up at the infinite sea of stars that decorated the cosmic ceiling above, pausing to drink in the majesty.

'No idea, she and her folks moved a week after she told me. Didn't answer the phone, didn't reply to my messages I sent, deleted me off of Face Space. Broke off contact.'

'That harsh,' Ramsey said, this time lighting a joint from his stash. Sweet smoke diluted out into the fire warmed night air.

'So you don't know either way?'

'Nope, she might have done, might not. I'll never know.'

'That's shit,' Ramsey inhaled one last puff and passed the joint onto Clark, who took it gladly. 'Who wants the last beer? I'll fetch the vodka as well.'

Ramsey pushed himself up and headed for the stream that had acted as their refrigerator for their refreshments.

'I'll have the beer,' Clark said raising his hand, 'Kelly can start on the vodka, he needs to drown his sorrows before they swim any closer to shore.'

Kelly smiled, and then looked into the distance.

'Hey I'm upset, but I don't want to think about it, I want to put her behind me and move on y'know. It's not like…'

'Guys!' Ramsey called out, his voice direct, altered from his jovial tone that he had maintained throughout the night.

'What's up?' Clark called back, craning his neck round to see what Ramsey was talking about.

Kelly and Clark faced each other with bemused glances, then got up and headed down the stream. Ramsey was stood, his gaze cast across the flow of water.

'What's up Rambo?' Clark asked.

'Look.' He pointed across the stream to the other side. Clark and Kelly followed the line of his finger as they came up behind him. Sitting patiently on the far side was a woolly looking dog. Traces of Alsatian could be detected in its features, as well as that of a wolf.

'Is that a wolf?' Kelly asked with a whisper.

'Looks more like a German Shepherd,' Clark added.

'It's a big fucker whatever it is.'

The Wolf cross sat contemplating them as one, it was a dirty white canine, but still stark against the moonlight darkness. The beast showed no emotion, nor did it flinch at the intruders in his territory. It simply stared, promising nothing but quiet and controlled menace.

'I bent down to get the booze and he was sat there. I almost…'

'Shat yourself?' Clark interjected.

'I was gonna say screamed like a little girl.' Ramsey passed the can of beer to Clark, 'Here's your beer. I dropped it when I saw the wolf.'

'Great,' said Clark, taking the beer. He tossed it once in the air, as if guessing weight, then without warning he flung the tin across the stream at the wolf. It glanced off its shoulder and thudded to the ground, rolling back into the stream. The rushing waters carried the can downstream and towards the lake.

With its dark coal eye that glinted back the firelight at them, the Wolf/Alsatian hybrid stared back, apparently unaffected by the blow.

'Well done dickhead!' Ramsey called out, 'that was our last can.'

'I was trying to shoo the wolf away,' Clark responded.

'Then why not chuck a rock or twig or something?'

'It's not just a wolf,' said Kelly, his voice low and thoughtful, 'I think I read about them, they're wolves that have mated with domestic dogs, that's why it looks like an Alsatian.'

'So what? It's still a wolf.' Clark replied.

'Yeah but the thing is they have the wild ferociousness of a wolf, while still harbouring the domestic dog's acceptance of man.'

'So what are you trying to say, a he-wolf fucked a she-dog?'

'Yes but he's not wary of us. It's not scared. At all. Hence…' Kelly gestured towards the Wolf/Dog.

'Shit. Couldn't your Daddy have fucked a Poodle? Or a Chihuahua?' Clark asked the Wolf/Dog.

'It's our own fault; man has been encroaching on their land for years. Dogs and wolves are essentially the same animal. They're genetically compatible. It was bound to happen at some point.'

'Where's the bear spray?' Ramsey asked, backing away towards camp.

'In my rucksack. Why?' Clark answered.

'Will it work against these things?'

'Maybe. Why not? It's only one. He probably smelt our stew,' Clark reasoned.

'I think we best get it all the same. Say, Kelly, shine your torch up on that ridge,' Ramsey asked.

'Okay.' Kelly did as he was asked and clicked the torch on. The beam travelled past the grey furred canine and up onto the ridge, twin points of light instantly glinted back. Then another. Then another.

Darkened forms began to rise from the gloom. Not stars, but something closer

'Are they…?'

Then another.

Then another.

All along the ridge, strange diamonds winked back at them. As if the stars above had descended upon the earth, settling and resting on the surface. Maybe a hundred or so deadly diamonds, fifty or so pairs of malevolent eyes stared down on the three friends from the ridge. Behind them the cliff ran parallel to the stream, the only way out would be up the incline to the Larch tree and then make their way onto the cliff side that way. The way they had come was no longer an option.

'Get the bear spray,' Kelly croaked.

Clark didn't move. He stood transfixed by the glittering display of illuminated eyes.

They started to advance.

'Clark, get the bear spray now!'

Clark awoke from the brief hypnotism and shuffled back towards the tents. Kelly followed his friend's retreat. The closest Wolf/Dog that had been sat patiently on the far side of the stream dipped his paws into the water and began to make his way across.

Clark dove into his tent and started a violent, searching rummage through the assortment of dirty clothes and food that filled his rucksack, searching with a definite urgency for the can of bear spray. Ramsey stood by the fire. He still had the vodka in his hand. Kelly watched as Ramsey undid the bottle and took a gulp of the strong liquor. His face scrunched up in distaste, he started to pace.

'Hey Ram, keep your head cool,' Kelly requested of his friend, 'I need you sober. Everything's going to be fine.'

'You sure Kell, they looked hungry to me? I knew we should have bought a gun from that last town. We're stupid. We're completely fucking stupid...'

'Clark, you found it yet?' Kelly interrupted.

'Yup.' Clark emerged from his tent with the red can of bear deterrent in his hand.

'Right, spray it round the tents, see if it works,' Kelly suggested. He bent down and picked one of the longer branches that he had collected as firewood, sticking the end of the five-foot limb into the base of the fire. Charring black engulfed the end as it set alight. Clark had already begun spraying the distastefully fragrant bear spray around the back of the tents when Kelly removed the wooden poker from the fire.

'What's that for?' Ramsey asked.

'What the fuck do you think? It's a hot stick to poke wolves away.'

'Good idea.' Ramsey bent low with the vodka still in his hand, grabbing a stick he too dipped the end into the embers, fashioning his own weapon.

A low growl resonated over the crackle of the fire; Clark rushed back from behind the tents, worry franking his face.

'They're getting closer, this stuff stinks but I think they know it's for Yogi Bear.' Clark forced a fake smile to hide the fear he felt.

Kelly clicked his torch on and pointed it at the gap between two of the tents. The torch's glare illuminated a pair of glowing eyes, bouncing, as they grew closer. A mass of fur and open saliva drenched teeth jumped out from the blanket of the night. It went for Ramsey as he was closest. The wolf's paws punched into his chest, it took his swaying, half drunk form by surprise. Ramsey dropped his ember-tinged stick and fell back. He still gripped the bottle tight as the Wolf/Dog sunk its teeth into his arm.

Ramsey screamed.

In trained unison the rest of the pack howled up into the watchful gaze of the milky moon.

Then they attacked as a single entity. Eyes wide, hackles raised and with many hungry mouths.

Kelly whacked and swung his burning stick, jabbing and searing flesh. The stench of burnt hair filled his nostrils as two wolves retreated in pain. Clark sprayed the can into the faces of any beast close enough. He edged his way towards his friend Ramsey, who by now was drenched in his own hot blood from the ragged bite wound on his arm. The Wolf/Dog held on tenaciously. Ramsey shifted his weight to and fro, rolling over on top of his attacker. The

78% proof vodka splashed out from the bottle, gurgling over the beast, trickling a tiny river trail towards the fire.

A fiery whoosh drowned out Ramsey's screams as the vapours of alcohol caught fire, engulfing him and the beast below him. The fire seemed to jump out and greet him, smothering him like a blanket, within a few seconds he was alight. Man and beast squealed, halting their attack on each other, they let go and fell apart.

Clark was mere feet from helping his friend when Kelly held him back. 'Leave him!'

Clark was about to bat Kelly away when the fire spread further, catching the floating fumes from the Bear spray, aerosol ignited in the air, leaping around their tents and belongings, creating a circle of vanquishing fire that dispersed the attack of the Wolf/Dogs.

Kelly grabbed Clark's arm and pulled him through the airborne flames. Hair singed and skin glowed red as the cloud of super heated gas kissed their faces. Clark was still facing his fallen friend, his other arm outreached and beseeching towards the now still, blackened form that he thought he could make out amongst the beautiful dance of flaming orange madness.

He called out Ramsey's name, adding to the cacophony created by the hungry howls of the Wolf/Dogs and the searing bright breath of flames that now ate hungrily at the contents of their camp.

By his collar, Kelly half pulled Clark up the hill, towards the tree. Where else could they go? The lake? They'd probably drown. The forest? They'd stand no chance running through the black of night. They'd be run down by the wolves for sure. Behind them the howls and snarls grew closer, literally snapping at their heels. Clark cried, and then tripped. Kelly went with him, his knees and palm impacted hard in the stones and pebbles of the trail. He looked back, only for a second. The camp was ablaze, the wolves had regrouped and had started to lope up the hill, yowling, whining and snapping at each other. Kelly could feel their blood wet teeth looming near his ankles, hot snarls puncturing the night air between them.

'C'mon Clarky, either I'll leave you and they'll eat you, or we can try and get to the tree.'

'But…Ramsey…' Clark bubbled, tears streaming over his raw pink skin. Kelly had never seen Clark cry, he was usually a hard ass, the one making the jokes. Not now.

Dropping his stick of ember, Kelly hauled Clark to his feet, half dragging, half running with him. They made the tree. The rough bark felt real and rough beneath his fingers, a lifeboat in a sea of fear. Clamber aboard before the waves of teeth washed over them in a tide of feral gnashing, eroding the flesh from the bones in a fraction of the time it would take the world's oceans.

Kelly wound the weather eaten rope around his shaking hands and began to pull his body up. The adrenalin helped him grip, digging his nails into his palms, he hoisted himself up, kicking his feet into the trunk, chipping away clumps of dead, dry bark as he levered himself up. The wolves reached them with a hungered snarl, the first clamped hold of Clark's shirtsleeve, pulling him to the floor. He punched at it, jabbing his aggressor's eyes until the tips of his fingers disappeared sloppily behind the fur and inside the dark wet sockets. The Wolf/Dog yelped and let go. More canines loped towards the base of the larch. Clark kicked away two more then jumped up as high as he could to grasp the rope. Kelly was near the top, one hand grasping the gallows branch that held the rope, the other still fervently holding onto the rope directly beneath the branch. When Clark took hold of the branch the rope pinged, sending a plume of mossy dust into Kelly's eyes. A snapping sound. Was it the branch or the rope? Could it hold them both, Kelly thought? He still hadn't a decent grip on the branch, should the rope snap they'd both fall. The rope pinged and creaked as fibres split and disintegrated beneath their combined weight.

'Let…go!' he pleaded with Clark who swung from the lower portion of the rope, fending off toothy attacks from below with swinging kicks from his walking boots.

'Climb up!' Clark screamed, his voice high and girlish.

Kelly couldn't proceed any further for fear of falling, the rope rotated wildly as Clark swung below. Kelly thought of his kid, the one he'd probably never meet or never know. He wanted to know her. He knew it was going to be a girl, he just knew. How could he not fight for this moment and every moment that followed? He had a child on the way. Some doubtful voice told that him that she would be born and he'd never get a chance to hold her in his arms. He had to avoid that potential reality at all costs.

Kelly kicked out below him, his boot kissing Clark's cheek with all the courtesy of a spank paddle. It took three more kicks before the tautness of the rope gave and Kelly was hanging alone from the tree.

A thud, a scream then a tearing of teeth into reluctant flesh.

Somewhere amongst the madness Kelly swore that he heard Clark curse him.

'*You bastard!*'

Call it luck, call it punishment, but there was just enough strength in the rope and his arms for Kelly to haul himself up onto the branch and into the boughs of the larch. Below the grim ripping of clothes and flesh continued long past the silencing of Clark's screams and dying whimpers.

Up close, Kelly could see that the skeleton still wore fragments of clothing that the brunt of nature had left behind. He still wore his walking boots, a plastic compass round his neck, a leather belt hung loosely around his empty hips. Beneath the skeleton's crotch, in a small bowl that nature had made as two of larch's limbs divided off into two separate angles, sat an unnatural object.

Kelly reached for it, weighing the rusted lump of metal in his hands.

A revolver.

He pried open the release and dropped the shells into his awaiting palm. Each one had been fired.

Clark threw the useless lump at the feasting wolves below. It hit one of them on the back of its head. It yelped, jumped and moved, shifted position then continued feasting on Clark.

With a frustrating shove, Kelly pushed the skeleton out of the tree. It fell and folded into a bony heap beside what was left of Clark. One Wolf/Dog sniffed it, and then carried on with what was left of Clark, who was clearly of more nutritional interest.

Kelly shifted along the branch and up into the skeleton's previously occupied position. He looked down the smouldering remains of their camp. He couldn't make out Ramsey among the blackened remains. A few white shapes of wolves sniffed around the dying embers of the fire.

Kelly cried out for help into the night. His pleading voice bouncing back from the lonely hills, his self answering his own calls reiterating his loneliness. He cried until he was hoarse. He kept checking his phone for signal, repeatedly sending out an SOS via text to everybody he knew. Each message came back failed.

No Network Coverage.
Please try again later.

He didn't sleep.

The sound of bones being gnawed and marrow sucked and tongued from cavities was nightmarish enough.

Dawn came and went. By then Clark was nothing more than a pinkish stain on the ground that the Wolves kept on licking in effort to conjure taste from the dust and rocks. Scattered around the bloody patch was a few chewed bones up and his boots that still contained the succulent flesh of his feet. A pair of cubs played with his boots, tonguing at the trapped flesh, nibbling away, morsel by morsel.

By noon he was thirsty, so thirsty in fact his voice dried up and went. The Wolf/Dogs remained, basking in the sun-baked ground below him; happy, content and full from their evening meal. Kelly figured they weren't finished.

They made no attempt to get at him, rarely looked at him, never barked or snarled. They showed no aggression whatsoever. Kelly figured they'd be patient for desert.

Evening came and went, so did dawn.

And again.

The Wolf/Dogs waited.

So did Kelly.

The earth circled the sun once again and still Kelly was alone in the tree. Too weak to call for help, he simply waited.

He counted the rocks and pebbles.

And waited.

They waited.

By the fourth day, the Wolf/Dogs grew bored and hungry at the waiting game and left their prey in the tree, they left as one, gallivanting and loping playfully across the plain, down towards the lake where they refreshed themselves with cool water and playful abandon. The scent of an injured bear caught their keen noses, miles away but still it warranted investigation. Again they moved proud though cautious, pouring over the rocky hills and valleys away from the sight of the skeleton tree.

Kelly waited.

He waited a long time for anybody to come and find him.

Nobody came.

Still he waits.

THE CHICKEN IN BLACK

Aves was more than used to these long, cold corridors; with the chipped floors painted a deep macabre red like old blood and buzzing fluorescents striping the ceiling, so he no longer shivered with the cold. He never even had to blow his nose nowadays. The newbies did though. They all did. After twenty-five years of working in the same old factory, Harold Aves had acclimatised to the cool hum of each corridor and clinical processing room. He had evolved to suit his environment and it was where he was happiest. Besides it was where he met her. His last and only true love.

His wife.

His only grievance nowadays was his trick knee in his left leg, which after a quarter of a century of pulling bulky Dolav containers around the factory floor was his only medical complaint. He was in tip-top medical condition otherwise.

Working at Agricorn was his life, and he prided himself greatly on his work, keeping the factory in good working order. He'd never leave; he was part of the furniture, a relic of the company's history. Last year, his bosses and the owner himself, Mr Reid, had admitted that he was the oil that greased the factory's gears and awarded him with a more than welcome ten percent pay rise.

He should have celebrated, but had no one to cheer with. He simply shook their hands and thanked them quietly then went home to an empty house, had chicken chasseur, then went to sleep in anticipation for his next twelve-hour shift at six am, like he had done every day since Daisy had died.

That was it, married for a year then she had died in childbirth, taking the kid along with her as well. He hated that selfish bitch for the pain she had caused him.

Hated, hated, hated and loved, loved, loved.

But after a time, he knew it wasn't her fault, but he had to blame her, he had no one else. It was hard to forgive the dead, but of course, we have to; as the dead can offer no defence for themselves.

The doctors had said it was just one of those things. *Amniotic fluid embolism* to be precise. So he looked it up in a medical dictionary. The baby essentially poisoned the mother from the inside, something about foetal cells and hair finding its way into the blood stream.

It happens every once in a while, they said.

Nobody's fault.

Whatever had caused it, he was alone now.

And he kept it that way for twenty-four years. His infinite sorrow had kept him single and celibate.

Harold rounded a corner, limping slightly as he pulled the empty Dolav through the thick strips of plastic and into Preparation Room Seven – Portioning, De-boning and Filleting.

He smiled as part of his routine at the short, squat Filipino cleaning ladies as they finished wiping and disinfecting each and every surface, giving them a polite nod as they left for the night. Not many English worked in the factories nowadays. All immigrants near enough. Out of the six hundred that worked here, less than a hundred were English. Aside from the bosses, most were college kids, all after some quick cash before university, the rest were from the continent or the Far East. They all seemed pretty nice, never caused any real trouble. Besides the eastern European ladies were nice to look at, not that he'd ever instigate anything, though he knew some were desperate for a husband and the green coloured card of opportunity that came with marriage.

As he positioned the sturdy grey tubs at the end of each production line, in his head he went over his mental list of each job he had to complete tonight. Setting out the trays of breadcrumbs and sauces for the next shift had already been completed in the Ready Meals Room. He had re-stocked the plastic gloves and tissues at the wash station in the Organic division; menial tasks that should have been completed by some layabout teenager, obviously too lazy to turn up for work. Now the job fell to lucky old Aves. He had been asked, and agreed without question. His entire list of tasks would take no longer than an hour; he'd be home before one. On Sunday nights the factory closed completely to let the machinery have a breather and for the cleaning ladies do a thorough job without having a workforce in the way of their mops and buckets

After the night cleaning crew had left and before the six am shift, the entire factory was alone to him. A security guard positioned at the front gate half a mile away was his closest and only human company.

Next on his list of jobs was a visit to the Slaughter Room, easily the singular most gruesome space on the whole site to any uninitiated newbies. After Aves' quarter of a century in the business, he had a constitution of iron. Tonight however, his stomach may be persuaded to turn otherwise.

***

The Slaughter Room was the most infamous, bloody and yet evidently the cleanest in the entire factory. The bosses were meticulous that this room be kept clean after each shift. Two cleaning crews came in one after another to mop up the blood and chicken shit that peppered the walls and floors.

At one end the room was the '**_Inbox_**' as the butchers referred to it, where the birds were hooked on, feet first to the upside down conveyer belt and immediately fed through a simple steel grey box. The first box effectively gassed the birds, starving them of oxygen in less than twenty seconds. Then they moved onto the second grey box where a series of conveniently aimed blades did the rest. The majority of birds fell within a certain height/weight/length ratio.

Some however did not.

These were known as un-classed birds. Not class one premium organic birds, nor were they class two birds that the poorer families bought. Un-classed; as in destined for dog food. It was here where the blades swept across the neck of the chicken, in swift and mostly painless motion. A chicken may struggle, be too big or too small for the machine. In which case the blades might hit them wrong. It either goes one of two ways. The blade cuts too high on the chickens' body and makes a mess of the whole bird or it cuts too low and the chicken is left with no skullcap, still flapping and bleeding when they appear out the other side. Any bird too mangled or bruised from the process are classed as unfit for human consumption and are thrown into a Dolav tub containing a thick polythene bag, ready to be shipped across the factory to the pet food division, basically a group of surly butchers with sharp knives and dull wit. Bones or anything else left on the carcass that can't be used, head for the power station across town as biomass, fuel for over thirty thousand homes in the local area.

Now vegetarians can't really complain about that when they're enjoying a hot shower, Aves had always reasoned.

Now the Slaughter Room was devoid of life. The dead remained in a grey Dolav brimming with bloody and dismembered birds in various stages of mutilation. The butchers had been so hard at work processing and plucking that they hadn't had time to move the gory grey container across to the other side of the factory. It was a fifteen-minute job at most. Hardly wincing his nose at the sight of several deformed Shire Whites that made it this far through the process, Aves covered the Dolav up with a plastic sheet and grabbed a nearby pallet truck, shifted the prongs into place and pumped the truck up beneath the Dolav, then pulled it out of the Slaughter Room and down the central passageway that ran the entire length of the factory floor.

Harold Aves sighed then continued his gradual trudge down the brightly lit three hundred-metre corridor. The oldie station that politely droned from a nearby speaker played a Johnny Cash song, '*One Piece at a Time*'. Not one of his favourites but still a good tune. He hummed and murmured along unconsciously, sending his memories back to his birthday a good few years back when over the intercom an urgent sounding voice called him to the cafeteria. This was back when he knew everybody's name. He was met with a surprise party, Cash's *The Chicken in Black* erupted from a record player and everybody cheered in smiley unison. Aves attempted a forced grin.

He said I'm sorry to tell you
But your body's outlived your brain.

168

They called him the Chicken in Black on account of the fact of three things.

1. He was a keen Johnny Cash fan forever singing or humming one of his many hits as he trundled throughout the factory floor.

2. He worked in a chicken factory.

3. He wore a lot of black. Aside from his white overcoat and blue hardhat, which were mandatory in a food processing plant. Aside from his pale, sun-starved skin, everything else visible was black.

The third point was more his deceased wife's fault rather than his devotion to all things '*Cash*'. He'd been in mourning ever since Daisy died. He'd never told his co-workers about his wife's death and didn't want sympathy back then or even now. He never really brought her up. At first people asked how she was doing and he'd reply quietly, avoiding eye contact.

'*Fine, Daisy's fine.*'

He carried the lie on for twenty-four years now and even his closest co-workers had never learned the truth. And they wouldn't. Quite frankly he was happy to keep up that pretence until he kicked this mortal bucket over once and for all.

From a side corridor, a stumbling figure approached, dressed in the same attire as him, blue hardhat and white overcoat; A young lad, slightly unsteady on his feet, moved forward with his slumped shoulder leaning on the wall for support, cheeks bulging, guilty eyes fixed like marbles.

'What shift you on?' Aves asked bluntly as they got closer to one another.

The young lad's iced blues were wide eyed, 'Sh...sh...shift?' his thick accent beckoned that he was born of the Eastern Bloc. Probably one of the new Poles that had arrived on site, Aves figured. The kid looked lost or maybe drunk.

'You been drinking lad? I can smell it on you.'

'Drinky I?' he responded like Aves had thrown a terrible accusation at him, holding a palsied hand to his chest.

'Yes... drinky you?' Aves sighed.

'I new here, I help the bootchas with chicks. End of shift vey make me drink. Initiation fur newboy vey say. I only have little bit. But very strong. I pass out in changing room, I wake everybody gone. Where vey gone?'

'Bootchas?'

'Err... Yeash Bootchas?'

Ahhh, butchers! They've gone home. You got a name?' Aves asked.

'Ahh... Tomas, my parents call me Tomas.'

'I'm wondering what the bootchas called you when you passed out.' Aves said under his breath, having noticed a thin, bile yellow stain down the front of Tomas's white coat.

'What?'

'Nothing, come with me I'll take you to clock out after I finish this. Though I doubt you'll get paid the overtime.'

Tomas stood still and clueless as Aves walked away. With a persuasive beckon of his hand he managed to get the wary Tomas to follow him onwards down the corridor towards the Pet Food Preparation/Biomass division of the factory.

Like the rest of the division, the large open room was deserted aside from a line of shelves on the back wall and the two worktables where the drones would hack away at any decent meat and toss the leftover giblets into a refuse bin.

'Right pay attention, this may come in useful to you one day. I've worked every department of this factory. From the Distribution Warehouse to the Cold Blast where we fast freeze the chicken, the Chicken Kiev line to bagging up turkeys for Christmas dinner. I've been everywhere and seen everything that can happen in this place kiddo. There's nothing I don't know, so the secret is to keep moving. Don't get stuck in one place. The managers are quite happy for people to chop and change jobs. It's business smart to have a workforce that can turn their hand to any department in case things get busy. Anyways, this is how we do things down this end of the factory.'

Tomas nodded blankly with eyes wide and red. Aves pushed the Dolav to the nearest table and with a hiss of air released the pallet truck from its weighty grasp. It settled upon the concrete with a satisfying *clump*.

'Now we need to put an additive on this chicken so it doesn't attract flies by the next shift, head over to that shelf on the far wall and fetch me some BIOSMATIC SYRUP, it should be clearly labelled. I'm gonna stack these crates.'

Tomas nodded with feigned diligence and headed over to the shelves on the far wall searching the rows of chemicals. Aves went about stacking a collection of red crates that some amateur had obviously dumped in here by mistake. From across the room Tomas held up a two litre red plastic carton, shaking it in his hand.

'Is this it Mistah?'

Aves paused from stacking the crates onto the pallet truck.

'Yes Tomas, very good.'

'But it's empty.'

'There should be a box beneath the shelf with a fresh shipment in.'

'I found the box Mistah.' Tomas hollered back.

'Good, good Tomas now bring it here and pour a little into the tub.'

***

Sliding the box out from beneath the shelf, Tomas tore into the plastic tape, his half drunken fingers struggling for purchase, and then finding an edge they ripped off the line of tape. The cardboard lid parted and revealed the red tubs inside. The inebriated Polish teenager lifted the first container out and read the label.

BIOHAZARD!

Had the old man said that word? His English wasn't fantastic but the word looked familiar.

Beneath this was more writing that he couldn't be bothered with, he just wanted to go home. And it seemed this old man wasn't going to show him out from this maze of corridors until he completed this meaningless task. Tomas headed back to the Dolav full of dead chickens, unscrewing the cap as he dragged his feet with moping indifference. The old man had his back to him as he reached up to stack the last of the crates. Tomas leant into the crate and poured the oily green liquid over the bird carcasses, making sure he covered every last one.

***

Aves turned and watched for about a second while Tomas drained the last drips from the container.

'**WHAT ARE YOU DOING?**' he screamed, not meaning to be as loud as he actually sounded. Tomas actually jumped at the outburst, dropping the plastic tub to the floor.

'I *said*, use a little bit, you've used it all! It only takes a little bit to keep the bugs away! It's a deterrent.'

'I sorry, I sorry mistah… mistah?'

'Aves, the name's Aves.'

Harold Aves gave a belated sigh then glanced down at the tub at his feet, then at the carcasses that were smothered in thick green sap.

'This stuff is usually clear. Why did they change it?' Aves bent down and picked up the tub for a closer inspection.

BIOHAZARD!
Trioxin 246
Not for consumption by mammals.
In case of accidental digestion
the use of accelerants over 400°F
is recommended for immediate disposal of subject.
For use in a controlled environment only.
Distilled by Kaltenbrunner Corp, Germany

Aves had never heard of Trioxin, or of Kaltenbrunner Corp. A wave of worry rapidly assaulted his brain as an over clinical odour registered in his olfactory receptors, his nostril hairs all itched at once, his eyes watered as if some evil invisible being had rubbed onion and chilli puree into the back of his eyeballs. He stumbled back towards the back shelf as did Tomas, both trying

171

their hardest to rub the stinging from their eyes with the cool palm of their hands.

They both seethed and hissed through gritted teeth.

Something unseen had attacked them, rendering them both blind with agony. In between heaving sobs, Aves could make out Tomas offering apologies in both his native and English tongue.

Now crawling on his hands and knees, Aves blindly felt his way towards the shelf. He needed the box from where the chemical came. He needed more information before his eyeballs melted out of his skull.

'PRZEPRASZAMY, PRZEPRASZAMY!' Tomas wept, 'a thousand nieośćobecn! PRZEPRASZAMY!'

'Tomas please shut the fuck up! I'm trying to think and your crying isn't help a great deal.' The weeping ceased… a little. Now the Pole sounded like a clucking chicken.

Aves slapped an outreaching hand atop the box that had caused the problem. Tomas continued to apologise quietly. Rubbing his eyes more severely didn't bring his vision back, it was then he remembered the eye wash station above the sink.

'Tomas we need to wash this stuff out of our eyes before it causes us any real damage.'

'*I'm sorry Harry; I think the damage is already done.*'

That was Daisy's voice in his head. Not ethereal or spookyfied in any way, but as if she was in this chilled room with him. She sounded so real. He almost responded 'I know,' but kept the thought hidden behind his pursed lips. It was good to hear her voice; it didn't panic him in the slightest, no matter how strange. Lack of sleep and the sudden stress he told himself.

But she sounded so real.

'Yeash Mistah Aves, we clean eyes make it bettah,' Tomas whimpered pathetically.

Pushing the box in front of him he continued his crawl across the cold factory floor. Tomas had ceased the sobbing apologies now, but was still intent on clucking.

'Right then Tomas, listen. Follow me across the room to the sink area. And stop making them damned chicken noises.'

He heard Tomas shuffle across the smooth painted floor, then say, 'I no make chick noise Mistah Aves.'

'Just hurry it up will ya!'

'*Right a bit Harry,*' Daisy said, '*you'll hit your hea…*'

The pointed corner of the metal table made contact with the dead centre of his forehead. A sharp bang swiftly followed by a curse that escaped the safety of his lips. An arrow of blinding pain shot into his frontal lobe.

Aves shifted right, continuing his shuffle until he reached the metal sink. Pulling himself to his feet he fumbled along the wall, his searching fingers finding the wall mounted bottle of eyewash. Popping the cap he tipped his head back and squeezed, allowing the fresh saline liquid to pool over his raging eyeballs. The whiteness of being blind soon grew to dull shapes, stars scattered about, objects moved about the floor hopping about in a random fashion. He made out the shape of Tomas and grabbed him by the hair, squeezing the eyewash into his grateful sockets. The young Pole gasped in surprise.

'Don't rub them, tilt your head back and let it do its magic. Blink it in.'

'*It will work*,' Daisy said as clear as day.

'I know sweetheart,' Aves responded out loud.

'You call me sweetheart?' a perplexed Tomas asked blinking out the agony.

'Not you. Is it working?'

'Yeash, I see colour. Tak. Dobre, Dobre. It is good, it is bettah.'

Aves' eyesight cleared enough for him to read the safety notice on the wall.

He bent down to the box and read what was on the side. A simple, stickered delivery notice;

Dispatch no. *73448601724*
Delivery to Ashbourne Barracks
Do not tip; keep box level at <u>ALL</u> times.
Attn: /Col Gulager Bio weapon division

A road sign appeared in his mind's eye, one junction down from the Chicken factory, *Ashbourne Military Barracks two miles*; probably the next call on the courier's route.

Ashbourne/Agricorn.

An easy mistake to make if you're in a rush.

Tomas made a mistake.

Mistaking Biohazard for Biosmatic. Anybody could. He had made a mistake in trusting the dumb Pole to find the right container.

'*It's not his fault*,' Daisy said sweetly in the teenager's defence.

'I know dear.'

'*It's not your fault either; I don't want you to blame yourself for this.*'

'I know sweetie.'

'You call me sweetie again. You like the men? You lika the cock?' Tomas asked, genuine worry fastened across his face.

'Your eyes better?' Aves answered, ignoring the Pole's question and pointing two fingers at him, 'I could make them worse.'

'Yeash sweetie,' the Pole responded with a smile.

'Don't get cute.'

Okay he reasoned, if we've got their delivery, then they've got the four tubs of Biosmatic syrup, a biological additive to keep flies and lurgies away from dead chickens.

A simple easy mistake.

Those five words worried him

NOT FOR CONSUMPTION BY MAMMALS.

They hadn't consumed it. The vapour had temporarily blinded Tomas and him; that was all. His eyesight was back. Nobody was the wiser. All he had to do was ensure that the Dolav full of contaminated chicken carcasses headed as biomass fuel to the power station instead of pet food. The company didn't want a lawsuit on their hands from customers complaining that their dogs have died in vast numbers. They trusted him with the keys to the factory. A screw-up like this could easily cost him his job, maybe even a little prison sentence.

He swallowed a tennis ball size of worry.

Harold Aves hobbled wearily over to the Dolav.

The chickens were gone.

He swallowed again; a basketball this time.

A few wings, legs, an assortment of heads, an occasional bloody feather and scrappy patches of white pimpled skin remained behind. But the whole crate of chicken carcasses had jumped ship, evacuated the immediate area; vamoosed.

Shit.

Maybe Trioxide or whatever the fuck it was called had melted the bodies. Maybe that's what is for, spraying on the Taliban from thirty thousand feet so they melted like toasted cheese in their mountain retreats.

Take that Osama!

Nah, Aves dismissed the thought with a slight shake of his head. Surely there'd be some evidence of residues left behind, bone fragments, a gooey, protein rich soup made up from dissolved chicken cadavers.

Aves pondered and then looked skywards, checking that the ceiling wasn't covered in flying fowl, a thin thought had occurred that the military gunk that Tomas had poured over the bodies had somehow given them the power of levitation.

No such luck.

He looked up. The ceiling was fowl free.

Then where were they?

'Go look.'

Aves turned back to Tomas, his lips hadn't moved. It must have been Daisy. She was right. They had to look.

***

They left Pet Food Preparation and followed a sticky green trail that scattered off up the corridor. There must have been a hundred chickens in that Dolav, maybe more. Dead birds don't dance was the only saying he could think of, even though it wasn't actually a saying.

Maybe, he thought, being as rational as he could in these strange times, they'd become unconscious during their temporal blindness and a group of feral cats had stormed the factory, taking every single chicken from the fat grey tub.

Don't be ridiculous. That's absurd.

He checked his watch. A quarter after twelve. He hadn't passed out, not for a second.

He had heard them. It wasn't Tomas clucking. It was the chickens. It must have been. Maybe they were stunned, maybe they weren't quite dead.

What all hundred or so? What are the chances?

A fault in the gassing machine perhaps? Nah some were missing heads.

You know what happened.

It happened as soon as Tomas opened that lid, the lid that held back the noxious fumes. Some chemical reaction had taken place when it came into contact with the dead birds, not supernatural, no nothing like that, it must be chemical. It must be.

You get it on your skin and…

The trail of gunge split off three ways, left right and straight ahead.

'Vich way?' Tomas asked.

Aves narrowed his sore eyes. 'You take the left, I'll head right. If you find a chicken, kill it. Even if it's dead.'

Tomas nodded with the most serious face he could pull then bravely bounded off down the left corridor. Aves turned and bore right towards the staff changing room. He plucked a fire extinguisher fro off the wall as he neared the door.

The green trail veered into the female changing area, before petering off to nothing. Aves pushed the half open door and entered. The changing room was swathed in hollow silence and the stale stench of after work sweat. He saw it almost immediately, sitting there beneath the bench. Shivering.

He blinked twice and shook his head as if to shake this apparition from his vision. It didn't go away. He knew it wouldn't go away anytime soon. The big chicken had no head, shoulders or wings for that matter. The blade had cut too high on its body, making it unsuitable for sale.

Without warning, the bird stepped out from beneath the bench and began swaying towards him.

A confident cock if ever he saw one.

It advanced.

It charged.

He felt his heart gain momentum in his chest as it anticipated the surge in adrenalin he would need to cope, a cool sweat broke out across his back and shoulders, his body telling him *"go on, it's okay, be scared"*.

Aves heaved the fire extinguisher high above his head and forced the thick red cylinder down onto the feral fowl.

Crunch.

But no splat. Not much liquid blood or giblets remained in the body of this beast, as it had already been gutted. Aves launched the extinguisher onto the twitching corpse again.

AND AGAIN.

AND AGAIN.

A frenzy of self-preservation overtook him; he had to prevent this thing from getting at him now and into further nightmares of the future.

The chest cavity had torn open, he was sure he had broken its back, yet it still jerked about as if electric was coursing through its corpse.

It was dead.

Or undead.

Well it wasn't moving about as much so Aves was as happy as he could be about that. He sighed, taking a lungful of cooled, stale air to bring him slowly back to a normal resting heartbeat. Things like this didn't happen. Maybe in experimental animal laboratories in cheapo Horror movies, but this was the North of England. The weirdest animal tale he had heard round these parts was someone releasing an exotic snapping turtle into a local fishing pond.

Aves looked down at the mess that was once a chicken.

One down, lots more to go.

His kneecap offered twinges from the sudden bout of exercise; he bent forward and gave it a welcome rub, back, front and sides. He played with his kneecap, pushing it left and right, stretching it a little. He flexed his entire leg letting the joint give a satisfactory pop, relieving the tension he felt building up.

He had once read a true story about a farmer, who one day took an axe and chopped off a chicken's head, dispatching the bird for his wife's cooking pot when the bird refused to die. It hopped off the chopping block and carried pecking at the ground as it always had, not fully realising it had no head. The farmer and his wife took the bird on tour around the USA as 'Mike the Headless Chicken' to mesmerised audiences, making a pretty penny off the back of it. The bird even had an agent. Aves certainly felt that Mike had nothing on his chicken problem. He certainly couldn't see himself going on tour.

Not yet anyway.

Now another strange but true story of headless chickens had come to light.

Picking the bird up by its twisted, snapped leg, Aves checked around and found no more chickens lurking in the sickly stale shadows. He hooked his fingers around the hose and took the extinguisher with him and headed back to where he had left the Dolav in Pet Food Preparation, slinging the chicken back where it belonged he scored a basket. He pumped the pallet truck back up and headed back to the corridor with the Dolav in tow.

He had a plan.

A vague one at that:

1. Find the chickens.

2. Kill *ALL* the chickens

3. Burn the chickens round the back of the factory with the help of Mistah Petrol can from the boot of his Ford.

Easy. Craftily burn the evidence in the security camera blind spot behind the factory. Then shovel the evidence in a sack destined for Biomass.

Perfect. He might save his skin yet.

Tomas screamed, cancelling all thoughts of getting away with this.

Leaving the Pallet truck and Dolav behind, Aves ran down the left hand corridor with the cumbersome extinguisher poised for action wishing it was an axe or baseball bat, something lighter and far easier to wield.

The trail and Tomas's screams led him to the Flavouring Room, where he found the Pole dancing round in a circle, beating off chickens with his hands as they attempted to mount him. Two clung off the back of his work overalls, cinching their beaks shut tight, their dead yellow eyes rolling around in primitive delight as they scraped at him with their talons. A couple more Mike the Headless chickens repeatedly ran into his shins like arrogant, troublesome toddlers, trying their very best to topple this giant that had summoned them back to life.

'**GETTAHVEMOFFMEEEE!**' Tomas screamed as he twirled like a bizarre, feather speckled whirling dervish.

Aves stormed in, raising his weapon and squashing the closest Headless Mike at Tomas's feet into a fleshy pink pulp. The second clueless wonder he dispatched in much the same way, breaking every evil twitching bone in its reanimated body.

Dropping the extinguisher, Aves span Tomas around; grabbing both of the attacking fowl by the feet then bashed them in unison on the blunt edge of the nearest worktop, thick trickles of maroon giblets and red gizzards dribbled out from the smashed birds, half jellified since death.

Tomas stopped screaming, and yet Aves kept smashing the chickens, using them as macabre drumsticks until the pimpled flesh fell apart in his hands, sticky spits of blood clashed with the white of his overalls, up the inside of his arms and over his front.

Breathlessly he ordered, 'fetch the pallet truck. Bring it in here.'

A quaking Tomas nodded erratic and white faced, doing as he was told he rushed back to the corridor.

A slight, airy squeak caused Aves to turn.

A portly, featherless cock with the top of its head missing sized him up from across the room and then charged.

Aves did the same, swinging his leg back he kicked forward, catching the chicken in the centre of its breast with all his might, screaming '**AVE IT!**' as he thrashed forward, compacting its ribcage. The poultry satellite lifted skyward upon contact with his steel toe-capped wellington boot, then pounded with a violent thump into the far wall with a single squeak, dropping down the wall to the floor, half stunned. Aves rushed over and gave it a thorough stomping.

When he'd finished, he turned round, a sheepish looking Tomas had arrived with the pallet truck.

'Vey attacked me. Vey crazy yeash?'

'Very crazy. We need to find every last one. And kill them…well the best we can. Understand?'

Tomas nodded duly, 'I see … dead chickens.'

Aves picked up the crippled cock remains and tossed them from twenty feet into the awaiting Dolav.

'And we'll need to arm ourselves if we're gonna choke these mother cluckers.'

***

In ten minutes they had assembled a small armoury, consisting of two filleting knives (one taped to a mop), a spare section of a conveyer belt covering (essentially a long metal club for bashing undead chickens to a pulp with) and the mop's long-term partner, a bucket (for trapping unruly and undead chickens).

Both Aves and Tomas had doubled up on extra large rubber gloves (to protect their hands from undead chicken bites/scratches.)

In the nearest Maintenance Room they had dug out a pair of plastic goggles each (to protect their delicate, essential eyes from the undead chicken bites/scratches/pokes). Their hardhats protected their craniums from any attacks from directly above. Tomas had found a sheet of clear plastic used as wall backing for the sink area, now they utilised it as a lid for the Dolav, in case any caught chickens got jumpy.

'Right let's finish what we started… before it gets any worse.'

Armed nervously with the makeshift spear, Tomas was charged with pulling the Dolav and pallet truck along, Aves made do with the thin metal club and the fillet knife stashed in the line of his belt. The bucket they kept ready on top of the plastic sheet on the Dolav.

They found two chickens straight away, simply waiting around the next corner, scrapping with each other in a fight to the undeath.

Quietly and with the cool precision of an African big game hunter, Aves stepped silently towards the two half headed chickens, who at this point in their undead lives seemed content with barging mindlessly towards one another and swiping talons to determine the alpha of the two.

Aves leapt forward with the club, screaming a determined '**HIIIIIYAH!**' he swept down twice cutting them both in two, equally four twitching fleshy parts, that still after a double death tried to fight each other.

Picking them up by the legs Aves tossed them back into the Dolav of Doom, back where they belonged.

'We're making progress now,' Aves said with a satisfied smile.

***

The night tore on. By three o'clock they had at least fifty more smashed up chickens back in the tub and they had only covered half the factory. The more they re-killed, the happier Aves became; strangely the happiest he had been in ages.

'*You're doing well,*' Daisy informed him, '*I'd say you were over half way.*'

They were approaching the Rotisserie Room when Tomas piped up from his silent stupor.

'Any chance we can get a drink? I'm getting a little thirsty.'

'Not yet!' Aves snapped from nowhere, rubbing his trick knee through his dark and now feathered trousers. All this time on his feet had taken its toll. He'd done more than a double shift with not so much as a half hour break.

'Not many more now, we have to get them all before the shift at six arrives, if we don't, we are both down the shit creek without a paddle or a boat.'

'Well I need something…'

A noise from ahead caused Aves to swing round with the club poised. Nothing moved. Tomas made a noise that caused him to turn back. The Pole had a cigarette on the go. With a rapid downward flick of the wrist, Aves knocked the offending white stick from Tomas's mouth and swiped the lighter from his hand with a singular motion.

'No smoking inside!' Aves barked before he had chance to protest. 'We're around the corner from the rotisserie ovens, a lot of gas in that room. One spark and the whole place will go kaboom! Understand? Kablamo! That's why we have the fag shelters outside.' Aves showed Tomas the lighter then stashed it in his top pocket, 'you'll get this back when we find that last chicken, okay?'

Tomas nodded glumly, and then spied a drinks machine further down the side corridor. He laid the spear on top of the Dolav and headed over to the machine, lifting his goggles off his face, resting them on his hardhat.

'Well I need a drink or something. You want anything?'

'Not yet.'

'Y'know, my friend told me to get job here. Told me, "good money," he say, "*ten pound an hour for evening shift packing chickens in plastic bags,*" I say that money is good, for ten pounds an hour I fuck the chickens.'

Tomas laughed at his joke and slipped a few coins in the humming machine and poked a button. A fruity looking can tumbled into the bottom tray. Tomas reached in and opened it, knocking it back thirstily. He belched a tropical, gassy aroma.

'I not so sure about working here now, tomorrow I quit maybe.'

From the corner of his eye, Aves had seen the white bird move on top of the machine, but in his tired brain it didn't register at first, by the time any words came out of his mouth, the sparsely feathered Shire White had reared up, stretching its three too many wings and dived bombed from atop the vending machine. The half drunk can of pop hit the concrete floor with a tinny resonance.

Tomas's curdling scream echoed down the deserted corridors and back again, an alien squeal that paralysed Harold Aves briefly to the spot. As the young man turned round he realised that the body of the mutated chicken was hanging from the poor boy's left eye socket. Its talon-armed feet scratched into his chest, the featherless five wings flapped independently, providing wriggling momentum, propelling it further and deeper into Tomas's skull. The terrified Polish lad's arms stood outstretched at his side, his fingers quaking in abject terror, unable to move.

Aves launched forward, grabbing the malformed beast bird by its scraping clawed feet. Upon arrival he found that the demon bird had not two, but three legs. A mutant. He'd come across them before. Unfit for sale, they were destined for biomass.

He pulled the bird free like Excalibur from the stone, except that mighty sword didn't have the mangled remains of an eyeball on the end.

Tomas screamed as the stringy optic nerve snapped with a fleshy ping as it was dragged out from his eye socket, what was left of the sensory organ wasn't worth saving, the hungry chicken had chewed it up to a useless mess of pulpy tissue.

Gritting his teeth and holding his tongue firmly to the roof of his mouth, Aves swung the devil fowl as hard as he could at the floor. Not once, not twice, but close to thirty times. After all this beating still the bird held up a fight. It seemed tougher than his previous quarries. It fought back more, it was stronger, a little more fight in the wee beastie. He felt bumps of grossly malformed flesh move beneath the pimpled flesh. Steroids, it must be the steroids they feed these things. That's why it's mutated like this. Five wings instead of two, increased muscle mass. All for profit. They must feed them all the same stuff. In the majority of birds it doesn't show, but sometimes a freak occurs. And here it was.

'GET BACK IN THE BOX!'

Aves lifted his size ten up and brought it down hard on the bird. It ceased its fight. He picked up it's bloated by steroids ravaged body and dropped it back in the Dolav. His knee gave way finally after the exertion of the stomping. Aves cursed and reached out to the tub grabbing on before he fell.

Damned knee.

Damned Chickens.

About ten of the big, bloated Shire Whites lined up halfway down the main passageway, all had their heads, a few had their necks broken, their staring faces brutally twisted to one side. More headless and mutated wonders piled in behind them as reinforcements, a good forty or so Mikes filled the corridor, clucking and shrieking. Hopefully this was them all.

'Tomas, can you walk?' Aves whispered, wide-eyed and urgent, still reeling from the avian ambush.

The young lad whimpered between halted breaths, and then achingly got to his feet, his quaking hand clutched to the bloody space where his eye used to be. Aves pushed him towards the Dolav. The poor lad was heading for shock. He'd seen a boy of similar age get his hand caught in a slicing machine once. He didn't say anything until the paramedics turned up. Even then he asked for his mummy.

'Follow me.'

Grabbing the pallet truck he pulled on down the corridor with Tomas straggling behind. The squawking monstrosities pursued them. Gaining the distance.

Aves barged through the next door, every other step his knee gave way, a painful explosion of searing agony flaming from his kneecap outwards. With the Dolav in the room he let go of the pallet truck sending it crashing into a preparation table, grabbing the club off the top before impact. Tomas sank to his knees, crying crimson tears out of his one good eye, the other side of his face had become a phantom mask of blood. The poor kid had given up and now seemed content with crying through the pain, his tears chalking a diluted line through the crimson flood on his face.

Aves didn't have time to rally him to his feet and left him behind to the mercy of the chickens, not that they'd show any. These chickens were evil and stupid like that.

Aves raised his club and swiped down at the first pipe.

After the reverb of the clang, a breathy hiss entered the Rotisserie Room.

The Shire Whites reached the crouched blubbering form of Tomas, setting upon him straight away. He didn't even bother to fight them off; he sat slumped as they pecked and scratched at his tender flesh.

Aves reached the second set of pipes further down the room.

Swing.

Clang.

Hiss.

He could smell it now as the ratio of propane to oxygen started to rise in the propellant's favour.

A couple of Headless Mikes ignored Tomas and found him instead. He didn't know how, but they'd found him. Aves launched a devastating kick at one, sending it soaring across the Rotisserie Room to impact with the far wall, the second he chopped down with the makeshift club, disabling, but not re-killing it. He hadn't time to finish it off. Soon he could wipe them all out with a single blow.

His knee burned from the kick, he collapsed. Forcing himself up with gritted teeth, Aves steadied himself to cover the last few feet.

Aves made his way to the third and final oven and swung down at the copper pipe, splitting it away from the joint that snaked inside.

More heady gas filled the room. The clucking, screeching and squawking reached a crescendo as they all hungered after him. Even without eyes or mouths they hungered after him. At the other end of the room Tomas lay still, covered in blood and feathers, they had done with him. Soon he would be done with them.

He slumped to the floor, dropping the club. It might have been his trick knee that blazed with pain from all the activity or it might have been the amount of noxious fumes that had now flooded into his bloodstream. The hard hat fell from his head; he pulled the misted, blood splattered goggles from his face and crawled into the corner beside the last broken pipe, letting the devil birds advance, getting them all close.

'*Hello Harry,*' she said.

A fat and heavily mutated Shire White jumped on his chest and began pecking at his face with ultimate belligerence, he was beyond caring now. He felt no pain; the gas took care of that, dreamily lifting him up to light headedness. He felt pleasant though nauseous; a column of bile rose up his throat. He held it down, clenching his mouth shut, saving his last breath for a couple more thoughts.

He could see Daisy on their wedding day. God she was beautiful. The dress hadn't cost them much but with her in it she sparkled like all the diamonds in the universe. Their wedding night had been the highlight of his life. That little hotel room in the Lake District, when she finally slipped off the pearly dress, letting it drop elegantly to the floor. Her words had made his day.

No, his entire life.

'*I've been waiting for you Harry.*'

Now she said those words to him again and they still meant as much.

The rest of the Shire Whites arrived; the first had started pecking out his eyes, yet he concentrated through the distraction of pain. It'll be worth it.

The 'Chicken in Black' up against the 'Chickens in White'.

The old tale of ultimate Good versus venomous Evil.

He was blind now, he could taste nothing but his own vomit, could hear only the hiss of rapidly escaping gas close to his ear and the tremendous cluckophony of the chickens pecking and darting randomly at his face.

Time for Zombiefried Chicken.

From his clenched hand he thumbed the flint wheel of Tomas' lighter, ignited Butane met and ignited Propane.

A warm and pleasant wind kissed his face with a deafening hiss.

Tickled him

Embraced him.

Engulfed him.

'*Hello Daisy.*

Colder than Hell up here

COLDER THAN HELL UP HERE...

Wearing a crimson velveteen Armani suit, maroon shirt and a rose tie, Mr. Nicolas Santos stood facing the snow swept glass, gazing out thirteen floors up from the surface of the frozen earth below; thirteen floors up inside the exquisitely decorated Lavey Building it had to be noted. Ultra expensive fine art by all the good, long dead artists adorned the walls, most works unknown to the general populace. Several bottles of Nun's Island whisky sat alongside unopened Wray and Nephews rum, nothing below fifty grand adorned the spirit shelf. The fridge held other treasures; fifty proof Samuel Adams *Utopia* at over one hundred times more expensive than regular beers, a case of Antarctic Nail ale, brewed with actual ice from the dissolving continent, a snip at nearly a thousand dollars per bottle. Sat on a shelf beside the fridge was an assortment of small stuffed mammals, red and grey squirrels as well as stoats and other road kill, each stuffed with a bottle of *The End of History*, another rarity from Scotland, fifty-five proof blond Belgian ale infused with highland nettles and juniper berries. Santos never touched any of them. He didn't drink. He liked to keep them on show to tempt those that were weak to the spirit. Though he never offered and they daren't ask, the various expensive bottles remained unopened.

Collecting earthly pleasures was a hobby of his.

One hundred and thirty cold feet below him, shoppers busied themselves in the precinct, gathering near last minute gifts on this chilly night before Christmas Eve, each beset by the unrelenting winter flurries.

The Bitter Cold bit them all.

It seemed nothing would cease their unfaltering lust for more things in their lives. In his business, this greed was to be encouraged.

Nobody could see as Santos's cool stoic pallor cracked into a self-satisfied grin.

With a slim finger he pushed the rounded spectacles back up his nose.

This time of year was his time of year. He drank it in droves. These poor proles; spending money they didn't have on presents their ungrateful spawn didn't need. The recession made people hungrier for a life they could only dream to lead.

If it were up to him, they'd all be in labour camps, working for nothing except his profit margins; like he had in his sweatshops in the Far East, children as young as two churning out plastic toy after plastic toy on a production line along with their parents and siblings. Over priced crap that people sought to have in their pointless little lives. It was this greed for pointless little things that fed his hunger. This deceit of the world was his business plan for domination, he'd tried before and failed, not this time though, this time he had a definite plan, a long term goal that he'd worked on for many a year.

The lie will hold, the deceit will continue. As ever.

Until...

One day…

He smirked, stroking the sparse collection of grey hairs on his wispy chin. Not long now, a few more Christmases and they'll all be beneath him in some way or another. He already owned or part owned 96% of the world's major businesses.

Banks, governments, countries, military regimes to name but a few; he had a knowing finger in many a tasty pie. The chances were that almost every transaction that had passed from one individual to another was directly involved with one of his corporations.

From cocaine refineries all along the Amazon basin, to the world's foremost frontiers of breakthrough medical research, he owned them. People didn't realise that he owned them, but he did. The names may change, but the ownership was the same.

He was the richest man in the world, not that you'd know it to look at his true self. A wizened old man, a decrepit frame supporting a sickly looking face, skin pulled taut like weatherworn leather over a bony skull. It was all about image. He paid handsomely to be left off the World's Rich List. He didn't want people knowing who he was. They could never find out. Not yet anyway. It wasn't time. They wouldn't understand, his takeover couldn't succeed just yet. The stars needed to be right, the correct alignment would guarantee his rise to power forever into the new tomorrow of his age. His time.

He hadn't the power yet.

But soon…

Their time would come.

A door opened behind him; big and heavy, furnished in the stretched leather of some exotic beast close to extinction. The light from the corridor filtered in, slicing through dead motes of dust as if some curious beam from another world, a signal from a different dimension.

'What is it Dunstan?' Santos didn't even bother to turn round. He knew who it was straight away.

'Your drink sir, and status updates from the field.'

'Business is *waaar*, Dunstan, let me know the casualties. I want *deeetails*,' the old man rasped.

'I know you enjoy them sir; I've picked the best. The rest you can read later after your duties.'

A small, bespectacled Dunstan pushed the tea trolley in, a clipboard under his arm. A clear glass container the size of a small dustbin sat on top of the trolley, a viscous yellow liquid wobbled from side to side as Dunstan trundled the trolley in towards Santos.

'Begin,' Santos ordered. Dunstan slowed the trolley to a stop and retrieved the clipboard from under his arm. He blinked twice, squinted rodent like, ran a nervous hand through his oily hair then read out the line on the list in his hand.

'Right, the GoGo Mega Cutie Pink Princess Super Castle is flying off the shelves, kids love it. We even had one case in the United States of two parents, a Mrs Wellington and a Mrs King actually gouging out each other's eyes because they both wanted the same toy.'

'*Ha Ha Ha*! Jolly good, which of the lovely ladies managed to take it home for her delightful cherubs?"'

'Err... neither Mr Santos. The toy had so much blood on it the police had to take it away as evidence. So nobody will get it I'm afraid.' A smile devoid of charm spread across Dunstan's face.

'That's what we like, fill the market with products people can't get their grubby little hands on, it leads to vast swathes of disappointment and demand. An infallible business plan if I may say so myself,' Santos grinned. He looked down at a group of boys engaged in a snowball fight on the street below. One slipped, breaking a rib on the edge of the kerbs, his breath forced from his lung in an exasperated gasp. The others rushed over, unsure whether their laughter was valid or not. Santos's malicious grin stretched further over his skeletal face, exposing worn and yellowed teeth.

Dunstan continued. 'The new diet pill has proved a massive success, as fast as we can source the herbs from the rainforest and refine it into a product; it flies off of the shelves just as quick. The additives have proved addictive to every genetic combination, so no race will be able to escape addiction.'

'What percentage are we running at for mere placebos?' Santos queried, this time he turned to half face Dunstan.

'Over eighty per cent of tablets are. We plan to maintain it at that level because, of course, people need to see results otherwise they wouldn't buy it now would they sir?'

'*Indeeedy*,' Santos chuckled. He liked numbers. Numbers made it all worthwhile.

'Now fifty-five percent of the Super Puppy soft quilted toy have the carcinogenic stuffing, would you like me to up it sixty?' Dunstan asked as his eyebrows rose in genuine concern.

'Why not? But no higher, we don't want any links to us ten years down the line when little girls womb's start falling out and boys discover that they can no longer piss straight because their *pee-pee* has ceased to function.'

'A wise choice Mister Santos. Give them the disease, give them the cure. Marvellous ingenuity.'

'Call me *Siiir*,' croaked Santos.

'Sorry sir, sorry to be so personal.'

'*Axe-cepted*.' Santos cracked his bony neck then cast a dry white eyeball over at the glass container. "Is it... warm?"

'Body temperature, fresh today.'

'*Hee Hee Hee*,' Santos giggled with vehement glee, 'Very well, any more news to brighten this winter night?'

Dunstan flipped the paper over on the clipboard, squinting in the dimmed light of Mr Santos' office. He always found it hard to read in here, even with the bulbs on the light never cast right, as if some void of darkness sucked the illumination from the room. And only this room.

'Erm, an airline pilot who couldn't pay his mortgage this month, crashed into the Mediterranean on route from Istanbul, two hundred and forty three on board, no survivors. His wife intends to claim on his life insurance to pay off her mortgage.' Dunstan looked up and smiled grimly, waiting for comment.

'*Deee…nied*, it's not Christmas every day you know, we have to turn a profit. Next.'

Dunstan returned his gaze to the clipboard. 'A care home in Northern Scotland has had its gas switched off as they couldn't keep up with payments, several of the residents have taken to selling their jewellery to online precious metal dealers in order to keep the care home afloat throughout winter.'

'Have they all sold their jewellery?' Santos asked with a knowing narrowing of the eyes.

'It looks that way Mis…Sir,' Dunstan corrected in time for a river of sweat to form upon his spine.

'*Huh huh huh…*' Santos raised a long, grey finger as if to make an important point. 'Return heating to them…, but *ooonly…* once every three hours. Then as the sun sets on Christmas Eve, turn it off completely. I don't want them completely without hope. Not yet anyway.'

'I'll arrange it sir.'

'Any more, Dunstan?'

'That would be the major ones at this very moment. The rest are mostly drivers skidding in the snow, crashing and blaming each other. A few have beaten other drivers to death but apart from that it's been mostly uneventful without our help. Oh… a Middle Eastern Terror Cell is planning a wave of atrocities across the globe upon midnight on Christmas Eve. Apart from that it's mostly quiet.'

'Why must they interfere? It's not even their holiday; couldn't they wait until New Year at least?'

'I can ask their leaders to postpone.'

Santos heaved a sigh. 'No, its okay Dunstan, let them have their fun. I suppose Christmas is the holiday for everybody to enjoy.'

'What time are you heading out tonight sir?'

'Ready to *slay*?' Santos rasped with an all too grim grin.

'As always sir, they are always ready; I trust you have plenty planned for this season?'

'Yes. Inform the minions I'm coming down the shop floor, I want them wetting their pants with excitement.' Santos turned and started to remove his rose coloured tie.

'Of course sir.'

'I don't want you watching me change Dunstan. It's not a pleasant sight at my age.'

Dunstan smiled sickly and left with his clipboard tucked efficiently beneath his arm. He bowed curtly then left the trolley with the yellow liquid in the centre of the room and closed the door behind him, locking Santos in with the dead dust motes.

The essence of light left the room.

Mr Nicolas Santos was alone.

He pulled the tie through his collar and draped it over his chair, then his crimson velveteen suit and still crisp maroon shirt joined the rose coloured tie. Shoes, socks and underwear followed. In less than a minute Santos was nude in his cold office, his ghostly white flesh remained un-goose bumped by the lack of temperature.

It would be such a shame to ruin such a lovely suit.

Santos gently removed the round glasses from the bridge of his thin bony nose and placed them on the edge of his desk.

His shoulders convulsed, his spine seemed to drum up out of his skin, rolling like a wave, cracking sickly as vertebra became dislocated and bones disrupted as they changed shape and dimensions. His flesh became flush as he became taller; a poppy hue eroded away at the white pigment, scarring his skin a rich deceitful red. Muscles seemed to breathe by themselves as they increased in mass, becoming more defined as they broke out of the mould the old man used to hide himself from the world.

Younger, stronger, stranger. The only words that would have fitted his transformation, Santos smiled with exquisite pain as his toes melted and fused together into two distinct blank hooves, fur started to sprout from his back, twin bony protrusions fought through bone and wormed their way out from his skull like twin, curling corkscrews.

Mid transformation Santos clumped his way over to the trolley and picked up the container, and brought the warm viscous yellow liquid to his lips. The mix of varied animal fats glugged greedily down into his wanton throat and into his hungry gullet. Several gallons of liquefied lard ingested in a matter of seconds.

Santos burped and patted his wobbling rotund tummy as his transformation continued, the horns upon his head leaned towards each other and began to entwine, thickening and rounding to a point, they became heavy, so much so the protrusions leaning to one side as they bulked. The fur upon his back lost its darkness, lightening to a thick, rich red, within a blink of an eye it covered his entire body, aside from his face and hands and feet. The cloven hooves rejoined each other, bleeding out a black oily shine, the soles thickened until they resembled a pair of sturdy winter boots. Tufts of white fur grew as the blood red bled away at the edges, at his wrists, down the centre of his chest, above his faux boots, along his crown and at the tip of his floppy conjoined horns, now also covered in thick red fur. Santos's pathetic wispy beard had thickened, now long, lustrous and white. He gave it a little tug to confirm its being. The beard held.

Santos fastened a thick leather belt around his waist and replaced the round frames upon the bridge of his podgy red nose.

Down stairs, the sleigh awaited.

'*Ho Ho Ho,*' he chuckled joyfully as he opened the door and left the cold office behind, heading downstairs to bask in the warm laughs of innocent and giddy, star struck children, disguised as any other ordinary department store Santa Claus, the lie he had told to the world every year for centuries now, continuing for one more joyful Christmas.

FALLEN

The Father and son watched the news, together and yet alone.

The pictures had to be believed.

Osaka, Japan was the first hit. One went straight into a downtown taxi rank.

A little township in the outback of Australia, found one there too. It landed inches from a four year old girl as she played in her dust bowl of a back garden.

Russia, numerous places. Most wouldn't be found with the white vastness of the Arctic Circle.

Africa; again, all over the place.

Hundreds, maybe thousands.

Little black children hiding their white teeth behind solemn smiles, warily poking the still bodies with sticks. A concerned parent dressed in charity sportswear pushes them back, scolding them before the camera.

All around the Mediterranean they washed up on shores of every coastal country.

Body after body.

With each passing hour they found more and more of them. They even showed amateur footage of one plummeting dead and twirling from the skies. Folks gasped and pointed.

France, Spain, Germany. Corpse followed corpse.

The bodily rain continued.

Britain as well. Then Ireland, numerous drops in the Atlantic, one even hit the deck of a container ship with a sudden clang that woke the crew from their bunks.

Across the width of America they fell from the skies, doomed by gravity.

Word was, in Mexico one hit a plane, straight through the mid section, heavy as lead.

236 killed.

They smashed into cars, tore through buildings, and thumped into the middle of fields. The majority however landed in the oceans and seas of the world, only time and the tides would reveal the true number

Hundreds?

Thousands?

Millions seemed a ridiculous word to be associated with what had happened. But from what they saw, it was starting to look that way.

It seemed everybody on earth had seen one fall, or found one.

They were everywhere.

All dead.

Except one.

The father looked outside the back window. Beyond his back fence the city bustled as it always had, even on this strange, eventful day. It would take more than a miracle to unnerve the rolling routine of humanity.

Silvery wings twitched on this windless summer day. A tired ebb of life fighting its last possible beat.

He hadn't registered the impact at first, but it had been six-oh-seven when they heard the house rattling thud. His son walked into his bedroom a minute later, tugging his duvet away from his anguish cragged face.

'I think a bird hit the house.'

'How would you know that?' His father twisted his eyes open to daylight, a tight grimace and a trying smile for his son. The same brave cherub face for the last seven months. It didn't affect him as much. He despised him a little for that. He'd taken it much better. The happy little twat.

'I heard a thud, then flapping. Then downstairs some feathers came down the chimney,' his son said.

'What were you doing downstairs?' the father started to chide.

Shy reluctance, then, 'I was making you breakfast Daddy. You've got to eat sometime.'

'I don't feel like eating, you know that. Stop asking.'

'You can't drink all the time, kids at school say things about you.'

His father righted himself, concern stiffening his spine, 'What things?'

'They say you look like a scarecrow and you smell like a pig poo.'

'Do they?'

'Yep.'

'Well, tell them that's how I like it.' The father scratched wearily at his unkempt beard.

The boy swung his shoulders. Words danced a jittery jig from behind his lips, 'you coming to see the bird?'

'What bird?'

'The big bird in the back yard. I've seen it.'

Reluctance, from the father this time, he sighed and sat up. He got out of bed, kicked a bottle with a clink, rubbed the expanding fuzzy growth on his face and stood up. He held out his hand to the boy.

'Show me.'

The boy smiled, took his father's hand eagerly and led him out onto the landing, where they stopped at the window.

The father saw it. His dry mouth dropped.

Downstairs his son had been trying to find a station with cartoons. But this morning every station was telling the same story. This was happening everywhere.

All dead. Every single one of them.

Outside in the garden, the great wing folded down to the uncut grass, then back up and open as if it breathed through the rising limb.

Maybe it was?

None had been found alive.

Except theirs.

The father looked from the thing in the back garden, then to the television, the phone, and back to his son. He repeated this debating routine for ten minutes, got up and went outside.

'Stay here!' he warned.

The son ignored the request and padded silently ten feet behind.

As he stepped barefoot onto the dewy morning grass, the father looked up at the roof. The chimney stack was scattered across the rooftop, obliterated and smashed on the driveway and onto the uninsured car he didn't drive any more.

In his mind he traced the thing's trajectory. It had come in fast and at an angle. The ones on the news had dropped straight down. This one it appeared had been trying to fly.

He approached silently, the great wing eased back and forth. It shielded the body from view apart from a lithe little foot.

As he stepped within three feet of whatever it was, (though he had an idea, he fully doubted this, as he considered himself relatively sane) the great wing flapped open, revealing a naked body of a beautiful woman.

Except she wasn't just a woman.

Her pure, blemish free, alabaster skin glowed as if diamond dust flowed beneath the derma. Even as he watched, it twinkled. A template created for all beauty.

She looked at him.

Her full eyes that revealed a shade of silver blue he couldn't dream or even imagine. Full red lips that quivered dually with pain and fear. Fine icy blonde hair floated hypnotically from her head, almost non-existent, but still there all the same, it had an otherworldly quality, moving slower than the traditional flow of time.

She held out a hand with long fingers that stretched towards him. Without thinking, he took it.

Her other wing was bent around her back at an unnatural angle. A dark, glistening liquid splattered up and over her back and neck, a raw graze decorated her forehead on one side. She needed help.

She might've been ethereal, but she was still broken.

He bent, slipped one hand behind her knees, the other under her back between her wings and lifted her up and carried her to the house. She felt light. As if the only thing he carried were his own clothes.

'Back inside,' he hissed to his son, who obeyed with wide-eyed wonder.

Although she had the shape of breasts and womanhood, no nipples or areola decorated her firm chest. She had no belly button hole, and from where he was standing, he could see no detectable sexual organs of any kind.

194

'Cold,' she whispered, and smiled at him.

For the first time in a hell of a long while, he smiled back.

Carrying her through the living room, the news anchor announced not to approach the bodies under any circumstances and to contact the police if you happen to find one. There seemed to be a vast backlog of reports according to the news.

'Turn that off,' he commanded.

His son obeyed; transfixed by the unearthly being that his father carried upstairs, her strange feathers scraping softly along the wall.

He laid her on the bed in the spare room, careful not to add injury to the broken wing, found a spare blanket and covered what modesty she had. She smiled a painful, yet grateful grin.

'I'll get you some more blankets,' he told her.

She smiled. He left.

His son was waiting on the landing, his face happy and pale.

'Is she…?'

'No,' the father cut in abruptly.

'She looks like…'

'It's not her.'

'Can I go talk to her?'

'Just stay away until we … I figure out what to do.'

'I just want to say hello.'

'You can't! Go downstairs and clean your toys up. That's an order,' he barked louder than he meant to.

Scorned, his son turned and moped all the way down the stairs.

His father followed, stopping halfway down the stairway to look at a picture of his wife, their son and he that hung on the wall portraying happier times. Her hair was shorter than the stranger in the guest room, eyes not as radiant blue, similarities sure; but then his wife had been dead for over seven months now.

***

He brought her more blankets and started the conversation.

'You got a name?'

She looked back, quizzical, dumbfounded, yet kept up the pretence of humility.

He pointed to his chest and told her his name. Then pointed at his son who spied in from the doorway and told her his name nodding eagerly while he said it, then he pointed to her, '…you?'

Her mouth opened as if her voice box had stalled, making an odd clicking sound, then finally she said in a calm and soft voice that shook him with one simple syllable.

195

'Eve.' She smiled

A torrent of tears built up behind him. He shook his head and left, barging past his beaming son, who crept into the room after he'd gone.

The father headed halfway down the stairs, grabbing the picture from the wall, ripping the hook out from the plaster. Tears flowed as he set himself down on the steps, stroking the image of his wife that had being cruelly robbed from them both. Again a one-syllable word evoked more raw emotion.

'Eve...' he repeated, blubbing away until night fell.

***

The son didn't waste time in embracing this stranger who looked remarkably like his mother. Minutes turned into hours as the evening cast its dark web across the night sky, the boy enjoyed the unending warmth that his mother emitted for as long as he could.

He asked her why she had returned. She smiled sweetly, kissed his forehead and said, 'for you, for him. I might've not had another chance.'

'Why did all the others fall with you?'

'A war above, a disease of minds, overcrowding then some bad people got through. Things collapsed. Soon we all had to fall. Everybody fell to somewhere. But time heals all things and I'll have to return to where I belong. I can't live here. None of us can. Only love can keep us alive down here. If we don't keep close to love. That's why we all tried to get back. But I found you, I was lucky to have found you and I'll wait for you both on the other side of that beautiful door. As long as it takes...'

***

Eve was asleep when he went to check on them. He had eavesdropped on their conversation. But the well of emotion was too much; he couldn't face her. She had gone, and that was that.

Dead.

Having a fully loaded cement lorry with bald tires plough sideward into your car at sixty miles does that to a person. Having to identify his wife by way of intimate beauty spots can crush a man. Moles could be a coincidence. She had no tattoos but her purple painted toenails and the toe ring from Hawaii had sealed the deal. It was the only part of her left intact.

He couldn't talk to her. He'd get attached again and he couldn't deal with losing her again. He was of sound mind and he knew that this couldn't last. The foundations of sanity were crumbling. He was an atheist. They both had been.

He feared if he fully understood this, the universe would tear itself apart.

His son was curled up on the bed by her feet like a dutiful puppy. He picked him up and carried him to bed.

He looked at Eve once. Her wing looked a lot better.

***

He awoke to a boom, then a rush of galloping breeze that thundered throughout the house and into his core. His son, who had apparently crawled into bed with him during the night grappled onto his arm, frightened. The clock read 3:37A.M.

The noise came from the back room.

They looked at each other, climbed out of bed and hurried across the landing.

The exterior wall was missing in the spare room, bricks were still falling, the broken joists above them hung down like dark teeth, giving the impression that they were both looking out from inside a monster's mouth onto the velveteen night sky. He could smell burnt hair, ozone and the freshness of a wet road after a rainstorm.

Eve's bed was empty; yet high above them, charging towards the cosmos was a bright white comet trail leaving the earth behind.

The father smiled, again for her. He held his son close, squeezed until his fingers hurt. His son didn't seem to mind. She'd come back for their son. Maybe help him understand and see forward in life.

She was gone now.

But this time she left them happy.

Even if it wasn't really her.

Even if it was.

He was still happy.

Because, despite the vast gulf of death that had existed between them; somehow, she had fallen back to him.

Reassurance was what he needed, and reassurance was what he got.

The father squeezed his son.

At least they had each other. He had that to be thankful for.

He now realised that you had to be grateful for what you had, despite what you've lost or think you've got missing from life. You can grieve for so long, but it achieves nothing. It doesn't bring them back, and it doesn't take you forward. To wallow is to let the loss win.

He had hope. More than enough.

DEVIL LET ME GO

Nathan Robinson lives in Scunthorpe, England with his wife and twin sons. His debut novel 'Starers' was published by Severed Press in October 2012 reaching #15 in the Amazon Kindle download chart. His short stories have appeared in numerous anthologies from Knightwatch Press, Static Movement, Rainstorm Press, Spinetinglers, and many more.

His tale 'Top of the Heap' has since been adapted into a short story podcast by www.pseudopod.org and was voted one of the top adaptations of 2011.

As well as writing he's the book reviewer for www.snakebitehorror.co.uk Find him at www.facebook.com/NathanRobinsonWrites www.facebook.com/DevilLetMeGo

Okay (deep breath), many thanks to everyone at www.spinetinglers.co.uk, www.pseudopod.org, www.snakebitehorror.co.uk, www.thisishorror.co.uk , www.severedpress.com , Mark Goddard, Marcus Blakeston, Kevin Bufton, Theresa Derwin, Theresa Curnow, Charlotte Emma Gledson, Theresa Derwin, Lyle Perez, Thadd Presley, Mandy DeGeit, Paul Johnson-Jovanovic, Nate Burleigh, Charlie Vaughan at Little Images, Heather Landry, Kayleigh Marie Edwards, Lauren and Nolene, Dan Henk, Jack Bantry, Jeff Strand, Emily May Mitchell, everyone who liked (and hated) Starers, my new fans on Good Reads, the Harlequin boys, Uncle Buck, Tom (RIP – The Chicken in Black is for you), Nanna Elaine, My brother Matthew, my Mum and Dad, my wife and my boys, Oscar and Henry, who terrify and delight me in equal measure every day.

And you, reading this, a big thank you. This couldn't have been done without you participation.

Nathan Robinson
July 21, 2013

This is a work of fiction. Names, characters, places and incidents either are products of the author's imagination or are used fictitiously. Any resemblance to actual events or locales or persons, living, dead or undead is entirely coincidental.

No chickens, monsters or summoned demons were harmed during the writing of this book.

"Zombie-fied Chicken" By Charlie Vaughan-
www.facebook.com/LittleImages

Imagine if you found yourself the attention of the entire world . . .

The dysfunctional Keene family awaken one Saturday to find several strangers and neighbours staring at their home. Events turn more bizarre when more hypnotised strangers arrive, all seemingly transfixed with those within the Keene household. As the ominous crowd gathers and grows larger by the hour the Keene's find themselves under siege in their own home. With hundreds, then thousands of bodies pressing against the walls of their home, a rising body count and grim premonitions plaguing their dreams, the family must work together to discover who or what is controlling the Starers.
Available on Amazon Kindle and in paperback.
ASIN: B009KC27CS
www.facebook.com/Starers

Made in the USA
Charleston, SC
30 July 2014